SANCTUARY FOR MURDER

A Natalia Hernandez Mystery: Book 2

Lauren Garcia

For Selma (Maw-Maw)
Our family's original bookworm. There are a few people in your life who you know will love and support you no matter what. Thank you for being one of those people for me. You've always made me feel loved and special.

"I was ashamed of myself when I realised that life is a masquerade party, and I attended with my real face."

FRANZ KAFKA

ACKNOWLEDGEMENTS

It has been such a rewarding process writing and publishing these books, and I've been so happy to hear from people about how much they enjoyed the first book. I always try to walk the line between a fun time with and hopefully an interesting plot while also developing characters who feel real and deal with real issues in ways that aren't always perfect. The fact that other people felt that too and it resonated with them has been really exciting.

Thank you, Isaac. You are so smart and sweet and kind. I can't believe how lucky I am to be your mom. The time we spend together is so much fun. That was one thing I didn't anticipate before becoming a mom. Just how much fun it would be. You're so funny and interesting. It's a privilege watching you turn into such a cool person. I love seeing the world through your eyes and hearing your take on everything. You teach me something new every day.

Thank you to Marty for being my first reader and friend. I appreciate everything you do. You're always so kind but honest in your critiques.

I am so grateful to have a husband that likes to talk and discuss everything. I don't know what I'd do without you. I can't imagine life without you. Thank you for always encouraging me and supporting me in everything.

Thank you to my aunt Mary and Maw-Maw who always modeled reading widely and showed me that a good book doesn't have to be boring.

Thanks to my mom for always reading to me and encouraging me to write. I am very glad you weren't like Natalia's mom, Blanca. I have a soft spot in my heart for Blanca with all her flaws. But I appreciate that you weren't her, and in no part is Blanca's character based on my own mother.

To my dad, I still miss you every day. You're never far from my thoughts. You're the reason I never gave up and am who I am today. I still want to call you all the time. You were the best dad anyone could have asked for. I just wish you were still here. I love you!

CHAPTER ONE

"**A**na, why don't you have a seat back in the office? Pacing is not going to make them get here any faster."

"Huh?" Ana asked. Her distraction over her upcoming wedding had been kicked into high gear with the impending arrival of her future mother-in-law.

"Go chill out and sit down," I ordered. "I've got the front for the next half hour at least, and I'll let you know if she comes."

"Well, if you're sure…"

"Yes, you're driving me crazy pacing like that. Go watch a cute kitten video or something."

"Okay, okay, I'm going," Ana laughed. "Just let me know when she gets here."

"Will do," I promised.

Ana disappeared into the back office leaving me alone in the empty lobby. I sighed, relieved. Miguel, the regular front desk clerk, had taken a lunch break. I'd eagerly agreed to cover the desk, so I could get out of the office and escape Ana's mounting anxiety, at least that had been the plan. It was the mid-afternoon lull, and nobody really had to be at the desk, but I welcomed the quiet. I surveyed the tidy, simple lobby with pride. I still couldn't believe after all these months that I actually owned a hotel with my two best friends. My grandma had left it to me after her death, but it still didn't quite feel real sometimes. Ana and her sister Lía had kept the hotel from shutting down, so I'd made them part owners too. Owning the hotel together was a dream come true, but that didn't always mean that it was easy.

Ana's fiancé, Carlos, pulled up and parked his light blue sedan directly in front of the hotel's glass door. Now it was my turn to feel nervous. I'd never met my best friend's future mother-in-law before, but it had been intimated, both by Ana and Carlos, that she was a force to be reckoned with. She was due to stay for the entire week of wedding festivities. *I really hope her personality has been at least somewhat exaggerated*, I thought, as she walked through the front door.

"What a charming little town you have here," the woman was saying. "You'll have to give me the complete tour of the rest of it later, Carlos. But right now I just want to lay down and relax."

"Well, you pretty much already saw everything there is to see, Mom." Carlos gave a nervous laugh. "I told you Santa Rita is pretty small. This is the main road right here." He gestured outside the hotel door and towards the church.

His mother raised an eyebrow. "Really? Well, I'm just not sure why you and Ana are so set on living here then." She shook her head.

Ana had exited the office and stood shyly behind the desk. "It's lovely to see you uh---"

"I told you, call me Sara," Carlos's mother instructed.

"Sara, yes well thank you for coming. It means so much to both of us." Ana smiled.

"All of us," I said. "I mean all of us here at the hotel and Santa Rita. We're so happy you're here, and we're definitely thrilled for Ana and Carlos."

The woman paused. "Who exactly are you?" she asked.

"This is Natalia. We grew up together," Ana answered. "Well she didn't grow up here, but when she was here– I mean we spent a lot of time together, and we're still friends. I didn't mean... Well, I--"

Carlos rescued Ana from her rambling. "Natalia is the main owner of this hotel. She's from the US and loves living in Santa Rita too." He was obviously trying really hard to sell his pretentious mother on our tiny mountain town in central Mexico. Carlos had grown up in the much larger city of León, just a few hours away, where his mother still lived. She was apparently the type who thought anything worth having was in a city, and if it wasn't there, then you didn't need it."

"You gringos really are strange ones, aren't you?" Sara's loud, long laugh echoed in the tiny lobby.

I bristled at the term. It wasn't exactly an insult. It was actually pretty common for residents of Santa Rita to use it towards me jokingly, even though both my mom and dad, whoever he was, were Mexican. But I'd lived the vast majority of my life in the US, and there were still some cultural differences that went over my head. The way this woman said the word, though, made me feel like an idiot who didn't belong anywhere.

"Well, I'll let Ana and Carlos get you settled in. They can answer any questions you might have. I've got quite a lot of paperwork, so if you'd please excuse me." I felt a little guilty about leaving so quickly, but not very. I reasoned that it would be better for their new family to spend time alone without my interference. I had a whole new appreciation for why Ana had been so nervous. I just hoped we could get through this wedding quickly, and I could avoid Sara during the entire process. After all, Carlos was a lovely person, and the last thing I wanted to do was insult his mother.

Back in the office, I was able to breathe a sigh of relief, but it didn't last long. The front desk bell sounded, so I hurried back out to the lobby again to see two young women in their mid-20's standing there fresh-faced and smiling, while a third was hunched over, her face buried in a screen.

"Are you Natalia?" The blonde one asked in halting Spanish.

"Yes, I am. How can I help you?" I responded in English.

"Phew, my Spanish is just awful, thank God. We talked online. I'm Jessica. This is Claire, and over there on her phone is Harriet." Jessica gestured to each girl in turn. My face must've still looked blank because she clarified. "We're the vegan Youtubers."

"Oh yes, of course," I said, the conversation starting to emerge from the recesses of my brain. With everything happening for the wedding, this was the last thing I needed. I remembered Jessica now. We'd agreed to show off some of our vegan desserts from the bakery on their channel. I thought their reservations weren't until after the wedding, but here they were right in front of me a whole two weeks early.

"Oh," I said. "I must've put your reservation in wrong. I thought you weren't due for another couple weeks."

Jessica furrowed her brow then turned towards the sour looking girl on her phone. "Harriet, do you know what date you put the reservation in for?" Harriet glanced up for a moment, shrugged, and turned back to the screen.

"Do you have a room for us?" she asked, glancing around the empty lobby.

"Oh yes, I'm sure we can figure it out," I said. The last thing Hotel Leticia and Santa Rita needed was bad publicity spewed all over Youtube for years to come, and since Carlos's relatives weren't actually paying full price, guests with money had to come first. Even Ana would have to agree with that.

I handed them their room keys and wished them well, but as soon as they'd disappeared down the hall, I flopped into the chair exasperated. A hotel full of out of town, snobby wedding guests and several Youtubers running around. *How could this get any worse?*

"You okay? I wasn't gone that long, was I?" Miguel asked.

I looked up to see him standing in front of the desk, a concerned look on his face. I pulled my head up, forced a smile, and let him in on the whole situation that had seemed catastrophic in my own head, but saying it out loud, it didn't actually seem so bad.

Miguel patted my shoulder. "It'll be fine. Don't worry. As long as all the guests stay alive, we're golden."

"Don't even joke about that," I groaned. "But you're right. We've got to keep things in perspective. One obstacle at a time."

"What obstacle? What are you talking about? Don't even tell me..." Ana whipped around the corner. I wasn't sure how much of our conversation she'd overheard, but she was already worked into a frenzy.

"Nothing's happened," I said. Strangely, Ana's extreme reaction helped to temper my own. I explained about the vegan Youtubers as calmly as possible. "It won't interfere with your wedding," I promised. "It's just extra work for me because I promised to show them some of our new recipes and around Santa Rita. Plus, they only speak English, so I might have to hold their hand a little bit more than other guests, but it's really nothing. I was just venting."

"It is a lot of work for you," Ana agreed, but she was visibly calming. "I'm sure they'll love everything, though. The Vegan Enthusiasts did, and your desserts are to die for."

"I'm sure they heard about us from the Vegan Enthusiasts." I laughed. I still couldn't get over the odd club name. "But they were just low-key bloggers who came to eat, hike, and type."

"Well, maybe these ladies will be the same," Ana said. "You said there were only three of them, right?"

I nodded. "That's true. How hard can it be?"

"Probably easier than my rehearsal party is going to be tonight." Ana sighed then checked over her shoulder. "I love Carlos. I really do, and I want to like his mother. I really do…"

"What is the rest of his family like?" I asked.

Ana shook her head. "I have no idea. I mean how can you ask someone that, 'Is the rest of your family as obnoxious as your mother?'"

I bit back a laugh. "Well, we'll get through it one way or another, I guess."

That night the party hall was teeming with people, the vast majority of whom I had never met before. I wanted to find a quiet corner to stuff my face and get out as quickly as socially possible. The rehearsal had gone fine, as far as I could tell, and probably wouldn't have been necessary, but I'd opened up my big mouth and told Ana about the tradition in the US, and since then she'd been obsessed about it, especially when I told her there was usually a dinner afterwards, which Ana had turned into a full-blown party for everyone. Thankfully, though, she hadn't wanted to import the bridesmaid tradition as well. God knows what kind of hideous dress Ana would've had Lía and me in.

She'd had to cut a lot of her more extravagant plans. Usually in Mexico the tradition was to have *padrinos* or godparents for each part of the wedding. Since there hadn't been any recent monetary windfalls, Ana had reluctantly agreed to forgo her own plans and rely on *padrinos*, and you couldn't exactly dictate your theme and decor to willing *padrinos* who'd agreed to handle their part and took great pride in doing so.

Except for the dress and rehearsal dinner, that had been all Ana and Carlos, mostly Carlos. They'd gone all out, and it showed. I was glad to finally see Ana happy. She'd planned everything for so long. I hoped it went by smoothly and quickly, for all of our sakes.

Balancing a plate on my lap, I headed for the far corner ready to devour it. But Sara stopped me. "You're uh what's her face, right? The owner of the hotel."

I bristled but forced a smile anyway. "That's me, what's her face, at least that's what my friends call me."

But Sara ignored my jab and shoved a cell phone in my face instead. "My ex-husband is late, as usual, but he claims he's lost. I can't find Carlos anywhere. Can you give him directions?"

"Well, I'm not actually very familiar with the roads outside of town. It might be better if…" But Sara had already walked away. She'd purposefully ignored me, and now this poor soul was relying on me to give him directions. If he wasn't in trouble before, he definitely was now.

"Hello, yes. This is Natalia Hernandez. I'm a friend of the bride. Your ex-wife said you were lost." But the voice on the other end sounded far away and staticky, not surprising seeing as the town was surrounded by mountains, but it made the task at hand even more challenging. I frantically searched, pacing the room, and looking for anyone I knew more qualified to help Carlos's father find his way. I spotted Nico over by the buffet line and made a beeline towards him.

"Nico," I said, out of breath. "Carlos's dad is lost somewhere, and his mom, Sara, asked me to give directions, but I have no idea. Could you--?" I passed him the phone. Nico was smiling, enjoying ever so slightly my frantic demeanor, but I didn't even care. He leaned over to give me a kiss.

"Sure, watch my plate *mi peluchita*." I smiled and blushed.

When I'd mentioned that Nico never used any pet names with me since we'd started dating, he'd taken to calling me his *pelucha* or stuffed animal. That wasn't exactly what I'd had in mind, but he thought it was hilarious.

He stepped aside, shoved a finger in one ear, and moved away from the hubbub of guests to take the call. He returned relatively quickly, a broad smile on his face.

"Good luck, he was almost here. He thought he'd passed the turn-off because he hadn't seen anything for so long, but we're right here, Santa Rita in the absolute middle of nowhere. I think we should put that on a sign. People would come from all over just to see it."

"I can't believe no one ever thought of that before. You are quite the marketing genius." I jabbed him playfully. "But thanks for helping. You were a lifesaver."

"Anytime," Nico said, while spooning extra salsa onto his plate.

"Now I just need to find Sara and give her phone back. Have you seen her?" I asked.

Nico furrowed his brow. "Sara? You mean the loud, obnoxious woman that my sister is actually choosing to be related to?"

"That's the one," I said. "But I'm pretty sure Ana is choosing Carlos, and Sara is just an unfortunate part of the package."

Nico shrugged. "I guess so, but it all makes sense now."

"What makes sense?"

"Why a well-off lawyer like Carlos would come all the way out to tiny Santa Rita to live. It was to get away from that harpy."

"You shouldn't say that. That's his mother you're talking

about and your sister's future mother-in-law."

"You're right," he agreed. "Carlos is a good guy. I shouldn't-- Oh, there she is over there." He pushed me lightly in the direction of Sara. "I'll wait over on the other side of the room," and with that, Nico disappeared.

I approached, phone outstretched. Sara had cornered the church secretary, Olga, who didn't bother to stifle a yawn.

"Sara, there you are. Your ex-husband should be here shortly. He was closer than he thought," I said, handing her the phone.

Sara pocketed the phone without even a thank you, but Olga had perked up. "Your *ex-husband*?" she asked. "Your son is a child of divorce then, a broken family. Did you inform Father Francisco of that?"

"What?" Sara sputtered. "Why would I inform the priest of anything? I'm not the one getting married, my son is. Are you saying the priest would call off the wedding two days before because of something that happened between the groom's parents?"

While I was happy to see Sara genuinely terrified and on the defensive, I was disheartened to have to agree with her. *What could this mean for Ana's wedding? Olga had to be overreacting.*

"Well, it's up to the priest's discretion," Olga said, "but we do have certain standards and morals to uphold within the parish."

Olga was reveling in the superiority now, and while it was fun to watch Sara being put in her place, I wished it could be about something else.

"Actually, I believe Father Tomás, not Father Francisco is performing the ceremony," I said. Father Tomás was quite a bit younger and more liberal than the older priest. "But whoever it is, surely there's no rule against..." But glancing over at Sara, I was unsure how to finish the question.

Olga furrowed her brow. "Well, I suppose not. It's not our job to judge, after all." She nodded in agreement with herself. "In the past, it might have been an issue, but now we are much more open-minded and recognize that the church is first and foremost a hospital for sinners even more than a shrine to the saints." It was obvious that was a line Olga had used before and enjoyed. She smirked in self-righteous satisfaction. "If you'll excuse me, I need to ask the Father about something I forgot about earlier," and with a nod, Olga was gone.

It took all of my strength to hold back the laugh bubbling inside, especially when I saw Sara, mouth agape, staring wide-eyed. To make Sara speechless, I had to hand that to Olga at least, even if I didn't agree with her content.

Now with Olga gone, it was just me and Sara. There was no other recipient for, a now very angry, Sara's barbs to be hurled at, but to my relief, her attention seemed to be focused elsewhere.

"Who is that with...?" she asked.

I turned to see what she was looking at and saw a man in an expensive-looking, black suit. Carlos emerged out of the crowd to hug him, so I assumed that must be his father. There was someone else with him, though, a woman in a low-cut, pink dress, and as she turned, everything went wobbly. If I'd been wearing heels, I would've keeled over. Standing next to Carlos's father was my mother, Blanca.

"What?" It was my turn to be speechless. How had she gotten here, I wondered, and why? She was living in a whole other country. Surely, she wouldn't hop on a plane and come all the way out here without warning me, and yet here she was, and with Carlos's father no less.

She saw me and started walking quickly over, enjoying the spectacle she was making of herself. "Oh Natalia, did I surprise you? Did it work? You told me to visit. I had to see what made you want to stay in this tiny town I couldn't wait to get away from. And when I found out that my old friend from high-school Luis was coming here for his son's wedding, it just seemed like destiny."

I remembered hearing that Carlos's dad had grown up in a neighboring town even smaller than Santa Rita, but it had never occurred to me that my mother would know him, and that if she did, she would've invited herself and decided to come now of all times.

"What a small world." Sara spoke for the first time, ice lacing her words, but my mother ignored her completely.

"So are you surprised?" she pressed me.

"Surprise isn't exactly the word I'm thinking of," I said. "But yeah, I'm definitely surprised."

CHAPTER TWO

My mother sauntering into the room with a barely-there, bright pink dress on the arm of the groom's father in a small, conservative town like Santa Rita sent the rest of my evening into a tailspin. I was thankful that at least Ana's actual wedding hadn't been affected, but I felt guilty just the same.

At least Blanca didn't expect me to entertain her and spent the evening mingling with *old friends*. Odd that in a town she had despised for years, there were so many old times she wanted to relive, laughing too loudly and being so touchy that I couldn't stand to watch her invade everyone's personal space as she worked the room.

"Are you hiding out too?" Nico asked. He'd found me watching the rehearsal through a large window outside.

"At least out here I don't have to listen to every cringe-worthy statement that comes out of her mouth, although I'm sure I'll hear enough about them later," I said.

"You don't have to stay, you know? There's no reason to torture yourself when there's nothing you can do about it."

I nodded. "I know. I was planning to duck out early, but now I feel obligated to stay. What if she does something really crazy? I'll have to step in to stop her."

"It's not your fault, and it's not as bad as you think." Nico nudged me. "But she is married, isn't she? She won't get into too much trouble."

I shrugged. "Last I heard she was, husband number five, but these things are fluid. She can drop a husband flat for no reason at all."

"But isn't this one loaded?" Nico asked.

I couldn't help but smile. "Good point, and I haven't heard any complaints about him, yet?"

"Well, then she's probably just flirting and likes to stir things up. Don't let it bother you." Nico patted my shoulder.

"That is Blanca's favorite pastime," I agreed.

"Blanca? You call your mother by her first name." Nico was surprised. I usually just said *my mother* in conversation because I knew it was odd, and most people didn't understand.

"She had me at 18 and didn't like the whole mother-vibe, so that's just what I got used to calling her. Plus, she's not the most uh… motherly figure."

"Oh, I see. Well, it looks like things are starting to wind down, if you'd like to brave it by going back inside?" Nico offered his hand.

"If we have to," I said. The room had already started to empty. Thankfully, it was a weeknight. I waved to Ana's sister, Lía, with her daughter and husband in tow, as they exited out the front of the hall. Blanca seemed oblivious and sat right in the middle of it all, hand on the father of the groom's shoulder, leaning into him, laughing. Sara stood off to the side scowling.

"Blanca, it's getting late. Would you like to go back over to the hotel with me?" I asked.

"What was that?" My mother looked over, slightly irritated at being pulled away from causing a scene.

"Let's go back to the hotel. It's getting late, and I know Ana and Carlos have a lot of work to do for the wedding in a couple days." So much for the questions. Someone needed to take charge here, I thought.

Ana sent a relieved smile in my direction whereas Blanca rolled her eyes. "I forgot how early everything ends in this little backwater place." Blanca laughed, but no one joined her. "I'll catch *you* later, Luis," she said, blowing a kiss towards Carlos's father, picked up her strappy pink heels that she'd left lying on the floor, and slung them over a finger. "Lead me," she said, grabbing my elbow.

"Would you like me to walk back with you?" Nico had a concerned look on his face.

"Actually–" Blanca began.

"No, we'll be fine. Thanks for offering," I said. The last thing I needed was my mother ruining my relationship. Nico and I had only started dating a few months ago, and the more time I could keep him away from my mother, the better. Plus, his sister Ana needed him right now more than I did.

"Are you drunk?" I hissed under my breath.

"Of course not. I'm just enjoying the night. I feel young again," Blanca responded.

I highly doubted that but chose to ignore her denial. "Well, you're not young anymore. You're a married woman, and these are Ana's wedding festivities that you're trying to ruin. Please, control yourself, or I'll send you right back to that husband of yours."

Blanca looked remorseful for a moment. "You're right. It was just a rehearsal, so I didn't think... but I know other people take this kind of thing more seriously. What about my luggage? It's in Luis's car. I need to–"

"I'm sure he'll bring it to the hotel tomorrow, and if not, I'll send for it. Don't worry. I'll find something for you to sleep in for tonight." I didn't need Blanca to dawdle around the rehearsal hall and stir up even more gossip than she already had.

It was unfortunate that both Blanca and Sara would be in the hotel together, but at least Luis wouldn't be there too. When Carlos had offered for his dad to stay with him at his apartment, I'd thought it was because they were so close and wanted to have some father-son time together. It hadn't occurred to me that he probably just wanted to keep his two parents as far apart as possible. There was some odd tension there, especially from Sara.

"You're right. I just don't get out much, and I guess I can't drink like I used to." Blanca stumbled slightly, but at least she was still coherent.

I bit back every retort bubbling at the surface and offered my own olive branch in return. "Are you sure you'll be okay walking back barefoot?"

"Of course, these heels are killing me."

"But the cobblestones might be worse. It's up to you, but–"

Blanca hesitantly stepped onto the sidewalk before rethinking her lack of footwear. "You're right. Let me strap these back on."

I waited while she leaned on me and reattached her shoes. Olga brushed past us in the doorway. I offered her a tepid good night, surprised that she hadn't already left a few hours before.

She turned to me, flushed. "And what's good about it? This wedding has brought a bunch of loose-moraled people to Santa Rita. If they think they can just behave however they want then..."

I sensed that Blanca was about to laugh and sent her a sharp look to silence her, which thankfully worked. "Did something happen, Olga? I'm sure nobody meant anything." She was very upset about something, and I didn't want to escalate it any further."

Olga shot Blanca a scowl, ignored my question, and turned back around to enter the hall. I thought about going in after her to help diffuse whatever situation might arise, but with Blanca on my arm and knowing her history, I decided against it. The best way to help was to get Blanca out of the way and into a hotel room asleep as soon as possible.

Once I got Blanca safely settled into bed on the other side of the hotel from Sara, I could finally breathe a sigh of relief. I stopped at the front desk to check in with Miguel and pick up Furby, my black and white kitten, who had grown quite a bit from the tiny ball of fluff I'd found huddled outside of the cottage when I'd first arrived in Santa Rita.

"Was he any trouble for you?" I asked Miguel, scooping up Furby and covering him with kisses.

Miguel shook his head. "He's been surprisingly quiet. Just curled up here and slept in the office most of the time."

"Well, thanks for keeping an eye on him. He would've been distraught alone in the cottage for so long."

Miguel smiled. "That is one lucky cat."

"Where is the line between lucky and spoiled?" I asked.

"Oh you crossed that a long time ago," Miguel said.

"I guess I can't deny that. Oh, by the way, my mother, Blanca Hernandez, is in room 308, upstairs. Someone might come by tomorrow to bring her luggage."

"Sure thing," Miguel said, but his raised eyebrow indicated he thought the whole situation odd but was too polite to say anything.

"Have you ever met my mother, Miguel?" I asked.

"Uh... No." He shook his head.

"Well, strap in. These next few days are going to be bumpy. Don't say I didn't warn you." I left Miguel scratching his head, trying to interpret my warning, but there was nothing to interpret. Chaos always followed my mother everywhere she went.

CHAPTER THREE

The next morning I rose so early it was still dark. The cottage my grandma had left me sat just behind the hotel and bakery and allowed for enough privacy when needed but was a stone's throw from both businesses. With all the various personalities staying at the hotel, it was nice to be nearby in case of any potential problems without being drawn into them unless absolutely necessary. I headed into the office with Furby under one arm.

I gave a cursory good morning to the night-shift desk clerk before closing the office door and dumping Furby onto the floor. His pride injured, he turned his back to me and furiously licked himself. I booted up the desktop and sighed. The silence of the early morning was calming, almost magical, but maybe it just felt that way because I rarely experienced it in a fully conscious state. I decided to tackle the emails and some bookkeeping first. With the wedding festivities in full swing, neither Ana or her sister, Lía, would have time to focus on much else. After being absorbed in spreadsheets for what felt like forever, the figures began to swim in front of my eyes.

I stretched. "Furby, I think we need a break and a cup of coffee. What do you think?" He blinked back with a disinterested scowl. "Oh, are you still angry at me? I'm sorry." I reached over to scratch under his chin, and he reluctantly accepted it and quickly became a motorized ball of fluff stretched out on the desk.

A tentative knock sounded on the office door. "Yes?" I called.

Miguel's shift still hadn't started yet, and the newly-hired front desk clerk stood in the doorway, silent and motionless.

"Andrea," *That was her name, wasn't it?* "Is everything all right?"

She nodded but still stood there not speaking.

"So, is there anything I can help you with?" I asked.

"Uh maybe… I think so, yes," she finally answered.

"And what would that be?" I tried to keep the exasperation out of my voice.

"Well, there is a uh guest saying something I don't understand."

"Really? What are they saying?"

"Well, I don't know. I don't understand them," Andrea repeated.

I couldn't help but sigh. "I understand that, but in what way don't you understand them? What are they saying exactly that you don't understand?"

"Words."

"So you don't understand their words?" I knew I sounded like a preschool teacher, but there was really no other way.

"Uh-hmm," she nodded.

"Can you repeat their words?" I asked.

She shook her head.

"So are their words in another language?" I prompted.

Andrea nodded. "I think they are speaking English, and they asked for you."

Finally, I tried not to roll my eyes. "Andrea, couldn't you have said that five minutes ago?" But she just shrugged her shoulders. I saw now why Lía had given this girl the graveyard shift.

"Okay, well thank you anyway. I'll go and speak with them." I stood and walked towards the front desk. Furby followed, eager to continue the cuddle session that had abruptly ended.

One of the Youtubers from the day before stood there waiting. I couldn't remember her name, so I just offered a cheerful greeting. "Hello, how can I help you?"

"Hi, my name is Claire." She looked down when she spoke, and I wondered how someone with a successful Youtube channel could be so shy. "Jessica wanted to know where we could get some picturesque early morning footage around town." Claire finally looked up.

"Well, Santa Rita is a colonial, historic town with great architecture. So all the empty streets are lovely early in the morning. The square around the church is also beautiful, and there are farms outside of town and trails through the mountains with a couple of vineyards. Honestly, I'm not much of a morning person or a photographer, but there is also not too much to Santa Rita to miss." Not wanting to disparage the town or business, I quickly added. "But it's very quaint and beautiful. That's its charm after all."

Claire nodded. "I figured that, but Jessica wanted me to ask anyway." Claire gave the impression of a human Eeyore, speaking slowly in a melancholy tone, the exact opposite of Jessica's over-eager, bubbly personality.

"I love your tattoos." I gestured to Claire's hand. Both her hands and wrists were covered. I normally wasn't much of a tattoo person, but Claire's really were a quite striking and unique style.

She smiled for the first time. "Thanks! I designed these

myself, and my friend inked them for me."

"Well, they're really cool." I knew I sounded like her grandmother instead of just a few years older.

"Thanks," she repeated.

I smiled. "Sure thing, let me know if there's anything else we can do."

Bubbly Jessica and sour Harriet bustled into the lobby. Jessica spoke loudly into her cell. *Who could she be talking to at this hour?* I wondered. But then I realized she must be recording something.

"I'm here at the Leticia Hotel in Santa Rita, Mexico. We got in yesterday, and today we're off to see what we can find and get some pics." Jessica shouted into the phone. *Was that really how loudly you had to talk*? After she finished speaking, she spent another good 10 minutes taking selfies.

I wasn't sure if I was supposed to hang around waiting or leave, but they really didn't seem to need me. Harriet's face was buried in her phone, just as it had been the day before. Jessica waved but didn't speak before heading out the front door. Claire gave a weak smile and wave before all three exited into the early morning darkness.

How were they going to appreciate or find anything to record glued to their phones like that? I wondered, accepting the fact that I had officially crossed over into old-person territory for good but not caring. I'd always loved listening to my grandmother's stories. They were much more interesting than any piece of technology could be. I wondered what she would've made of the foreign, vegan Youtubers, especially quiet Claire covered in piercings and tattoos.

I tried picturing grandma attempting to interact with them through language, cultural, and generational barriers. I laughed at the idea. Andrea was still standing next to me. She jumped at the sound of my laugh, giving me a sideways glance.

"They are quite the strange crew, aren't they?" I tried to sound light, but she just stood, staring.

"Yeah I guess." Andrea rolled her eyes and plopped back into the front desk chair. *Even for the graveyard shift, couldn't Lía have found someone better?* I'd never felt the need to physically shake an employee before. But I ignored her and headed back into the back office to finish up.

"Why do emails take forever?" I asked Furby, stretching. I wasn't sure how much time had passed, but it was well into the morning. I'd made a decent dent in the workload, but my rumbling stomach said it was time for breakfast. Furby yawned and stretched as well before sauntering over for a pat. "What a hard life you lead, sir?" Furby purred and rubbed my hand in agreement.

"I guess I'll go over to the bakery for a quick bite to eat. You stay right here." I pointed at the roly-poly cat, but he only blinked back, stretched, and flopped onto a pile of papers. I wasn't able to make it past the front desk, though, before I found Carlos's mother, Sara, yelling excitedly at the regular front-desk clerk, Miguel.

"Is there some kind of problem?" I asked, knowing full well there must be by the sound of things.

"No, nothing is wrong here." Sara clammed up.

That was suspicious. I glanced over at Miguel. He gave an impish smile and a wink. I relaxed. It must not be anything too serious then.

"Well, if you must know." Sara huffed. "I was trying to get some information from this young man." She pointed at Miguel. "I wanted to know what room your mother, Blanca, was staying in, so we could talk. I had no idea she knew *my* Luis." Sara's voice had a thin veneer of sweetness that disguised nothing.

I looked back at Miguel. He nodded. "Yes, among other things," he confirmed behind a smirk.

Sara glared at both of us, impatiently drumming her fingers on the desk. "So...?"

"Well, I..." My patented response towards guests didn't seem right when dealing with family and friends all staying for the same wedding. My thoughts raced trying to put something together that seemed credible. I wanted to avoid Blanca and Sara having direct contact as much as possible. Ana and Carlos deserved to have a peaceful ceremony with minimal drama. But just then a chipper, singing Blanca came swinging around the corner. *The best laid plans*, I thought with a sigh.

"Well, hello, Sasha was it?" Blanca greeted her newfound nemesis.

Sara opened her mouth to correct her, but Blanca continued on, uninterested. "Could you direct me to your son Carlitos' apartment? Luis still has my things in his car, and with all the fun of last night, I forgot to get them." Blanca laughed, which caused Sara to visibly tense even more.

"Of course, I would be thrilled to show you where my son's home is," Sara said through gritted teeth.

"Excellent," Blanca pressed on. "Please forgive me for not being more put together." She looked Sara over. "Well, I can see that you know how it is." Blanca laughed again.

Sara's face and body had become so rigid that I knew I needed to step in and try to mitigate any more problems.

I looked pointedly at Blanca. "Don't be so rude," and offered Sara an apologetic smile.

"Let's all try to get along for the sake of Ana and Carlos. The last thing we need around here is a crime scene." I laughed, but nobody joined in.

Claire, one of the vegan Youtubers, ran into the lobby out of breath, flushed, and staring vacantly. She raced over, clutching my hands so tightly it hurt. She tried to speak but could barely gasp anything out. "There was a uh– we found– Oh my God!" She put her hands over her face.

I helped her over to a chair, rubbing her trembling shoulders. "What is it?" I asked. "What's wrong? Is someone hurt?"

She shook her head, sobbing now. Claire didn't strike me as the publicly sobbing type. A lump formed in my throat. Something was seriously wrong.

"I was in the church with Father Tomás. He was showing me around. He speaks a tiny bit of English, and I had Google translate, so we could communicate, you know. The church was amazing."

"Yes?" I prompted trying to get her back on track. Obviously that wasn't the reason she'd entered hyperventilating.

"We– we uh found..." She gulped. "There was a dead body under one of the pews," she said.

CHAPTER FOUR

"What?" A collective gasp came out between Blanca, myself, and even Miguel, who understood enough English to piece together Claire's statements, leaving just Sara in the dark.

"What? Somebody tell me what happened," she demanded. "Is Carlos okay? What is it?"

I ignored her questions and kept focus on Claire. Trying not to tremble, I asked, "Who was it?"

Claire shook her head. "I'm not sure. I didn't get close. It was a woman, I think." She choked out another sob. "They were under a pew, so I couldn't see very well. Father Tomás knew her, I think. He was really upset. He said he would go get the police, and I didn't want to stay there. I didn't know what to do. I don't know where Jessica and Harriet are. We all split up to get footage of different locations. So I just came back here, and– Oh my God!"

"You did the right thing." I patted her shoulder.

"Somebody better tell me what's going on here." Sara yelled, angry that she didn't understand what was happening but even more furious at being ignored. No one responded to her demands, so she pushed past us and out the front door of the hotel. I couldn't help but be relieved to see her go.

Miguel offered Claire a cup of water. She gratefully accepted it, still shaking, but it had dulled substantially.

I heard my cell ringing back in the office. "Can you stay with Claire, please?" I asked Blanca.

Blanca nodded and took my place next to Claire, rubbing her shoulders.

I didn't want to leave Claire without anyone she could communicate with easily, and Blanca was the only other person I knew who spoke both English and Spanish fluently. "Don't leave her," I demanded.

"Of course not, what kind of monster do you think I am?" Blanca said.

I rushed back into the office to pick up the phone. It was Ana. "Finally," she said without greeting. "Did you hear what happened?"

"Kind of," I said. "Claire, one of the foreign Youtube girls, is here. She said that she and Father Tomás found a dead body under a pew in the church."

"I can't believe this. I feel like a selfish twit because it's bad enough that someone died, but the day before my wedding. It has to be postponed. I can't have my wedding in the middle of a crime scene." I heard Ana shudder over the phone. "I'm going straight to hell, I know, but I am sad she died. I really am. Don't get me wrong. I just–"

"Ana, hold on. Before you continue with your self-flagellation, who exactly was killed and what happened? Claire didn't know, so I really didn't get any other information."

Ana took a breath before continuing on. "It was Olga, the church secretary. Father Tomás called. We were on our way over to start decorating for tomorrow. He said it looked to him like she'd been hit over the head and shoved under a church pew, so no one would see it right away. I can't believe this. How could this happen the day before my wedding?"

"Why don't you come over to the hotel," I said. "I don't want to leave Claire alone right now, and we can talk it over. Everyone else is safe except poor Olga, and we can just take this one step at a time, okay?"

Ana sighed. "Okay, I'll be right over."

"Oh, and uh... could you bring something to eat? I'm starving."

"How can you eat at a time like this?" Ana asked.

"Me starving isn't going to do anyone any good," I said. "Oh, and try to bring something vegan for Claire."

"I'll do my best," Ana said.

Back in the lobby, Blanca still sat next to Claire. Both were silent. Furby rubbed Claire's leg with the side of his face, energetically purring, while Claire scratched him behind the ears, and Miguel sat at the front desk, awkwardly glancing around the lobby.

"Everything okay?" he whispered, pointing towards my phone that I still held in a vice grip.

Stepping closer to the desk, I kept my voice down. "Ana called. She said it was Olga that they found." I nodded in Claire's direction.

Miguel's eyebrows shot up. "Really? Who would want to hurt Olga? That church is her life. Maybe it was an accident."

"Maybe." I shrugged, remembering Olga's acid tongue at the rehearsal yesterday. It wasn't too much of a stretch that she'd probably pissed off her fair share of people over the years.

"Hey Claire," I said softly. I wasn't sure why we were all tip-toeing around and speaking in hushed voices. Claire might still be in a fragile state, but when exactly did it become a little ridiculous?

Blanca didn't have any qualms about hurting anyone's sensibilities and snapped out of the caring, mother-figure, as she always did. She stood abruptly and asked loudly. "So did you learn anything? Whose body was it?"

Everyone jumped, including Claire, but other than that, she didn't seem upset by the question.

"Ana called. Father Tomás warned her not to come over to decorate the church because of the uh.." I cleared my throat, "incident. Ana said it was the church secretary, Olga, who was found um... deceased."

"Oh my God!" Blanca gasped and crossed herself dramatically. "And imagine we were just talking to her last night. That's crazy. So was she stabbed, shot, bashed in the head, what happened?"

I recoiled at the vulgar questions and the morbid curiosity gleaming in Blanca's eyes. "Come on now. That's not appropriate. Olga was a person, not entertainment."

Claire, who seemed to have fully recovered now, chimed in. "Did you guys know her very well?"

"I really only met her last night at the wedding rehearsal for my friend Ana. But she did seem a little upset," I said.

Blanca snorted. "To put it mildly." She turned to Claire. "You know the kind of person who always has a massive pole shoved up their–"

"Hey!" I glared at Blanca before continuing. "Ana was going to bring some lunch. You're welcome to come over to the cottage," I told Claire. "It's just back there." I gestured towards the back door of the hotel. "Or if you'd rather just go back to your room and wait for your friends, I understand."

"No, that sounds great." Claire smiled. "I'm feeling much better, but it would still be nice not to be alone right now. I hope Jessica and Harriet are okay. I keep calling and texting them, but they don't answer. You don't think–"

"No, no, I'm sure they're fine." I waved my hand to illustrate how ridiculous that unfinished thought was, even though the exact same worry had occurred to me more than once, and the fact that Claire couldn't get ahold of them raised even more alarm bells. "But maybe we should... you know just in case–"

"Hold on. " Claire gestured at her phone. "Someone just texted me. It's Jessica." Claire smiled. "She found Harriet out by the winery. They didn't have any cell service, but they're on their way back now."

I tried not to sound as relieved as I felt. "That's excellent."

"Yeah," Claire bounded to her feet. "I'm awfully hungry."

"I'm glad I'm not the only one," I said, scooping up Furby and heading out the back door towards the cottage. I paused, remembering Blanca. I glanced back unsure if I should invite her or not. She was my mother after all. "Would you like to–" I started.

But she quickly shook her head. "I need to go over and see Luis. He has all my stuff."

"Yeah, yeah, of course, but you know you're always welcome," I said, not meaning it. I'm sure Blanca knew I wasn't being 100% sincere, but she seemed to appreciate the gesture anyway. She smiled, a little sadly, and I nodded before turning to leave.

Ana was already waiting for us at the cottage. "I brought tacos de canasta. They're potato." She held up the bag.

I had to heft Furby up onto my shoulder in order to unlock the front door. He complained angrily once inside, furiously bathing himself. Ana appeased him with a piece of taco. He looked up at her with pure adoration.

I quirked an eyebrow. "Miss I-don't-like-cats, huh?"

Ana smiled. "It's not that I don't like them, but Furby is so much smarter than all the other cats. Aren't you?" Ana scratched Furby at the base of his tail. He offered his adoring subject a squint of delight.

Claire was still standing awkwardly in the doorway, so I motioned her in. "This is Ana," I said, switching to English. "She's the one who was supposed to be getting married tomorrow and brought us some tacos. I'm pretty sure they're all potato inside, no meat or anything from animals. That's right, isn't it?" I asked Ana.

"What?" She glanced up mid-pet.

"Sorry," I said, shaking my head and switching back to Spanish. "They're all potato no meat, right?"

"Yep," she promised before heading over to the sink to wash her hands.

"Thanks," Claire's shyness from earlier this morning seemed to have returned. She looked down, and her voice was barely audible.

This was going to be one interesting lunch, I thought, translating between the semi-silent Claire and bubbly Ana who never shut up. I wondered how much I could get away with not translating for Claire without seeming rude.

I dug into the plate of tiny tacos, piling them on my plate. "Help yourself," I directed Claire.

Ana poured everyone guava water and golden silence ensued, broken only by Furby's intermittent taps as he went around to each person requesting his due.

"Oh, that was so good," Claire said, leaning back. "I didn't realize how hungry I was."

I nodded. "Stress and adrenaline do that. At first you're not hungry at all, and then you're ravenous, at least that's what happens to me."

Ana's phone buzzed. She had to wipe off her greasy fingers before grabbing it. "I'm so stupid!" she exclaimed, dramatically slapping her forehead.

"I'm sure you're not, but what is it?" I asked.

"I already called the florist and told them to hold the flowers until we know more, but Maritza is in the bakery now decorating the cake. She has a question about the icing, and... and... Oh no, I need to go talk to her."

"I can't believe no one told her what happened," I said. Normally the Santa Rita gossip mill was more efficient at dispensing information than any social media network could ever be.

"Well, you know how Maritza is when she's working. She probably didn't want to talk to anyone, and stupid me didn't... Oh geez, I got to go." Ana grabbed her jacket, gave Furby one last scratch behind the ears, and offered a "Sorry," to Claire in heavily accented English.

"Ana forgot about the cake for the wedding that was supposed to be tomorrow," I explained. "So she has to run over to the bakery and tell Maritza, the baker."

"But aren't you the owner of the bakery?" Claire asked.

I nodded. "It's not great that she forgot to tell Maritza, but it's not the end of the world either. Ana's part owner too, so technically she's Maritza's boss."

I was sure neither Ana nor Maritza had ever thought of their relationship in that way, though. Maritza ran the bakery with an iron fist and could be a little intimidating, but she was also incredibly talented, organized, and quite sweet once you got past her gruff exterior.

With her hunger satiated and in a calmer atmosphere, Claire began to relax and speak more. We moved over to the couch, and Furby, having a new set of hands to worship him, set about wooing his new subject with rubs and constant attention. Claire proved to be an easy mark. She eagerly rubbed and scratched Furby in return, allowing him to settle contentedly on her lap.

"I'm sorry about Furby. He can be a little demanding. Just push him off if he's too much, or if you don't want to be covered in cat hair." I could swear the cat opened his eyes just to scowl at me.

"Oh don't worry." Claire laughed. "I have two cats back home. A little cat hair doesn't bother me."

"Well, you're in the right place then. So are your cats vegan too, or how does that work? Sorry if that's a dumb question."

Claire shook her head. "No, not at all, they eat regular cat food. Cats can't really be healthy and vegan, but a lot of our subscribers don't agree with me on that." Claire laughed. "The vegans online can be a tough crowd."

It was odd to me how such a shy, self-conscious person as Claire could face the masses head-on, especially the vegan masses, which even I knew from limited experience could be quite enthusiastic with their opinions.

I shook my head. "I don't know how you do it, put yourself out there like that online. It must be hard to face all that criticism."

"It can be. It definitely was at first," Claire agreed. "But we started in high-school, Jessica and I. We just made different recipes, and we were so small that nobody really cared to criticize us. Also, we had absolutely no idea what kind of landmines we were stepping into, or I probably never would've done it in the first place. It was only in the last couple years that the channel blew up, and Harriet handles most of the behind the scenes stuff and all the mean comments too. So I don't really have to see them, especially the vile ones, and nothing much phases Harriet."

"I can see that," I agreed. "Harriet doesn't seem very connected to the world around her."

Claire nodded. "She works really hard, and she's not always the most tactful either. But she's been great for the channel. We hired her once it became too big for us to manage everything ourselves, and last year when Jessica was sick, Harriet was a lifesaver. There's no way we could've done it without her."

"Jessica was sick?" I asked.

Claire nodded. "She doesn't like to talk about it a lot, but last year she had ovarian cancer. She's in remission now, but it was pretty rough there for a while."

"That sounds awful. I can't imagine..." Claire began to shift nervously again, so I decided to change the subject. "How long have you and Jessica been friends?"

"Since middle-school. Jessica didn't have the easiest of childhoods, so she spent a lot of time at my house, and that's how the channel was born. Jessica always loved animals, got me into being vegan, and then we were bored and decided to film ourselves making recipes and laughing, mostly laughing. Our first videos are so cringey now." Claire smiled. "But they were so much fun. I keep thinking maybe someday it will be fun like that again, but once it's a business— well there's only so much fun to be had."

A sudden knock at the front door revealed Jessica and Harriet back from their excursion. Jessica entered first and ran towards Claire.

"Oh my God! I just heard. Are you okay? I can't believe–"

Claire waved away the concern. "I'm fine, really. I was rattled at first, but I'm okay now. I just feel bad for that poor lady."

I offered both Jessica and Harriet refreshments, but they refused, preferring to settle themselves on the couch next to Claire. I wanted to find Ana and see how she was holding up with all this unforeseen stress. I was sure she had a list a mile long that I could help her with.

I glanced around my tiny living room. I had three hotel guests, who I barely knew, occupying it when they already had perfectly good hotel rooms. *How could I tactfully get them to leave?* But Harriet broke into my thoughts.

Looking at me directly, she asked, "I guess we go over to the bakery now to film, right?"

"What?" I wasn't sure if she was asking for my permission or trying to order me around, but surely Claire wasn't interested in filming after what had happened today. Jessica and Claire both stopped speaking and appeared equally as confused as I was.

"Today?" Jessica asked. "I really don't think Claire–"

But Harriet tapped her phone. "We have a schedule and a limited amount of time here. In order to keep to it, we need to film today." She looked over at me. "Online we spoke about it, and you said your baker could demonstrate some of your vegan desserts, and you'd translate."

Yes, I'd agreed to that but not the day before my friend's

wedding right after a murder. "But today…" I bit my lip, trying to hide my irritation.

"Unless you'd prefer we ask around about the murder. Actually, that'd be a lot more interesting for the channel," Harriet said, considering it. "It's not really our brand, but hey it would really bring in the views. That's for sure." She shrugged her shoulders. "We also need a workspace. Do you have a conference room for guests, a place for us to work?"

A conference room? Couldn't they just use their hotel rooms? "Well, we have a multipurpose room. You can use a corner of that if you'd like. I'm not sure when the wedding will be, but that's the only time it won't be available."

"Harriet, I think it's too soon for that," Claire said, glancing nervously over at Jessica for guidance.

Jessica worried her lip, glancing between her two friends. "I don't know. It could be interesting, but we need more information first. After all, the police haven't even interviewed Claire yet. That is a good idea about the workspace, though, Harriet. Could I make smoothies there?"

"Smoothies?" What was this girl talking about? It wasn't a kitchen. "It's not exactly set up for–"

"Just green smoothies, I like to make them every day for health. I brought my own blender." Jessica smiled.

I sighed. "As long as you don't leave a mess or make them when most guests are sleeping, I guess it's okay."

"Your smoothies are disgusting," Harriet said. "She makes us drink them every day. It's awful."

"Well, neither of you have gotten cancer yet, have you?" Jessica asked, looking affronted at the criticism.

Claire ignored her friends' back and forth. "Talk to me?

Why would the police want to speak with me?" Her voice trembled.

Jessica shrugged. "They always want to talk to whoever it is that finds the body."

"But I don't think– Do you..." Claire looked towards me, her eyes large.

"I wouldn't worry about it. Even if they do talk to you, it will be pretty informal. They'll just want the facts of what you saw," I said. Claire nodded, but she didn't look convinced.

"So should we go over to the bakery now?" Harriet asked again.

I nodded. The last thing the hotel needed was bad publicity. "Let me just send a quick text," I said. I didn't want Ana to think I'd abandoned her the day before her *maybe* wedding. I still didn't know if she was going to go through with the party or transfer the venue for the ceremony or postpone everything altogether.

But there was already a message waiting from Ana. Stay away from Maritza. It read. She's in a foul mood. You've been warned.

I turned towards Harriet. "So you don't speak any Spanish at all?" I asked.

Harriet shook her head.

"Excellent," I said, brightly.

"Why is that excellent?" Harriet asked, but I ignored her question.

Thank God for language barriers, I thought. The less these girls understood what Maritza was about to say, the better.

CHAPTER FIVE

As we approached the back of the bakery, I could hear Maritza long before I could see her.

Even Claire asked. "Who is that yelling?"

"That's Maritza," I said between clenched teeth. It's not that I was afraid of her or that Maritza would be rude to me. I was her boss, and I'd gained her respect over the past few months. But she was an imposing character, and even though I knew I could get her to do the segment, she wouldn't be happy, and I didn't feel right asking her to put her face on, from what Claire had said, a rather large online platform if she didn't want to.

You're talking about pastry, not politics, I told myself. *Chill out, and if anyone says anything out of line, pull the plug.* But the whole thing felt rushed and awkward. Why had I ever agreed to do this?

By the time we were inside, Maritza's tirade had abated, and she even smiled when she saw me, although it turned into a quizzical squint when she spotted the three guests next to me.

"Give me one moment, would you?" I said to the three Youtubers and walked quickly towards Maritza before they could respond or follow.

I motioned Maritza over to the side, away from any potential eavesdroppers. Thankfully, she followed without any protests. "Those are the vegan Youtubers, right?" she asked.

I nodded, not sure where to start but decided that the best course of action was just to explain everything plainly. "That dour looking girl on her phone over there wants to either do a baking segment or some kind of murder tell-all for their Youtube channel. I know this has been a horrible day, but please

Maritza, if you could just show how to make one of our vegan desserts for a segment on their channel. I'll translate everything. You would be a lifesaver."

"Sure," Maritza shrugged.

"What?" I was shocked at how pleasant she sounded. "But you were just yelling, and Ana said you were really angry." I was saying too much, so I stopped.

"Yeah, but it's not your fault. It looks like your day's been rougher than mine anyway. Why would Ana say that? I wasn't happy about being told at the last minute not to do a wedding cake, especially when everyone else seemed to know, but it's not like I jumped down her throat or anything."

I raised an eyebrow. "Really?"

"Well, maybe at first, but that was before Ana told me about the murder. She just said she didn't need the cake but didn't explain why. I thought it was some flakey reason, but once I knew what happened…" Maritza shrugged her shoulders.

"Great, well uh.. I really don't know anything about their channel except that they're vegan, and I think it's mostly cooking. But are you okay with being on it? If you're not, that's totally fine. I don't want you to feel–"

Maritza held up her hand. "As long as I'm just baking, I really don't care what's on their channel. I don't think baking a cake with someone means I endorse everything they've ever said." She laughed, but I shook my head.

"Maritza, Maritza, Maritza, have you ever *been* on the internet?"

"You're so dramatic," Maritza said. "You really think I care what people think about me." She laughed drily. "That is not one of my burdens in life."

"Okay, okay, let's get this thing over with then." I motioned the Youtubers over, but it was just Claire and Jessica.

"Harriet went to grab the equipment," Jessica explained, flipping her shiny blonde hair behind one shoulder.

Of course they needed equipment. Why hadn't I thought of that before? Obviously a large Youtube channel like theirs wouldn't record on a phone. "So why was Harriet so eager to get us all out here, if she wasn't even ready yet?" I asked, feeling slightly annoyed.

"Well, we need time to go over the segment," Jessica said. "I'll be doing it with you. After Claire's stressful day, I think it would be best. Don't you?" I'm not sure who Jessica was asking, but she didn't wait for a response from anyone. Instead she addressed Maritza. "*Yo quiero* uh *make-o uno cake-o uh.. con–*"

Maritza looked at me, ignoring Jessica, and rolled her eyes. "What kind of language was that supposed to be?" she asked.

"I'm not sure," I admitted. Hopefully, Jessica's passive Spanish skills were just as awful as her speaking ones, or she was going to get offended by Maritza real fast.

Switching to English, I turned to Jessica. "How about you just speak in English, and I'll translate for Maritza. That will probably speed things up a bit."

Jessica shrugged. "That's fine."

After over 20 minutes of translating between the two, Jessica had finally paused to touch-up her makeup. My brain felt muddled, and I could tell Maritza's nerves were starting to wear thin too.

"Where is that other girl with the stupid camera?" Maritza asked.

When I didn't immediately translate, Jessica glanced up from her compact. "What? What was that she asked?" looking at me for clarification.

"Uh, Maritza was just wondering when we might be getting started," I said.

"I'm sure any moment now. Actually, why don't I go look for Harriet." Claire stood up. She might not be bilingual, but she could read the emotional language of the room.

Jessica, on the other-hand, seemed like her social skills were just as poor as her Spanish ones, or maybe she just didn't care. "Oh, don't worry about it, Claire. That's what we pay Harriet for."

"But what about Maritza I'm sure she–" Claire started to say.

But Jessica cut in. "And that's what she's paid to do, wait and cook. Plus, I'm sure this is a thrill for her." She turned back to studying her face in the mirror.

"What did she just say?" Maritza asked. She knew a little English, but after working with the public for so long had become completely fluent in complaintese, so there was no point in trying to fool her.

"Well, Jessica was being a little bit rude honestly, but hopefully this thing gets underway soon," I said, walking the fine line between honesty and glossing over the specifics to avoid conflict.

Jessica looked up, probably at the sound of her name, and squinted quizzically. Now she knew how Maritza had felt. I smiled innocently and was just about ready to postpone this whole thing when Harriet entered hauling several pieces of equipment with her.

"Alright, let's hurry up and get this thing started," Harriet demanded, as though she were the one who'd been kept waiting. I was starting to wish that I didn't understand English either. Right now it would've made my life a whole lot easier.

After what felt like hours of setting the lighting up, we were finally ready to go, according to Harriet.

"How do I look?" Maritza asked.

"Oh, I thought you weren't burdened by the opinions of others," I said.

"Touché, so how do I look?"

"Beautiful, as always." I sighed. It was true, even in a chef's smock, Maritza's olive skin contrasted with her gray green eyes, and her shiny black hair was swept up into an intricate braid. I never understood how people could braid their own hair like that.

"Do I have anything on my teeth or face?" I asked Maritza.

She laughed. "You look fine, better than fine actually." She wiggled her eyebrows.

"Ha-ha, very funny." I snorted. "I'm keeping the bar low over here. I'm just the translator after all. You're the main attraction."

"I'm pretty sure that's Jessica," Maritza pointed out, and it was true. Not only was it her channel, but Jessica had the kind of features and body-type that women paid thousands of dollars to get. She could command any room or camera shoot she wanted, the kind of girl who would've made my life miserable in high-school.

It was hard to believe just looking at her that she'd been on death's door just last year. That could be why Claire was so deferential and treated her with kid gloves, I thought, and

43

immediately felt guilty for my attitude. Who knew what Jessica had been through? The least I could do was to have a little patience with her.

Maritza locked the bakery door to keep any potential patrons from ruining the take. "And stay quiet," she barked at Lupe and Rosa, the two other bakery employees. They pretended to be busy cleaning the bakery shelves, but were obviously watching the spectacle at hand, and who could blame them?

"I don't want to do this stupid thing 500 times if I can help it, but God knows we probably will with these morons in charge." Maritza pointed at Jessica as she spoke.

"Everything okay?" Claire asked, glancing between Maritza and Jessica nervously.

"You bet!" I said. "Maritza is just so excited to get started." Maritza snorted, exposing my translation for the lie it was.

"Chill out," I whispered to Maritza. "We're almost done. Just hold it together for a little longer, okay?"

"I'll try. I'm just not the most patient person, and these people are getting on my last nerve," Maritza said.

"Well, that's no newsflash." I gave her arm a playful jab, and Maritza actually smiled.

The video started with Jessica recounting their trip to Santa Rita so far, minus the murder, which is always good. But it was awkward just standing there next to her while she spoke for minutes on end. Did Maritza and I really have to be here for this? Was the camera even on us right now? I couldn't tell since Harriet was behind it and had given zero direction to either Maritza or myself.

"Okay, so now we're here with Maritza, the head baker at Hotel Leticia's bakery with some absolutely delicious vegan desserts. The owner, Natalia, will be translating for us. So what will Maritza be showing us how to make today?" Jessica asked. Her bouncy tone hid all of the earlier sharpness.

"A strawberry, chocolate cake," Maritza answered, not needing the simple translation.

The demonstration continued. Once Maritza started baking, her previous frustrations seemed to dissipate. The only difficulty was speaking quickly enough in order to translate everything. I'd never had to switch back and forth between languages before for such a long period, and it was trickier than I thought to remember who to repeat what to, especially in front of the camera, but everything was going pretty smoothly, I thought, giving myself a metaphorical pat on the back.

"So are you and the baker vegans too?" Jessica asked.

I translated for Maritza, even though the question had been directed at me too. I decided to ignore that part.

"No," Maritza answered plainly.

"So you enjoy murder and torture, but you just added the vegan dishes to make a profit. Is that it?" There was a glint in Jessica's eye.

"What?" Jessica's change in tone caught me off guard.

Claire appeared shocked as well. She sat there slack-jawed, but Harriet just continued filming, so I had to keep my cool.

"What did she just say?" Maritza asked. I translated for her.

"What the–" Maritza started, but gathered herself. "Look, I'm a baker, so I'm showing you how to bake. We try to make food for everyone. It doesn't matter what a baker eats but what they bake. If you want to talk about philosophy, you can go over to the university and debate it there. Got it?"

I had just started to translate Maritza's statements when a

loud pounding started on the front door of the bakery.

"What now?" Maritza demanded, ignoring the camera and everyone else around her.

"Why don't you stop rolling, Hare." Claire directed Harriet, who thankfully listened without complaint.

Maritza sent Rosa to go open the door. "Send whoever it is away. Stupid people can't read a sign."

But moments later Rosa returned followed by Santiago, Santa Rita's very own, very incompetent acting police chief.

"Sorry to bother you," Santiago said, not looking sorry in the slightest. "I'm here to speak to a..." He looked down at his pad of paper. "A Miss Claire Anderson about the body that was discovered this morning."

Claire blanched at the sound of her name. "What does he want?" she asked.

"He says he wants to talk to you about the body," I said.

"What? What does he want to know? Do I need a lawyer?" Claire asked, tears gathering in her eyes.

"I'm not sure," I answered honestly. "I really hope not."

Santiago motioned for us to follow him. "You won't mind translating, will you?" he asked me.

"Of course not," I agreed. "We can use the hotel office if you'd like."

"That would be just fine," Santiago said.

"Claire doesn't need any type of attorney, does she?" I asked.

"Oh, I don't think that will be necessary." Santiago smiled in such a way that made me immediately reach into my pocket to text Carlos.

CHAPTER SIX

Carlos was not only Ana's fiancé but also a lawyer. We needed to buy some time. Santiago was not above lying, and there was no way Claire and I were going into that room alone with Santiago without some legal guidance.

"If you'll excuse me, I need to use the ladies' room." I gave Claire a pointed look hoping she'd understand.

Thankfully, she did. "Me too, I guess it was all that coffee." She smiled.

"Make yourself comfortable in the office. If there's anything you need, just ask Miguel at the front desk, and we'll be right there." I smiled at Santiago but didn't give him an opportunity to argue and ducked into the employee lounge with Claire. After waiting a beat, I slid the lock closed after us.

"What's wrong?" Claire's shiny eyes had grown even larger than before.

I looked down at the phone I still held clenched in my right hand. Carlos's message was simple in all caps. STALL! I'M ON MY WAY. I sighed. There was only so long we could stay here without angering Santiago. Maybe he did just want to get a statement from Claire, and if that was the case, I had no intention of getting on his bad side unnecessarily.

But with Carlos on the way, we had someone to not only advise Claire but to also make sure that Santiago minded his p's and q's. Santiago knew that Carlos had friends in high places, and Santiago was lazy more than anything else. The last thing he'd want was to go toe to toe against Carlos and be humiliated once again, or at least that's what I was banking on. I sent a quick text to Nico as well. He wasn't a lawyer, but it would be nice to have his support. Plus, he and Santiago had gone to school together, and it would be nice to have him to mediate just in case.

"I'm just trying to buy us some time," I said as lightly as possible. "You remember my friend Ana? Well, her fiancé is a lawyer, and I just think it would be best to have someone with us who knows the law, but you know police can be touchy about that kind of thing, so…"

Claire nodded. "But you don't think he wants any more than my statement, do you? After all, we just got to town yesterday, and I don't know anyone, much less have a reason to kill them."

I nodded. "I think it's more likely he just wants a statement, but better safe than sorry, right? Carlos is on his way now. He lives just down the road, so maybe I'm being a bit dramatic, but it can't hurt." I shrugged. Claire nodded.

I heard voices out by the lobby, and at the sound of my phone glanced down at Carlos's new text.

"Thank God." I breathed. "He's here."

But in the lobby of the hotel not only had Carlos arrived but Ana, Blanca, and his dad Luis were also with him. Carlos smiled at me apologetically.

"Wow, I wasn't expecting a whole caravan of people." I looked at Blanca, but she ignored my not so subtle barb.

"Sorry, I knew time was of the essence, and my dad and Blanca both wanted to come. Ana and I tried, but we just couldn't shake them," Carlos whispered. He looked over at Ana for confirmation who nodded enthusiastically.

"It's okay. I'm just glad you could come at such short notice. Santiago's in the hotel office."

"Let's go. I'd be shocked if Santiago really wants anything more than a simple statement." Carlos smiled.

I nodded and explained the plan to Claire. "The police are going to ask some simple questions about what happened. Carlos is just here to make sure everything is kosher. If he sees any problems with the questions, he'll interrupt, and if you have any questions about anything that's said or want any clarification, just ask."

Claire nodded. She looked remarkably calm compared to earlier. Santiago was already seated behind the large desk. All my piles of chaotic organization had been swept to the side. I had to bite my lip to hide the irritation.

"Hello, Santi," Carlos extended his hand. Santiago looked surprised and irritated at the attorney's presence but shook his hand, nonetheless. Carlos continued. "Miss Anderson isn't familiar with Mexican law, so she said she'd be more comfortable if I were present, and I knew you wouldn't mind. This is just a routine statement after all." Carlos's voice didn't even hold a tinge of the animosity that I felt emanating from Santiago.

Santiago offered a tight-lipped smile. "Of course." He nodded towards Claire. "But as you said yourself, Carlos, this really is just a routine statement, and I don't think you'll be needed for anything."

"Well, that's excellent, makes my job a whole lot easier," Carlos said brightly and settled himself into one of the straight-backed chairs opposite the desk.

"I'm sure you will translate everything properly." Santiago looked at me. "But just to make sure there's no discrepancy and for the record, I will record everything. Please speak your translation loud enough for the recorder to pick it up," Santiago said, and when I had finished translating for Claire, I nodded assent.

"I'll be making a second recording too," Carlos chimed in, pointing to his phone. "Two are better than one, and in case yours gets lost, we can rely on mine." Carlos smiled innocently at Santiago who just scowled and ignored Carlos's comment.

"Well, let's get started then," Santiago said, pressing the play button on his ancient-looking recording device.

Claire gave her statement about what she had found that morning with Father Tomás, indicating that she wasn't certain who the woman was or what exactly had happened to her.

"I just know that there was a lot of blood, and it was so horrible. I ran back to the hotel right after," Claire said and looked down. She was shaking again, so I placed my hand on hers.

Even Santiago seemed to feel compassion. "Well, thank you for your time Miss uh…" He glanced at his paper but gave up. "I don't think anything more will be necessary at this time." He switched off the recorder, and Carlos followed suit.

If this guy can't even remember a name, how is he going to find an actual murderer?

"Well, thank you for your time and your statement. I know this was a very horrible experience for you, and I'm sorry you had to be a witness to an awful accident such as this." Santiago finished and stood to leave.

My translation caught in my throat, but Claire was staring at me waiting for me to finish, so I did. I turned to Santiago before he could leave.

"What do you mean, accident? Surely you don't–"

"Nothing is official yet," Santiago clarified. "But given the statements of both witnesses, Olga seems to have been a victim of a terrible fall on a slippery floor, after which she rolled under the pew. It's very tragic, but no one is at fault, and we'll be able to close this case and allow her family to grieve properly. Excuse me." Santiago moved towards the door, but the glint in his eyes gave away the perverse pleasure he took in the power he had to shock.

"But Santiago, you know you're not supposed–" Carlos tried to interrupt.

"I know, I know. It's nothing official, but I'm just letting you know because I saw how upset the witness was and wanted to put her mind at ease."

I realized I hadn't been translating, and Claire's confused face gave me a pang of guilt. I wasn't the lawyer, Carlos was. I should let him do his job and get to mine. I finished translating as much as I could remember for Claire. Her surprised face echoed my own.

Carlos didn't respond. He appeared deep in thought, thanked Santiago, handshakes went all around, and Santiago left through the front door, a slight hop in his step, pleased with the mayhem and gossip he'd left in his wake, and the fact that this bombshell would require him to do zero work, apart from filling out a few more forms and reports, was probably just the icing on the cake. The bile rose in my throat. I'd never wanted to smack someone's smug face more than I did right then.

Nico arrived breathless. "Everything okay?" he asked. "I came as soon as I could."

I nodded woodenly, still shocked at what had just transpired. Ana's brow creased in concern. "Are you sure? You guys don't look all right."

I turned to Carlos. "I have no idea what just happened in there."

Carlos shrugged. "Santiago took the statement and

revealed that he is going to label it an accident."

"An accident! Olga's head was bashed in. How is that an accident?" Ana was shouting so loudly even Carlos looked uncomfortable. "Carlos, isn't there anything you can do?" she asked.

"I'm not sure yet, but I'll look into it," he promised. "Let's focus on the wedding first," trying to pacify his bride-to-be, without luck.

"Don't focus on it?" Ana shrieked. "How can we have a wedding if there's another murderer running loose around town? Don't you have a heart?"

Carlos looked stunned and hurt by Ana's accusations. I decided to step in. "Ana, let's all try to calm down," I said. "Carlos did his best in there, and I'm sure if there's anything in his power to do to get justice for Olga, he will. He's no coward."

Ana visibly began to calm. "You're right. I'm sorry." She reached over to hug Carlos.

Nico stepped towards me and put his arm across my back. His rhythmic rubbing helped to calm my own nerves. I leaned into him.

"Well, I think I'm going to go lie down," Claire said awkwardly, interrupting the brief silence. "I woke up pretty early today, and after everything, I'm just bushed."

I was relieved. I liked Claire, but it was difficult having a grown adult I barely knew and had needed to babysit all day. It would be nice when this whole wedding and vegan Youtuber week was over.

"Maybe it really was an accident." Blanca shrugged. I'd almost forgotten she was there. She'd been so uncharacteristically quiet.

"What?" I was annoyed at her inserting herself into something she knew nothing about.

"Well, you don't know. You're not a doctor, none of us are. None of us really knew or liked Olga. I think we should just enjoy our visit, and Ana you should have your wedding. There's no reason to sit around angry and scared because someone had an accident in the church. If anything, we should learn that life is short and have some fun while it lasts. I know I am. I'm not going to sit around pretending to care about someone I didn't even like." Blanca laughed, but no one joined in.

"Well, I'm not surprised to hear something like that from *you*," I practically spat before I'd realized what had come out of my mouth.

"And what does that mean exactly?" Blanca put her hands on her hips at the accusation.

I wished I could take it back. It wasn't worth it, but I couldn't. I continued on like a train you see coming down the tracks but can't stop in time. "Just because you didn't like Olga, you don't think she's worth anything, and you think everyone is just as shallow as you are. That's not surprising, though, because you didn't even think your own mother was worth visiting or even coming to her funeral." Tears gathered in my eyes. I blinked them away. I knew I'd been angry about my mother's refusal to attend grandma's funeral, but I hadn't realized it had been this intense until now.

"Funerals are for the living, not the dead. She didn't even know if I came or not. Plus, what's the point? It's not like she left me anything. You got it all. You were the daughter she'd always wanted. She wouldn't have wanted me to come anyway, so what did it matter if I enjoyed myself instead of calling off my vacation midway through? How would that have helped anybody?" Blanca flipped her hair.

In the past I would've continued to argue, and we could've gone back and forth for hours, upping and upping the ante until one or both of us cried, but glancing around the lobby– my lobby, I knew it wasn't worth it anymore. She'd never see anything wrong with her behavior, her selfishness on display 24/7, and probably never would. So instead I gave a tight-lipped smile and ignored her barrage of lies.

"I guess we all have our point of view. Let's not let this get out of hand. I need to go feed my cat and have something to eat. Are you guys hungry?" I left the question open-ended, glancing at everyone, but mostly Nico, Ana, and Carlos, praying that Blanca didn't want to come over. Thankfully, my prayers were answered. Both Blanca and Luis begged off the invitation.

Luis yawned. "I'd love to, but I have a pile of work I need to get to, but Carlos you stay out as late as you want. Don't let me get in the way of your fun. I'll just hang out back at the apartment."

"I need to get my beauty sleep. Maybe we can do something tomorrow, a mother-daughter outing," Blanca said. Her edge had been replaced with a saccharine sweetness that wasn't much better than the daggers of outrage she loved to throw, but I didn't care.

But Nico, Ana, and Carlos agreed, so we headed back. I needed to know from Carlos what recourse we had, if any, to get this case back on track towards justice.

CHAPTER SEVEN

"So what can be done?" Ana asked once we were all seated around my small kitchen table.

Carlos shrugged. "I'm not really sure. Maybe we can make some noise to get more national attention, but that takes time, which cases like these don't have, and seeing as we are not family or related to the deceased in any way." He shrugged again.

"Let me go check on the pizza. I can't think on an empty stomach," Ana said, heading outside. "Nico, did you tell them to bring it to the lobby or the cottage?" she asked.

"The cottage of course," he said.

"Well, I hope so, but I'll check anyway." Ana looked doubtful. "Because if they take it to the lobby, we'll never see a single slice."

I turned to Carlos. "Do you think it could have actually been an accident? Maybe Claire was mistaken. She was pretty shaken after all." *Maybe we were getting too far ahead of ourselves? Accidents did happen after all, even strange ones.*

Carlos nodded. "It's very possible. Claire isn't a medical authority, and I do know that head wounds can bleed an awful lot, which could give the appearance of a severe blow to the head.

Nico patted my shoulder. "I know you and Ana love playing amateur detectives, but I really think you should leave this one alone, especially with the wedding. That's enough for everyone to handle, and unless Olga's family needs help, maybe just let it lie.

Before I could respond, Ana entered piled with pizzas and

breadsticks. "Nico, did you order a large pizza per person?" she asked, her face and voice obscured by the pile of boxes.

Nico grinned and rose to help his sister with the unwieldy load. "Never can have too much pizza. It's even better the next day," he said.

After a couple slices, I decided to turn the conversation towards a less gruesome topic. "So, Ana, what are you going to do about the wedding?" I'd been hoping she'd bring it up on her own, but she hadn't even alluded to it yet.

"I'm not sure. Father Tomás said I should come by the church tomorrow to discuss it, but I really don't know what to tell him."

"Well, I'm happy to go with you."

Ana smiled broadly. "That would be excellent, and it gives Carlos more time to spend with his mother, which reminds me; please talk to her. Sara asked me three times when you're going to spend time with her and not just your dad."

Carlos nodded. "I will."

"So are you planning on postponing the wedding?" I pressed Ana, who still hadn't given an answer.

"Well, it gives me the heebie-jeebies that Olga just died there for whatever reason, and everyone's going to be talking about it. I don't know."

"Ana, it's a really old church. When was it built, 17-something? I'm sure plenty of people died there. Who knows what horrible things happened in that building during the inquisition and colonialism or the revolution."

"Are you trying to make me feel better? Because it's not working?" Ana narrowed her eyes at me.

I laughed. "I'm not trying to make you feel anything. I'm

just giving you the truth. It's a really old building with a lot of history, which makes it interesting and beautiful, but a lot of history– most of history isn't good. That doesn't take anything away from your day, though. Everyone is going to be there for you."

Carlos nodded. "I agree with Natalia. The day is for us. We could also talk to Father Tomás about having it outside?"

Ana shook her head and laughed. "In Santa Rita even Father Tomás wouldn't agree to have the ceremony outside. Can you imagine the scandal? People would be up in arms. But you're right. We should just go forward. What's the use in waiting now?"

I nodded, glad that Ana had finally seen reason. "So tomorrow we'll meet with Father Tomás and get the whole thing rescheduled then, excellent!"

I couldn't help but show my relief. It would also give me the chance to ask the priest more questions about Olga's body and what kind of investigation had been done. Father Tomás was no doctor either, but he'd probably seen his share of dead bodies in the course of giving last rites and visiting grieving families. Maybe he could put the whole murder investigation to rest while we were at it, at least I hoped so.

Ana and Carlos took advantage of their free evening, leaving Nico and I alone, finally, except for Furby. The black and white cat took the opportunity to jump on my lap and stare Nico down when he tried to sit on the couch next to me.

"It looks like I have some competition," Nico said, reaching over to scratch Furby, who accepted the attention but continued to glare.

"He's a little protective," I agreed. "He wants to be the only man in my life. Do you really think it could have been an accident?" I asked.

"What accident?" he asked. "Oh Olga, well we really don't know, do we? And even if we do, there's not a lot you can do about it, unless you could get the person to confess outright or something," Nico said before turning red. "Not that you should do that. Please promise me that you and Ana aren't going to go snooping around trying to find a murderer who may or may not exist. It's dangerous. If Olga's family isn't concerned, why should you be?"

"It just happened. We don't know that they won't pursue more answers. Plus, Olga's family didn't speak to Claire right after she saw the body. I did, and I don't think it was an accident."

I knew it could be a long shot, and maybe Nico was right. But why would Olga have just suddenly fallen down for no reason in a church she'd worked at for years? And the injuries didn't match a common fall.

Nico leaned in. "Well, I won't ask you to stop thinking about it, because I know you can't. But can you at least wait until you talk to Father Tomás tomorrow? Maybe he can clarify things. After all, how well do you know Claire? Plus, when people are stressed, they don't always remember details well."

I nodded. "I think I can do that."

"Good, and we can enjoy our time alone for the first time in ages," he said, leaning in for a kiss.

The next morning Ana arrived bright and early to walk over to the church together. "I want to miss any lookie-loos in the sanctuary," she explained.

I agreed. Olga had been a fixture of Santa Rita's namesake church, which was the literal center of the community, and everyone would have their own theory and ideas about what had happened.

"Okay, but let's go out the back way," I told her. "We don't need to run into Blanca or Sara. They'll slow us down and may even want to come along."

Ana reluctantly agreed. Normally, we passed through the bakery on our way to any errand. I knew Ana was looking forward to the fortification of a nice pastry, but it was also the most likely place to find Blanca, Sara, or the vegan Youtubers, who probably wanted to finish their baking segment, and any one of those people could derail our plans.

We ambled down the main, cobbled street past the many closed shops and a few vendors selling atole and tamales. Ana and I crossed the main square overflowing with manicured trees, bushes, and flowers, birds chattering overhead. Older women crowded the benches, eager to have their morning atole and gossip session with friends before heading out to purchase fresh bread and produce for the day. The main municipal building sat next to the church. We followed the walkway lined with ornate wooden doors on one side and arches leading back out onto the square on the other. The path ended right outside the back entrance of the church. This was where we'd hopefully find Father Tomás and avoid any gawkers idling around the main sanctuary pretending to be zealous parishioners.

Ana tentatively knocked, and when no one answered, knocked a little stronger. "I really hope we don't have to go around front," she said, echoing my own thoughts. But thankfully the door was pulled open a crack, barely revealing a face and then was opened wider, but instead of easy-going Father Tomás, we were greeted by a surly Father Francisco.

"Can I help you?" he asked, not sounding as if he wanted to help anyone for any reason, least of all us.

"Yes, my name is Ana Gallardo. I was supposed to get married here today by Father Tomás, but after yesterday's events, it didn't seem uh, uh..." Ana was floundering, and Father Francisco didn't move a muscle to assist the situation, so I decided to step in.

"Ana was supposed to meet with Father Tomás. Do you know if he's available?" I asked.

The priest's eyes narrowed further, making him look even more like a human toad without a neck. "No, he's not, but you can come in and wait for him, if you'd like." Father Francisco still didn't move and made it evident that *he* wouldn't like us to come in at all.

But we had every right to be here, especially after the arm and leg the church was charging to use the sanctuary. It was robbery, as far as I was concerned, in this tiny, religious town of predominantly working-class residents to charge so much just to use the sanctuary. The least that this cranky priest could do was let Ana sit down and wait for her meeting with Father Tomás.

"Thank you. That's so kind," I said, pushing towards the door, forcing Father Francisco to take a step back with a deep sigh.

"If you must," he acquiesced.

The back area of the church consisted of a few offices and a miniscule waiting room with wobbly, mismatched furniture that looked like donations from the 1980's. Father Francisco gestured towards the waiting area and, without a word, closed and bolted his own office door.

"Well, wasn't that a Christ-like greeting," I said loud enough for Father Francisco to overhear.

"Shhh," Ana said, looking horrified.

She, like a lot of the residents in Santa Rita, were way too willing to kowtow to Father Francisco. It's true he was a man of the cloth, and he'd been in Santa Rita for forever. He'd been the only priest in town when I was kid, but it was also well-known that his cleaning lady, Silvia, was also his longtime mistress, while he looked down his nose at everyone else for any minor sin. I remembered one Friday during lent he had caught my grandma buying beef for the next day and started to lay into her, but she'd had none of it.

"And who will be cooking your fish tonight? Silvia, I suppose. I know Silvia is an excellent cook, and from what I hear she does so many things excellently for you, Father, doesn't she?" The priest had grown red at the insult, and my grandmother had walked away, her head held high. She never cared about what anyone did in their private lives, but at any whiff of hypocrisy, she could be savage.

After that Father Francisco had had a particular hatred for my grandmother, so much so, that she had made anyone who would listen promise that Father Francisco wouldn't say her funeral mass and that she'd rather not have any at all than to let that hypocrite speak. "Not even over my dead body," she always said. I smiled remembering her feistiness. Maybe I'd picked up more from her than I'd realized, or perhaps it was just lack of sleep that had done it.

Ana glanced at her phone. "Father Tomás said he's on the way," she said, flashing me the screen.

I nodded. "Thank God, this office gives me the creeps."

"Really? Why? Oh, you don't think this church is bad luck now, do you?" Ana asked.

Why had I opened my big mouth? "Not like that." I tried to backtrack. "There's no such thing as bad luck, and like I said, I'm sure Olga's death isn't the first bad thing that's happened in this church or any other old building. That's what gives them character."

"I guess you're right," Ana said. "After all, the important thing is that Carlos and I get married, right?"

"Of course," I said, nodding enthusiastically.

Father Tomás breezed in, a thermos of coffee in one hand, keys in the other. "Sorry to keep you waiting." He unlocked a small office door next to the one Father Francisco had entered. "Please come in." He smiled and stood to the side ushering us in.

His office held a small desk, several chairs, and a bookcase. The walls themselves were completely covered with every type of crucifix or holy picture imaginable, crowding out any bare space of wall. I guess not surprising for a priest, but it still took me off guard as I stared around the room for several moments trying to take it all in.

"I'm so thankful that you were able to take time out of your schedule to come down and speak with me today, Ana. Please let me extend my deepest apologies for the unforeseen circumstances yesterday. I know today was supposed to be your wedding day, and losing Olga the way we did has broken everyone's heart. She was such an intricate part of the church. We're lost without her, and for you to lose your wedding day that you've been planning so long is a particularly hard blow. You've been very gracious about it. Thank you for that."

Father Tomás looked sincerely into Ana's eyes, and the way his long brown bangs fell over his deep green eyes made him look more like a movie star than a priest. If Father Tomás ever wanted to leave the clergy and pursue more worldly goals, he'd be able to have any woman he wanted, or if he walked the Father Francisco path, he could do both. But Father Tomás's sincerity made that course seem highly unlikely.

"I wasn't sure what to do about the ceremony," Ana said. "I don't want to be disrespectful, but we also have all these out of town guests, so I'd like to reschedule for the next available date." Ana's words came out all in a rush.

"I know it must be difficult for you. Since we don't have

Olga anymore, everything is in a bit of chaos. Is there a specific day you'd prefer?"

Ana shook her head. "Everyone is already in town, so the sooner the better."

"Yes, of course. I'll check with Silvia and have her get back to you with the soonest date."

My ears perked up. "Silvia? Do you mean Father Francisco's Silvia?"

At least Father Tomás had the decency to blush. "Well, she has worked with Father Francisco for many years, yes, and she's familiar with the goings-on in the church."

"I'll bet she is," I said before biting back the rest of my retort. I needed to find out more information from Father Tomás before we were quickly escorted out of his office, and I lost my chance.

"I'm sorry. I don't mean to be disrespectful. It's just Olga was everything here. I don't think anyone can replace her, especially so soon and suddenly. Nothing will be like it was." I shook my head mournfully, and while there were some dramatics to my answer, it was also true. For whatever Olga was or wasn't, she had been extremely organized and ran the church like a machine, at least that's what everyone had told me.

Father Tomás nodded knowingly. "I didn't realize that you'd known Olga so well." I felt a twinge of guilt at his assumption but didn't correct him.

"She will be dearly missed. She was never afraid to share her opinions, but I respected her a great deal," he said. The slight smile alluded to disagreements I'm sure he'd had with Olga, but his care seemed genuine.

"Do you really think it was an accident, Father?" I asked in a stage whisper, watching his face intently for any leaked emotions.

Father Tomás swallowed. "I'm not sure. It was very unpleasant to come across."

Isn't that the understatement of the century, I thought. I really needed this priest to be more forthright if I was going to glean anything from the conversation.

"Claire, one of my guests who was with you at the time, was quite shook by it for hours. She said there was blood everywhere and didn't see how it could've been an accident," I said.

"There was a lot of blood," Father Tomás agreed. "And I don't know how someone can fall that hard and then roll under a pew in that way, but I'm a priest, not a physicist or a detective or any kind of medical professional." He looked me square in the eye. "So I think I'll leave those speculations to them."

What a political answer. "Well, we also have the brains God gave us, I guess, and we're supposed to use them. I'm not planning on stepping on any toes, but if something did happen to Olga, don't you think she deserves justice?" It was my turn to look Father Tomás square in the eye.

"Maybe you're right," he said to my surprise. "Perhaps I have been too placid in my response, but I really don't have any more information. It was obvious she'd already passed. The body was under the pew and difficult to see. We only noticed it because of the puddle of blood." He shuddered.

"Thank you, Father. I'm sorry to be so intense about the matter." I offered my own olive branch.

"I understand," he said. "Emotions are running high right now. If I had known you and Olga were so close– Oh, that's right I forgot. Olga's sister-in-law, Lupe, works for you, doesn't she? I'm sorry. It can be difficult to remember all the intricate pieces in a small town like Santa Rita."

"Oh yes, yes," I nodded, even though I'd had no idea until that exact moment that the Lupe who worked in our bakery had any direct connections to Olga. It wasn't surprising in Santa Rita, though. I sent Ana a sharp look out of the corner of my eye. She was supposed to be a guide to the ins and outs of Santa Rita's intertwining connections, but she just shrugged. Apparently she'd been in the dark as much as I'd been.

"I know Olga and her brother hadn't been on the best of terms as of late," Father Tomás continued oblivious to my ignorance. "I kept telling her. Family is family. You should make amends with your brother while you can." He shook his head sadly. "We never know when we'll be called home."

A knock sounded at the office door, and a slightly heavier, slightly grayer Silvia than I remembered from my childhood poked her head in. Her voice was tinged with an arrogant sweetness that grated.

Father Tomás asked Silvia to give Ana a date for when the ceremony could be rescheduled. "Oh, please come out to the desk, and I'll attend you there," Silvia said, retreating back towards the waiting area. We followed her into the waiting room. It was obvious Silvia was no typist and had barely used a computer before, but what she lacked in expertise, she made up for in unjustified confidence.

"The next available date we have for you is a week from Thursday," Silvia finally announced.

"What? That's almost two weeks away," I said. How could this little chapel get off postponing Ana's wedding so long?

But Silvia simply shrugged. "I'm sorry, but that's the soonest available date." She smiled, not looking at all disappointed.

"But couldn't something else be bumped, like a baptism or quinceañera or something? They aren't as important as a wedding with out of town guests waiting. Couldn't you at least ask someone if they'd be willing to reschedule?'

Silvia smirked. *She smirked!* "Well, baptisms are usually on Sundays, but the chapel can be reserved for many different reasons, and those reservations should be respected. That's very important to us."

"Important when it suits you. Are you sure it's not because you–"

"Next Thursday would be fine," Ana cut in. "It will give us time to visit with family and reorganize everything for the big day. Thank you!" Ana spoke brightly to Silvia and sent me the *please shut up look*, and since I was supposed to be Ana's support system on this venture, I obeyed. Was being around Blanca making me turn into her? God I hoped not.

Silvia entered the date into the system and handed Ana a small card congratulating her on the *big day* like it was the first time it had been arranged. I needed to get out of this church before I really told someone off.

We turned to leave just as Father Francisco opened his office door and breezed past, bumping my shoulder without acknowledgement, like I was some ghost haunting his parish.

"Excuse me for being in the path of Father Pharisee," I said before I could stop myself. I couldn't help but take pleasure in the genuine shocked look on both Silvia and Father Francisco's face before Ana hurried me out the door and onto the square.

"What got into you in there?" she asked. "Apparently, nervous Natalia is no more. I think I did too good of a job at stoking your confidence." Ana pretended to be upset, but a small smile tugged at her mouth.

I shrugged. "I'm not sure. Maybe I'm more stressed than I realized."

"Father Pharisee, where did that come from?" Ana asked.

"I don't know. It just came out. I never liked him as a kid. He was always so mean during confession and the situation with him and Silvia. I guess I just–"

Ana couldn't contain her smile any more, and soon we were both doubled over with laughter. Even those passing by were stopping to stare.

"I can't believe you. Did you see the look on their faces?" Ana asked when she could finally catch her breath. "I can't wait to tell Lía and Nico. Lía will be so bummed she missed it. She even offered to come today too, and I turned her down." Ana wiped the tears of laughter from her eyes.

I pictured Ana retelling our exploits to her siblings and felt my face grow hot. This story would be added to the Gallardo family lore in perpetuity and would soon get around to scandalize and entertain all of Santa Rita in a matter of days at most.

"So what do we do now?" Ana asked. "Father Tomás didn't have much to add to the whole Olga situation."

"Of course he did. I feel more certain than ever that whatever happened to Olga was no accident."

"But what do we do about it?" Ana asked.

"First we find Lupe. We know her, and she's related to Olga. There's got to be something she can offer that will get us closer to the truth."

"*Us?*" Ana asked. "You know I have a wedding in less than two weeks with a bunch of padrinos to organize, right?"

"That's plenty of time." I laughed. "But seriously, you don't have to tag along if you don't want to. It's Lupe's day off, so I'm going to go over and see her. But I know you have lots of guests to attend to. I'm sure your future mother-in-law, Sara, would love to have some bonding time." I smiled.

Ana turned slightly pale at the mention of Sara. "Well, we really should go over and pay our respects to Lupe and her family. Plus, after that display in the church, I'm afraid of what trouble you could get yourself into alone."

"So it's off to Lupe's then. Do you have any idea where she lives?" I asked.

Ana nodded.

"So you know where she lives, but you didn't know she was Olga's sister-in-law?"

"I'm not Santa Rita's family historian," Ana said. "It's difficult to remember everything and everyone, but once Father Tomás mentioned it, I did vaguely remember the connection."

"Okay, so it's off to Lupe's then," I said.

CHAPTER EIGHT

Ana directed the taxi to a small house on a dirt road at the outskirts of town surrounded by overgrown, empty lots. A cow stood in one of them watching us while munching grass.

"Hopefully Lupe's home," Ana said, asking the taxi driver to wait just in case.

"Shouldn't we get his number too?" I asked. "If we get stranded out here, it will be one heck of a walk back to town."

Ana laughed. "It's not that far out, Miss City. Plus, there's a bus that passes every 10 minutes or so a couple of streets over."

"Really?"

"Yes, and there's electricity and indoor toilets too."

"Ha-ha, very funny," I said, but the look on Ana's face showed that she *did* think it was pretty funny.

Lupe in an apron with a bucket in one hand opened the door. The shock of seeing Ana and I at her front door on her day off seemed to paralyze her for several moments before she finally answered. "Hello, is everything okay? You're not– I'm not–"

We should have thought this plan through better. Who wanted their boss's boss to show up at their house on their day off unannounced? I thought about just turning around and piling back in the taxi, but wouldn't that just seem even weirder? Thankfully, Ana had better social skills than I did.

"Oh, don't worry, Lupe. We're just here for a visit. I was meeting with Father Tomás about the wedding, and he mentioned that you and your husband were related to Olga. We just wanted to come by and offer our condolences, but if it's a bad time, we certainly understand and wouldn't want to intrude."

"No, no please come in. Thank you. I was worried you'd come here to fire me or something." Lupe laughed. "Please come in." She passed us through. Her land was surrounded by a wall, creating a small patio cluttered with an outdoor sink, stove, a small washer, and plastic tubs filled with water for various cleaning needs. Clotheslines were strung up across the entire patio. Inside her tiny house, little light was able to enter. The small room didn't have much, but from the polished concrete floor to the brick walls, everything was impeccably clean.

"Can I get you some coffee and something to eat?" Lupe asked, gesturing towards plastic white chairs set around a tiny table.

"Oh, you don't–" I started.

But Ana cut in. "We'd love that. I'm starving."

Lupe grinned. "Excellent, just give me a moment. Let me put some water on."

My refusal would've been taken as an insult if Ana hadn't wisely interceded. I smiled a thank you.

"See, you need me," she whispered back.

Lupe returned with a cup of coffee for each of us and a plate piled with beans and rice, nopales, a bowl of salsa, and plenty of tortillas. "Sorry I don't have more on hand. I didn't get a chance to stop by the butcher's yet."

"Oh no worries." Ana's eyes lit up at the spread.

"Sorry to just run in on you like this," I said. No-knock calls were a part of everyday life in Santa Rita, but it was something I'd never get used to, even though I'd just instigated one.

"Oh, it's nice to have visitors. Beats being here alone all day with my housework."

"This really is delicious," I said, ladling more salsa onto my rice, bean, and nopal taco. Why was it that simple food in fresh air always tasted better than fussy food in over-priced restaurants ever could? It was a mystery for the ages.

"Really?" Lupe looked skeptical. "I wish I had some meat to offer, but–"

"Oh, don't apologize. You should call it vegan. People will pay five times the price for everyday food without meat or dairy if you label it that. It's all the rage now. Those vegan Youtubers at the hotel make quite a bit of money just talking about it."

Lupe shook her head. "I guess growing up we were practically vegan then, but we just called it poor."

Ana laughed. "My mom said the same thing. I had to explain the whole vegan thing to her three times before she understood it."

"Today was supposed to be your wedding, wasn't it?" Lupe asked Ana. It was an obvious ploy for information, but I couldn't blame her for being curious at our unexpected arrival.

Ana seemed to expect the question too, nodding. "We went to talk to Father Tomás to reschedule it for the Thursday after next."

"So long?" Lupe raised an eyebrow.

Ana shrugged. "Silvia, you know Father Francisco's uh– well you know who she is. She's the new secretary now that Olga– Well, that's the nearest date." Ana was so flustered I couldn't help but smile.

Lupe smiled too. "Oh, I know what you mean. I'm not surprised she swooped in so soon after Olga was murdered.

Silvia's been eyeing that job for years. If Olga hadn't been so efficient, they would've found an excuse to kick her out, but in just a few days that church is going to be in complete disarray with lazy Silvia at the helm. Olga could be a little harsh at times and slightly judgemental. Lord knows we had our disagreements, but she wasn't lazy. That's for sure."

"Do you know when the funeral and wake will be?" Ana asked. It was customary to have prayers, songs, and refreshments in the family's home each evening after someone died. After a couple days, a mass and burial would be held then more nights of prayers, and an additional mass after the nine days was complete, much more involved then the short, simple wakes and funerals I'd grown up around in the US. But due to the unusual circumstances, I wasn't sure if the family was waiting or forgoing the tradition altogether. Funeral traditions weren't as strong as they used to be, even in Santa Rita, but seeing how traditional and religious Olga had been, I expected her family to keep up the custom.

But Lupe shook her head. "I'm not sure who will host Olga's wake and prepare her funeral. I talked to Esteban about it and told him we should step in, but he said that's the last thing Olga would have wanted. He's probably right. I don't think she'd want Esteban or me to organize her service."

"So Esteban was Olga's older brother, right?" I asked, trying to keep Santa Rita's family trees straight.

Lupe nodded. "But they haven't been on good terms for years, ever since their father died."

"Really? That's so sad. I had no idea," Ana said.

"It is," Lupe agreed. "I don't know all the details. I didn't want to get involved in Esteban's family business, but Olga had a little house off the main street in Santa Rita. She and Esteban grew up there. But she lived there her whole life in that very house and took care of their father. He was sick for a long time. Esteban did what he could to help, but honestly it wasn't much. And after their father died, Esteban wanted to sell the land and the house on it and split the money, but Olga refused.

"There was no will, and it would've been a fortune to take to court, so it was just left to fester. I told Esteban to drop it. It was her house, after all. She'd always lived in it, taken care of the house upkeep and both their parents by herself. I told him he was just being greedy about the whole thing. I think he recognized he was in the wrong later, but by then it was too late, and they're both so stubborn." Lupe shook her head. "So many things were said. It's hard to go back after that. I wish I had done more to have a friendship at least with her, but she was a difficult person to get along with in her own right."

I nodded, remembering my brief encounters with Olga. "She was no shrinking violet, that's for sure."

"Exactly, but Olga wasn't as tough as she appeared. I think she did it to protect herself, the *get them before they get you* approach to life."

"Did she have any other family or close friends that you know of?" I asked.

Lupe shook her head. "None that I know of, but like I said, we weren't exactly on the best of terms, so maybe she did. I just didn't know about them."

"But if you and Esteban don't take care of the funeral, who will? What will happen with the body?" Ana asked. I could see the wheels of concern turning in her head. There was no way Ana was going to allow Olga to be laid to rest without a proper send-off.

Lupe shook her head. "I really don't know."

"We'll have to work something out then," I said,

tentatively.

Great, just what I needed, another time-sensitive responsibility heaped onto my already full plate.

"So what's going to happen with Olga's house now?" I asked. Ana's eyes grew wide in surprise at my question, but I wanted to see Lupe's reaction to the mention of the house since that had been the source of their falling out to begin with. I didn't think that Lupe had been as innocent as she pretended to be.

"Oh, I hadn't thought about that." Lupe's lack of foresight on the matter wasn't sincere to me. *How could she not have thought about it at least a little?* "Well, it would depend on the title, but I assume it would go to Esteban since there's no other family to claim it."

"So Esteban doesn't feel bad about how his sister died after years of arguing over a house that he's going to inherit anyway?" I asked.

Ana shook her head vigorously, making cut motions with her hand, but I ignored her. I knew I was on the line, if not fully crossing over into the offensive, but I wanted to get a better sense from Lupe about how deep the family resentments really were, or at least I hoped to.

Lupe pursed her lips at my comment but, not surprisingly, was in no hurry to argue with the owner of the bakery where she worked. "I don't want you to get the wrong impression of Esteban. He's not a bad man, but he's old-fashioned, and he doesn't talk a lot about how he feels. I know this is hard on him in his own way, but he doesn't like to show it."

"I know the type. They think it's weak to show how they feel or God forbid cry." Ana laughed hollowly in an attempt to lighten the mood.

"Exactly, I'm glad *you* understand," Lupe said in a not so concealed jab at me. But I didn't mind. I was more interested in watching her emotions and reactions play out than in smoothing things over, at least for now.

So far Lupe and Esteban seemed to be the only ones that had something to gain by offing Olga. Justice took precedence over anyone's feelings, especially since Lupe didn't seem to be in the midst of any type of grief that I could discern. She leaned back languidly sipping her coffee.

"I'm not sure if Esteban still wants to sell Olga's house, or maybe we could live there. It might be nice to live downtown. Honestly, I haven't really thought about it." Lupe smiled in a way that made it obvious that it was definitely something she had already considered.

I stood, not trusting what words might come out of my mouth if I stayed. "Well, we came to comfort Olga's family members and see if we could help in any way with the services, but seeing as Olga's family," I looked pointedly at Lupe, "is not going to do anything for her. I guess now we have to plan a wedding and a funeral. So if you'd please excuse us, we have a lot of work to do." I stood to leave.

Ana reluctantly followed. I could hear her apologizing for my behavior in hushed tones. "I'm really sorry, Lupe. I don't know what's gotten into Natalia. She's not normally like this."

"Maybe she just can't handle stress," Lupe whispered loudly.

I'm sure I wounded her pride and shamed her with my harsh criticism, but sometimes people needed to be shamed to pull their heads out of their own rear-ends. The lack of concern Lupe showed for her sister-in-law, especially when she and Esteban both stood to gain the very thing they'd wanted and fought over all these years, made me want to give her an even bigger piece of my mind, but instead I offered a polite thank you and goodbye to Lupe before heading back out onto the dirt road.

"Which direction did you say that bus stop was in?" I asked Ana. She pointed, and I stomped off down the dirt road so quickly that she had to jog to keep up in order to avoid the plumes of dust that puffed up in my wake. I waited for Ana's reprimands but none came. She'd wisely decided now wasn't the time to address any rudeness on my part. I knew I should have handled the conversation differently. A lot of my anger was misplaced and should have been directed at Olga's brother, Esteban.

My anger abated somewhat walking the half-kilometer down the dusty road in the afternoon heat past small walled houses and empty grass filled lots before finally stopping in front of the bus stop that sat adjacent to a tiny convenience store.

"You want something to drink?" Ana asked. I nodded, surprised she still hadn't taken the opportunity to at least express surprise at my behavior.

She returned a moment later with a soft drink in each hand. "You're just like your grandma, you know?" she said, handing one to me.

"Really?" That was the last thing I expected to come out of Ana's mouth.

She smiled. "So now we have a funeral to plan before my wedding. I guess we'd better get started."

CHAPTER NINE

"So what do you think? Can we handle it?" Ana asked. Instead of taking the bus back to the hotel, Ana and I had decided to go to her house and explain everything to her mother. Beatriz sat silently, listening, not betraying a single emotion on her face. I tore a paper napkin to shreds while I waited for her to speak. I knew I'd been in the right to criticize Lupe, but I wasn't sure if Beatriz would see it that way.

"Well, I guess we'll have to, won't we?" Beatriz finally said. "Olga has to have a proper burial, and if her family won't give her one, then we will." She shrugged. "It's not a lot to do really. We'll have pastries from the bakery, and we can use my house for the visitation. I'll just need to have some extra chairs on hand and plenty of coffee."

"That covers the visitation, but what about the funeral masses?" Ana asked.

"Where's Lía? Find her and bring her over here," Beatriz directed Ana, who hopped up in search of her sister. The entire Gallardo family including Nico, Ana, and Lía lived on the same piece of land.

Usually in Santa Rita when a child became an adult, instead of moving out on their own, they'd work together to build a house next to or on top of the already existing buildings on the familial property that was itself encircled by a wall, if they got along and had enough space to do so that is. So most houses tended to be on the smaller side, but there was no mortgage or rent to worry about, and you could always add more rooms as you needed them.

Lía's house that she shared with her husband and daughter sat just across the patio from Beatriz's, and within moments she'd joined us at the table.

"So this is how it is then, everyone just ignores me until I'm needed? I see," Lía said.

Ana started to protest. "We just got here. I swear. I told mom because I have no idea how we're going to handle everything between–"

"I was joking," interjected Lía, giving her sister a pat on the shoulder. "But I do want to hear all the juicy details. Ana said Natalia really laid into Lupe about not wanting to plan Olga's funeral."

I felt my face grow hot at the mention of the interchange. My righteous anger had cooled significantly, and now I just felt regret. I could only imagine the story Lupe would spin about what had happened.

Thankfully Beatriz stepped in and brushed any awkward conversation away. "There's time enough for that later. Do you think you could supervise the planning of Olga's funeral masses, Lía?"

"We'd all help, but you could be the funeral coordinator." Ana probably wanted to reassure her sister and offer her an important title to sweeten the deal, but Lía laughed good-naturedly.

"A funeral coordinator, is that something I can add to my resume?" she asked. "What a morbid career that would be. But it should be simple enough. I just need to reserve the church for the priest to offer both masses and order some flowers, contact the cemetery about a burial plot and transport of the body, and we could have a simple meal back at the house here afterwards. We'll worry about the tombstone later."

Apparently Lía's version of simple and mine were not at all in alignment. There's no way I could've pulled this off by myself.

Beatriz nodded in approval. "That sounds excellent, simple but respectful. I think even Olga would have approved."

"Well, I don't think Olga would've approved of much of anything," Lía said. "But it's the best we can do on such short notice and with a wedding on the horizon to boot."

"Actually, I think Olga would be thrilled," Ana put in. "Imagine how bad this is going to make Lupe and Esteban look, especially when they're moving into her old house. They'll get to experience the disapproval of Santa Rita on full display for years to come."

"That is not the point," Beatriz said, her face serious. "But you're not wrong." A smile escaped her tight lips. "It really is cold for her only living relatives not to lay her to rest properly, especially when they're going to inherit her home."

"Maybe Esteban and Lupe couldn't afford it, and they're too proud to admit it," I said, remembering the tiny house on the outskirts of town. "After all, a house isn't ready money." It hadn't occurred to me before, and I started to feel slightly guilty about my abruptness with Lupe, but Lía quickly squashed any need for that.

"That's really the whole point of the nine-day visitation, though, to get money. The donations are used to pay for practically everything, and what we can't pay for from those I intend to scare out of Father Francisco and the church." Beatriz let out a surprised gasp, but Lía continued on, undeterred.

"If they even try to charge for use of the church–" Lía snorted. "They should be thankful we're not related to Olga, or I'd have them in court. She was murdered at work after all. If her family didn't want to have the funeral, then the priests should have, especially for all the work she's done for the parish all these years." Lía shook her head. "But her brother is just selfish and unfeeling, Lupe too. That's the only reason they're not organizing the funeral, end of story."

"Now we don't know that for sure," Beatriz said. "But it certainly does seem that way, doesn't it?" I smiled at Beatriz's indirect criticism. "But the point of the visitation isn't for money, Lía. It's to pray and mourn."

"Oh of course, I thought that was a given," Lía nodded. "But the money sure helps."

Ana nodded too but whispered under her breath. "Don't listen to her. The real point is definitely the money." I stifled a smile.

"The situation with Olga's brother is highly suspicious, if you ask me," Ana added. "I don't think Lupe is capable of violence, but the fact that Esteban stands to gain so much and doesn't even want to take the time to organize a funeral makes him my number one suspect."

"Suspect?" Lía's mouth hung open. "I heard that the whole thing was an accident."

"You are out of the loop then. There's no way that was an accident," Ana said.

"Please girls. Let's take this one step at a time. The police said it was an accident, so let's leave it at that. No more sleuthing, please," Beatriz said, looking at me for support.

I shrugged, trying to keep Beatriz happy but still remain truthful. "I have to agree with Ana. I don't think it was an accident, but I'm not sure there's much we can do about it if the police aren't even investigating, unless we can get an actual confession or some incredible evidence."

Beatriz threw up her hands. "Oh Lord help me! These girls are going to drive me to an early grave."

My phone chimed. I glanced at the screen. It was Maritza. My stomach sank. Hopefully there wasn't a problem at the hotel or bakery. She almost never called. I excused myself before stepping outside onto the patio.

"Hello?" I offered hesitantly.

"Did you really go over to Lupe's house and lay into her for not burying Olga properly?" Maritza's words sounded accusatory, but her voice had a hint of a smile to it. Well, at least there wasn't any big issue at the bakery, or Maritza wouldn't have started off with this line of questioning and definitely wouldn't have been so jovial about it.

"I wouldn't say I laid into her, but it did seem a little cold to me. That's all." I felt defensive about whatever imaginary version of our encounter Lupe had repeated.

But Maritza laughed. "I'm glad you're finally getting a backbone. I've told Lupe for years that she and Esteban weren't right for trying to kick Olga out of the only home she ever knew just to possibly make a little money, and that's if they can find a buyer at a decent price. It's good she heard that they're greedy from somebody else. But when Lupe called, she was crying. She said she didn't know if she was fired or not, so that's why I'm calling. I need to know if I should hire somebody else or what I should tell her."

"Fired? No, of course not." The thought had never occurred to me. "I'd never fire someone for personal reasons, and I definitely wouldn't do it without talking to you first. Lord knows we need you, Maritza, and we need you to be happy." It didn't hurt to butter Maritza up a little bit.

"Flattery will get you everywhere." Maritza laughed, recognizing my ploy immediately. "I told Lupe as much, but I promised I'd double check. Oh, and these vegan people keep coming into the bakery, and they're trying to talk to me about something. I have no idea what they're saying, though. The blonde one thinks she's speaking Spanish, but it's no kind of Spanish I've ever heard before."

"They probably want to finish filming." I groaned.

"Probably," Maritza said. "I know. I don't want to either, but we did agree, and the sooner we finish the better, don't you think?"

"Yeah, you're right. I'm at Ana's now. I'll meet you over at the bakery, and hopefully we can get this thing over with quickly."

"Sounds good to me. See you soon."

I hung up with Maritza and ducked in to tell Ana and Lía about the call. "Let me know how things go with the church and what help you need," I said before running down to the corner.

It was possible to walk from the Gallardo property to the hotel, but the bus was faster than walking and cheaper than a taxi. I'd thought about getting a car, but the expense didn't seem worth it in such a small, slow-paced town. Unless someone needed a car to travel out of town or for their business, like Nico, it was more common than not that residents in Santa Rita chose to walk or take the bus with the occasional taxi. The mild climate also made it a pretty attractive option and a nice way to stay in shape with all the pastries and good food I scarfed down every day.

To my chagrin I found the vegan Youtubers and Blanca sitting at one of the bakery tables chatting amicably together. I cringed. Maritza was standing behind the counter with a similar reaction plastered across her face.

What was Blanca doing here? I'd hoped to at least chat with Maritza before facing the Youtubers, and now I had to contend with Blanca too. Oh well, we just needed to get this thing over with. But before I could decide who to talk to first,

Blanca spotted me and ushered me over. Our argument from earlier was completely washed away in typical Blanca fashion with no residual anger, at least until the next altercation when she'd bring up all her old complaints again, but until then she was like a person with argument amnesia.

"Hi, sweetie, where have you been?" Blanca asked in English, coming over to plant a kiss on my cheek. I stiffened at her approach. She'd never called me sweetie, at least not in recent memory, and whenever she put on the pretend mother act, nothing good ever followed.

I smiled weakly and acknowledged the three Youtubers who sat around with half empty paper cups of coffee in front of them.

"We've been waiting for you all day," Harriet said, the same scowl settled on her face, but this time directed at me and not over a screen.

"Oh sorry about that. We had to reschedule a wedding and then found out we needed to plan Olga's funeral since her family doesn't seem too interested in it." I tried to keep the edge out of my voice.

"That sounds awful," Claire said, pulling over a chair for me.

"I'm not surprised about that," Blanca butted in. "Who *would* want to have a funeral for that self-righteous–"

"So how are you feeling, Claire?" I interrupted Blanca's incoming tirade.

Thankfully, Claire took my prompting and ran with it, going into enormous detail about what they'd done that day and photographed around town. "We just ran into your mom here about five minutes ago, and I was asking her about Olga and what she was like."

I restrained myself from rolling my eyes and smiled instead.

"Yes, yes, yes, I was giving them all the gossip about everyone around town here." Blanca laughed. I cringed.

"And Jessica was just talking about her cancer battle. I can't believe you had to go through that at such a young age." Blanca clucked her tongue melodramatically.

"Claire mentioned your cancer journey," I said. "It really is amazing you've overcome so many obstacles."

"Oh thank you." Jessica was beaming. "I couldn't have done it without my bestie. She gave Claire a slap on the shoulder.

I glanced over at Maritza. She was still waiting behind the counter. *Time to get this thing over with.* "Well, I'd hate to waste any more of your time. I really am sorry, Harriet, for making you look for me all day, if I had known…" I offered a contrite smile, which Harriet accepted with one of her own. *The girl could actually smile. Amazing.*

"I'll get the equipment set up," Harriet said, pushing her mousy brown bangs out of her eyes.

Claire sidled up next to me while I watched. "You okay?" she asked.

"It has been a tough couple days," I answered honestly. "I know you guys need this segment, but after we finish, I just want to crawl into bed."

Claire laughed. "You and I both. I told Jessica to lay off of the, *everyone has to be vegan* rant she went on last time. I'm sorry about that. She's just very passionate about her beliefs."

"Thanks," I said, but before I could say more, Harriet called me over.

"We're ready, Let's try to make it snappy this time, Jessica. Everyone has better things to do than to listen to you prattle on about nothing." At least Harriet and I were on the same page for once.

"So how are we going to organize this segment?" Harriet asked, glancing around the room.

A sudden thought came to mind, an idea that would save the afternoon, at least for me anyway. "Why don't you have Blanca translate this segment instead?" I suggested. "She can translate as well as I can, probably better."

"That's an excellent idea. Blanca looks way more put together too, no offense, Natalia," Jessica said, smiling at my mother in her expensive red heels and tailored dark blue pants. I grimaced but didn't complain.

After all, it was true. Blanca spent way more time on her looks than I ever would. Everything from her makeup to jewelry, even her nails, were impeccable. They always had been, but now she had the money to do it right. I never really noticed or cared, but for someone like Jessica, who valued things like that, she was probably an inspiration.

"What's happening? Are we going to record, or what?" Maritza asked, confused, so I switched to Spanish.

"I was just suggesting that Blanca do the translating for the next segment instead of me," I explained.

Maritza shrugged. "I don't care who does it, but let's get this thing over with, so I can go home and soak my feet. They're killing me."

The bakery had already been closed early for the day, and after a short preamble from Jessica, Maritza was soon baking in front of the camera while Blanca translated. Jessica asked inane questions, thankfully steering away from any questions about personal dietary choices, and the segment finished without a hitch.

"Thanks, Maritza." I walked across the bakery. "You did great. Hopefully, this pays off for the business," which I was seriously starting to doubt. "If you want to, you can head out. I know it's been a long day."

"Thanks." Maritza nodded. "I want to get out of here quick before they think of some other crazy confection and ask me to whip it up in front of the camera."

"Yes please hurry. I want to get home too. See you tomorrow," I whispered back. I looked up and saw Nico standing at the back of the bakery quietly surveying the situation.

"What are you doing here?" I asked. Finally, a nice surprise to round out this awful day.

He reached over for a hug. "What? Do I need an invitation to come over and see my girlfriend?" he asked. "With the goings on these last few days, I feel like we haven't had time to just relax together, except the other night." His eyes danced.

"Shhh," I silenced him, glancing around, but the only people nearby who could've overheard and understood were Blanca and Maritza, neither of whom would have cared or been shocked by my love life, quite the opposite, actually.

Nico ignored me. "Now what do you say we head back to your place–"

"Nico, please!"

He shook his head. "You have a dirty mind. I was going to suggest that we enjoy some of these tacos I have here." He shook a plastic bag in one hand filled with tacos al pastor.

"You are speaking my language." I stood on tiptoe to kiss Nico. "They smell amazing."

"Ah, go get a room," Maritza yelled across the bakery with a wide grin. She had her purse and keys in hand.

"Well, don't mind if we do," Nico said, stepping to the side so I could walk past.

Blanca and the Youtubers exited after us. I turned, trying to be polite and conversational with Blanca, but she ignored my attempt at chatting. Her entire focus was on her new friend Jessica, following her through the back of the hotel as though no one else existed.

It was odd that Blanca still hadn't wanted to come over and visit me at the cottage. Maybe she was still angry that grandma had left it to me instead of her, but I'd thought she'd at least want to go through some of the photo albums and keepsakes from her childhood and take them back home with her. She was avoiding it for some reason. I just wasn't sure why.

"So who are those Youtuber girls? Are they big?" Nico asked. "I've never heard of them."

"Well, you're not exactly their demographic, or are you a closet watcher of vegan Youtubers in English?"

"Maybe I am," Nico joked.

"Well, let's check them out while we eat. I'm curious myself. I haven't actually seen any of their videos yet."

Since grandma's TV was ancient, I set my laptop on a nearby table, so we could enjoy our tacos while we watched. I didn't know their channel name, but I just entered vegan Youtuber cancer and found a range of videos during Jessica's struggle with cancer. Thankfully, their videos had subtitles in Spanish too, and we clicked through some of them.

"Wow, I had no idea that girl... What's her name? Jessica? That she almost died from cancer," Nico finally said after we'd polished off the majority of the tacos.

I shook my head. "I know. It's incredible." I hadn't realized how long Jessica had struggled either, or how bad it really was. There was video after video, usually in her bedroom with Claire talking about veganism but also discussing her cancer treatments. "Their followers were really generous too. Look, according to this, they raised almost 100,000 dollars for the cancer center. That's incredible. It almost makes you trust in humanity again."

"Almost," Nico agreed.

"Jessica believes she was cured because she was vegan. Do you think that's true?"

Nico snorted. "I'm sure a healthy diet of any kind doesn't hurt, but she mentions a ton of medical treatments in these videos too, so it wasn't all broccoli and brussel sprouts."

"Well, her fans definitely think it was the veganism." I glanced through the comments on the video where Jessica announced she was cancer-free. "Look at all these," I said to Nico, translating a few of them, so he could get the gist. Comment after comment about how her diet had saved her life.

"Everyone believes what they want." Nico shrugged. "These girls believe in eating plants. Olga believed in following archaic rules that even the most religious Catholics don't take to heart."

"And what do you believe in?" I teased.

Nico looked at me, desire in his eyes. "I believe in... tacos," he said.

"I believe in tacos too," I said in the same faux-dramatic voice he'd used, and we both burst out laughing.

CHAPTER TEN

I popped into the bakery to pick out my customary morning pastry. I meticulously looked over every option. I finally decided on a chocolate dipped rebanada and a cream-filled beso and eagerly headed over to a far empty table to enjoy my sweets and caffeine in peace.

But just moments into my peace, it was shattered. *I should've taken my food back home.*

"This seat taken?" Harriet asked.

Startled, I looked up and reluctantly shook my head. I was stuck now. There was no way to gracefully exit the conversation without at least talking a little bit.

"So how are things?" I asked Harriet. I was surprised that she'd even wanted to sit and talk with me. It's true she'd been slightly happier yesterday, but prior to that, her entire visit she seemed irritated and nonplussed by everyone and everything around her.

Harriet shrugged. "Oh, you know how it is. Work sucks. People suck. Life sucks."

I wasn't sure at all what Harriet was referring to, but I didn't want to ask. There was a lot of subtext behind those statements that I had no desire to delve into, and thankfully she didn't feel the need to explain further. Instead she popped a chocolate donut into her mouth.

"You know, Harriet, I don't think those donuts are vegan," I said nervously, expecting her to spit it out and start berating me about false advertising, but to my surprise, she just laughed.

"Oh, that's Jessica's shtick. I fell off that wagon a long time ago. Now I'm what you might call a part-timer." She laughed again.

"Really? Does Jessica know about that? What about Claire? Is she a part-timer too?" Claire had seemed so genuine when we'd spoken.on the day she'd found Olga. She'd never mentioned it as some kind of ploy for the channel.

Harriet shrugged. "As far as I know, Claire is all in. She does whatever Jessica tells her to, and Jessica is *obsessed*. When I came on board, I was genuine at the time. But it was also a job, mostly just a job, if I'm honest." Harriet stared at me through her large owl frame glasses, her plain brown bangs were a little too long, and the fringe hung down slightly obscuring her eyes.

"But Jessica read Maritza and me that whole riot act about being hypocrites for just serving vegan food. Doesn't she do that to you too?" I asked.

"Sometimes, I don't really listen, though. I do many things that irritate Jessica." Harriet chuckled.

"I was watching some of the videos last night from when Jessica had cancer. It seems like you helped her get through a really dark time– well you and Claire." I tried to change the topic and compliment Harriet at the same time, but she just laughed again, this time so loudly that everyone in the bakery turned to look in our direction.

"Okay," she finally said.

Okay? What a weird response! How could I back away gracefully? So I pulled the most amateur stunt in the book. I took out my phone and glanced down at it, careful to angle the screen away.

"I'm really sorry, but there's something I have to attend to at the hotel." I stood to leave. "I'll see you around. Let me know if you need anything."

"Absolutely," Harriet said after a sip of coffee, still chuckling at some joke that only she seemed to be in on.

Today was the first day of Olga's visitation. I still wasn't sure what I needed to do, but seeing as I was the main catalyst that had caused everyone to take on the responsibility, I shot a quick text to Ana to see what I should bring. She suggested pastries, so I headed over mid-afternoon with a load of pastries.

Every single one of my cloth shopping bags was filled to the brim with sweet bread from the bakery. I should have taken a taxi, but I was over halfway to the Gallardo family property by the time I realized that. I'd opted for walking rather than the bus, thinking that it would be easier to carry everything without incident but that it wasn't so much as to require a taxi. Obviously, I was wrong. I stopped to rest when a large pickup truck pulled up beside me.

"Can I help you, miss?"

I glanced over to see Nico leaning out of the driver's side, a large grin across his face. I'm sure I looked crazy, but I was too tired to care or tease back.

"You're a life-saver." I climbed into the truck next to him.

"I try. But why were you lugging all of that stuff by yourself on foot?" Nico shook his head. "Taxis in Santa Rita haven't gone that high, have they?"

I laughed. "I wasn't thinking, obviously. I thought it wouldn't be too hard, and I could get there faster. I was just starting to rethink that decision when you pulled up."

"Well, why didn't you call me? I would've been happy to drive you over. I was on my way anyway. Mom wanted me to bring some extra chairs." Nico gestured towards the bed of the truck heaped with wooden chairs he must've brought from his carpentry shop downtown.

"I didn't think about it," I answered honestly. I'd always been self-sufficient and not used to others even wanting to help me.

Beatriz's kitchen/living room had been cleaned from top to bottom. Lía's daughter, Nora, was only seven, but apparently Beatriz had roped her into helping as well. She stood stirring a pan of milk on the stove. Her miserable expression intensified when she realized she had an audience.

Beatriz emerged from the back bedroom. "There you are, Natalia. I thought I heard someone arrive." She reached over to offer a hug.

"I brought pastries, and Nico's here with a truck full of chairs." I gestured and pulled pastries from the bags onto waiting platters.

"Excellent." Beatriz clasped her hands in relief. "Tell him to bring everything in here. It'll be a tight fit, but we'll make it work." She glanced around the small, spotless room. Everything had been moved to the side or out of the room altogether to make space.

"Looks good," I said. "And if too many people come, we can always move it outside on the patio."

"Exactly," Beatriz agreed, stepping towards Nora to see how the stirring was going.

"I come bearing chairs and pastry, lots and lots of pastry." Nico entered with a chair in one hand and the rest of my bags of pastry in the other. He leaned down to kiss his mother before placing them all on the kitchen table.

While they were chatting, I headed back out to the truck to bring in as many chairs as I could. The more seating the better. I really hoped people would come to Olga's visitation, especially the generous ones.

Surprisingly, Father Tomás was one of the first to arrive. He poked his head shyly through Beatriz's kitchen door, a bouquet of flowers in his hand.

"Oh thank you so much, Father," Beatriz said kindly, accepting the flowers and handing them to her husband. "Please find a jar and place these on the table," she instructed. Roberto quietly obliged with a small nod towards the priest.

Father Tomás stood awkwardly for several moments. "I want to apologize on the parish's behalf. Lía and your whole family have been extremely generous in organizing all of this for Olga. I'm sure she's more at peace because of your efforts. Father Francisco's behavior this morning was unacceptable. I apologized to Lía, but I wanted to apologize to you directly."

"What behavior?" Roberto asked, speaking up for the first time. "What did that old priest say to my daughter?"

"Roberto, shhh," Beatriz cautioned. "Now isn't the time."

"Then when is the time?" Roberto asked. "Father Tomás just brought it up, so I don't see why I can't ask about it."

Father Tomás, who had been nervous before, now looked ashen and fidgetted even more, like he wanted to bolt from the room. I felt bad for him, but I was more curious to hear his answer than empathetic for his predicament, so I made no move to help.

"We can ask him about it later." Beatriz glared at her husband. "Right now we have a wake to plan. I'm sorry about that, Father. Please forgive Roberto. He's very protective of his children, no matter how old they get."

Father Tomás sighed and offered a tight smile. "Not a problem, I completely understand. It really wasn't that much of an ordeal." He looked over at Roberto. "You know how Father Francisco is, and when Lía came to ask for help with Olga's funeral expenses, he was less than charitable, let's say. But it's all worked out now, no problem."

"Well, thank you, Father. I appreciate you helping to mediate. Things are a lot better around Santa Rita now that Father Francisco isn't the only priest at the main church." Roberto's voice sounded gruff, but it was sincere. I couldn't wait to hear Lía's side of the story and glad I wasn't the only one to tell Father Francisco off this week.

Ana entered more bubbly and excited than anyone should be at a wake. "Hey Mom, did you decide where to put the body?"

"Ana!" Beatriz's face turned red. "What kind of way is that to talk? We decided to put Olga in your father's old work shed out back." Beatriz gave a pointed glance towards Father Tomás seated behind the door. I hid my smile behind a sip of coffee.

Ana had the manners to look thoroughly embarrassed. "Oh Father, I didn't see you there. I'm really sorry. I didn't mean to sound–"

"Not at all," Father Tomás said. "It's very kind what all of you are doing for Olga. It really warms my heart to see such Christian charity."

I was starting to like Father Tomás more, but he was still too much of a sycophant for Father Francisco for my liking. I took some pity on him, though. "Father, excuse me for my ignorance, but if you'd like to pray over the body or whatever it is that you do, I'd be happy to show you where Olga is uh… lying in state," I said.

Those were not the right words at all. Olga wasn't a political figure, but I couldn't remember a nice way to put it, and *'do you want to pray over the corpse'* didn't seem like a very nice turn of phrase. But Father Tomás instantly took me up on my offer. I was relieved. We'd gained valuable information from him last time, and if I could get him alone, maybe I could get even more questions answered.

CHAPTER ELEVEN

I led Father Tomás towards the small stone building that Olga had been laid out in. It was where Roberto had started his carpentry business before Nico had taken over and expanded everything downtown.

I stood awkwardly next to the priest as he recited prayers. I'd always been less than a casual mass attendee, so I just mumbled when there were words I recognized and followed the sign of the cross whenever Father Tomás utilized it.

The small workroom had been fully transformed and meticulously cleaned from every speck of dust or loose nail. Fragrant flowers filled the room, and every statue or religious symbol from the surrounding houses on the Gallardo family property were up for display spread out both on the walls and various tables.

Ana had been right about the attendance for Olga's wake. I could already see a line of people weaving themselves through the main front door across the patio towards Beatriz's house. They noticed us through the window. It was now or never. I had to get some more information out of Father Tomás before anyone came over to interrupt.

"Ana and I went to talk to Olga's sister-in-law, Lupe," I said. "But Esteban wasn't there. I had no idea that they'd been on such bad terms. They were going to let Olga be buried as a pauper."

The priest shook his head sadly. "I didn't know that either until Lía came by. Olga complained about her brother sometimes, but I didn't realize it ran so deep. We would've never let her be laid to rest that way, though, I can assure you."

I wasn't sure I believed the young priest. The most Father Francisco would've allowed the church to do, with pressure, is pass the collection plate around for her during mass. Santa Rita would've paid for it, but Father Francisco wouldn't lift a finger for free, unless he was badgered or shamed into doing it. But I nodded anyway.

"Was there anyone else who Olga complained about besides her brother?" I asked. "Did she have any enemies that you know of?" I knew I was laying it on thick, but time was of the essence, and I needed the priest to be clear.

"Not that she told me about. Olga was a very… passionate person and not afraid to share her opinions. There were always those that she offended without meaning to and vice versa but no one especially that I know of."

Did priests take a PR course at seminary, I wondered. "Yes, yes, I understand, but what about in the church? Father Francisco is also a passionate person. Did he and Olga ever have any disagreements right before she died, or anyone else close to the church?" I thought about using Silvia's name but decided against it. It was already too difficult to keep the creeping frustration out of my voice.

"Oh that," Father Tomás chuckled. "She and Francisco did butt heads at times, especially about…" He glanced around before whispering. "Silvia. Olga did not approve, but since nothing was openly spoken about, and he was the priest, she didn't really complain. Olga thought I was much too liberal and represented everything wrong with the church too. But the most I ever heard Olga ever say was that she was praying and concerned for us and hoped we'd find our way back to the truth of the church."

"So why don't you say anything– about Father Francisco and Silivia, I mean?" I asked. "I don't care what people do in their personal lives, but it's so hypocritical, and he's insufferable about it." I was afraid I'd overstepped my boundaries, but Father Tomás didn't even flinch, and I understood now why he was so popular. He had the air of a therapist about him, like you could reveal anything, and he wouldn't be shocked or judgemental.

"What good would it do?" he said simply. "Everyone knows. It's been an open secret for years. I'd just make my main coworker angry with me, and he could have me transferred to another parish. How would that help people in Santa Rita?" He shrugged. "Maybe I'm too pragmatic. I'll pray about it." He touched my shoulder. "I really will."

"I shouldn't monopolize your time. Thanks for speaking with me," I murmured before nodding and thanking the other attendees as they threaded their way towards the priest. I passed back into Beatriz's kitchen, now crowded with people, to see what else needed to be done. But Beatriz had everything in hand.

An elderly neighbor who attended wakes as part of her weekly social schedule grabbed my arm, eager to give her analysis. "This one is very nice, but I went to one on Libertad Street last week, and it was so beautiful. They gave generous portions of shrimp soup and so many flowers, all kinds."

I nodded and smiled patiently as she listed the number of mourners at each wake in the last year. When I heard some raised voices on the patio, I stiffened. *What now?* But it quickly changed from minor annoyance to full on de-escalation mode when I heard Blanca's voice in the mix. She was my responsibility, and I did not need her making a scene at a wake of all places.

"If you'd excuse me, please." I turned to the older woman and then rushed out the door onto the patio to find Blanca already in a heated debate with Sara.

Well, at least she hadn't added someone new to her list

of enemies, I thought. *What was Sara doing here?* Blanca hadn't been fond of Olga, but at least she'd known her. Apart from one intense argument at the rehearsal party, Sara hadn't known Olga at all. Well, neither had I, actually, and here I was helping to host the visitation. But still why would you show up at a wake just to make a scene? I suppressed a sigh before wading into the fray.

"Please," I said softly, trying to utilize a trick my teachers had always used with disruptive classes. "Whatever issues you two have, now is really not the appropriate time."

"Not the appropriate time." Sara turned to me red-faced. "And who are *you* to dictate to me the appropriate time? This woman" –she jabbed a finger in Blanca's direction– "has been running all over town with *my* husband, and now I find out she's *married*. What are you, a prostitute or something?" Sara practically spit her words at Blanca.

I could feel the heat rising in my own chest, but I squeezed my hands and tried to push it down. Screaming would only add to the fire, and I needed to diffuse it. I looked around hoping Carlos would come and handle his mother.

"Prostitute?" Blanca was yelling now. "It's none of your business anyway seeing as he's your ex-husband, and I don't know you from a hole in the wall. And who do you think you are yelling at my daughter that way? She's been gracious enough to let you stay in her hotel for practically free, and you have the nerve to scream at her. You are an ungrateful, spiteful–" Blanca glanced around before lowering her voice. "Well, I won't curse here seeing as it's a wake and all, but I can see now why Luis divorced you."

Blanca flounced past me and into the house away from Sara, who stood looking slightly abashed as the realization seemed to dawn on her that she'd just made a spectacle of herself at a visitation.

"Thank you for coming, and you're welcome to stay, but I think it's best for you to stay away from Blanca, please. This is supposed to be a night for mourning and remembering Olga, not for hashing out petty grievances." I kept my voice low and as neutral as possible, pretending as though I was speaking to a spoiled child who didn't really know any better, and maybe that wasn't far off with Sara.

I had to find a tactful way to tell Carlos that he needed to hang around and control his mother. After all, that's what I was doing with mine, and if he couldn't control Sara, how was I supposed to? Hopefully, Blanca would make herself useful and keep her distance. I was proud of her for actually taking the high-road for once.

But there was no time to find Carlos. The three vegan Youtubers walked through the main door of the Gallardo family property. There would be no rest for the weary, apparently.

Claire reluctantly approached. "I hope it's okay that we came. I wanted to pay my respects to Olga. I never met her, but I thought it might help after finding her that day. I..."

"Of course, of course," I patted her arm. "There are refreshments in the kitchen, through there." I pointed across the patio. "And if you would like to see the body and pay your respects directly, it's in the small building behind the main house, but you're not obligated to. Whatever you're comfortable with."

"Thanks." Claire nodded.

"Plus, when else would we get the opportunity to attend a Mexican funeral," Harriet said, her voice inappropriately excited.

This was apparently just another cultural experience to check off her vacation agenda. I just hoped they didn't do any filming. *Surely I didn't have to tell them that, did I?*

"Harriet!" Jessica hissed in Harriet's direction. "I'm sorry about that. She has absolutely no tact whatsoever."

"So where are the skeletons?" Harriet asked, ignoring Jessica.

"What? I'm sorry I don't think I understand." I really needed to get away from this girl.

"Well, you know, like Day of the Dead, there are skeletons everywhere. Do people take them from funerals or bring them?" Harriet wouldn't back down. She glanced around with a gleam in her eye.

"No, they're not real. Just like people in the US don't really hang skeletons in their yards. They're all either plastic or sugar. *This*" –I motioned around me– "is called a wake, visitation, whatever. We aren't monsters. We don't just carry around real skeletons for fun when someone dies."

"Sorry, I wasn't trying to offend you. I didn't realize you were so sensitive about it." At least Harriet had the courtesy to look embarrassed.

"I'm really sorry." Claire's face had turned a shade of red that I didn't think was possible on a human. "Let's just go," she whispered loudly towards Jessica and Harriet and tried to pull them back the way they'd come in. "This was a bad idea."

While I would've been relieved if the three of them left, it wasn't that big of a deal, and I didn't want Claire to feel badly about something that she'd had nothing to do with.

"Don't worry about it." I touched Claire's arm. "If you'd like to stay, you're all welcome to." I looked towards Harriet and nodded. "There are refreshments in the house. Please stay as long or as little as you'd like."

Claire smiled broadly, and Harriet mumbled, "Thanks."

Jessica shot an irritated look at Harriet, but I couldn't read it. Something was going on between those two, but I didn't have the energy or interest to care, as long as they kept their drama outside.

I spotted Lía across the patio, excused myself, and hurried towards her. "How's everything?" I asked.

"So far, so good for the first night at least. I went by the church today, and we've got almost all the funeral organized and paid for." She winked.

"I heard about that. Father Tomás apologized for Father Francisco as soon as he arrived. He made it sound like there was some big blowup."

Lía shrugged. "Father Francisco didn't like to hear that the church shouldn't charge for use of the sanctuary, that they should actually be contributing towards Olga's funeral arrangements, and thankful that they weren't being sued."

"You said that?" Lía was always practical but equally diplomatic in her approach, at least at the hotel. This was a side of her I'd never seen since we were kids.

"Well, it's true. Olga wasn't my favorite person either, but it was the literal least the church could do, and Father Francisco strutting around there like– Anyway, I said it, and I don't regret it."

"Well, good for you, and thanks for all your help. I feel bad about roping everyone into doing this, especially with the wedding and all."

Lía shrugged. "Well, it has to be done, and it's not that hard. Plus, my mom would've agreed to host it no matter what. That's just how she is."

"Let me see if she needs any more help," I said. "I saw Blanca go into the kitchen. Hopefully she's not making Beatriz's work any harder than it needs to be."

Beatriz's kitchen was overflowing with guests, and Blanca was quietly providing refreshments. Had Beatriz just performed a miracle corralling my mother like that?

Blanca smiled shyly. "You want some coffee?" she asked.

"Sure, thanks." I accepted the steaming styrofoam cup.

"You want me to help?" I asked.

"That would be nice, thanks." Blanca passed me the carafe before busying herself to boil more water.

Blanca was calm, not yelling, not trying to steal the show, just quietly helping. It was so unlike her. I didn't know what to say. It was easy to find the words when I was frustrated or wanted to reprimand her, but now in this quiet moment, I was coming up empty.

"I'm glad you came," I mumbled. Blanca nodded mutely, and I couldn't think of anything else to add.

CHAPTER TWELVE

"What are you doing here?" I looked up from my hated bookkeeping duties to see Ana standing in the hotel office.

Ana shrugged. "Well, the wedding's been postponed, and everything's been dealt with until then, so I thought I'd come and see if I could be helpful here."

"I'm sure your future mother-in-law has plenty of ways for you to keep busy," I teased.

But at the mention of Sara, Ana visibly tensed. "Oh, please don't remind me. Carlos should be happy I love him so much, because if not..." She shrugged.

Furby languidly stood from the pile of papers he'd been laying on and stretched, arching his back and rubbing against Ana. She offered a small smile and a pat.

"Carlos is a great guy, but you need to tell him to control his mother. Did you see her last night at the wake? And he was nowhere to be found," I said.

"I didn't see her argument, but I sure heard it," Ana agreed. "Carlos wasn't there yet, and I wasn't about to go and argue with her."

"Well, I can't say I blame you. Luckily Blanca took the high road and was actually helpful the rest of the evening."

"I saw her. Maybe she's turning over a new leaf."

I shrugged. "I'm not going to get my hopes up. But except for that hiccough, everything went smoothly. The Youtubers showed up and were irritating, or at least Harriet was, but other than that, no other issues."

"I saw them. Honestly, I was pretty surprised that they showed up at all. I saw the blonde one and the one with the glasses, sorry I don't remember their names, really going at it. Why would you go to a wake for someone you didn't even know on vacation just to stand there and argue?" Ana shook her head. "Well, I guess that's what Sara and Blanca did too. People are weird."

"It is strange," I agreed. "I kind of get why Claire wanted to come. She's the one with the tattoos. She found the body and was pretty freaked out by it, but the other two– at least leave your bickering at home."

Furby, bored with our gossip, decided to occupy himself with a paperclip on the floor, chasing it back and forth under the desk. I looked down at my phone as it announced an incoming text from Maritza. Lupe called in sick. Can you please come by the bakery and help? We're swamped.

I jumped up, eager to do anything that didn't involve spreadsheets. I showed the text to Ana.

She frowned. "That's not a good sign. Do you think Lupe's planning on quitting?" Ana didn't actively accuse me of anything, but the implication was there.

"Well, I guess it's up to Lupe whether she wants to quit or not." I shrugged off the question.

Furby meowed loudly and rubbed my leg. "Maritza won't let you near her bakery, sorry bud." I gave him a scratch behind the ear. "But you can hang out here, and I'll come back for you, okay?" Furby arched his back, stretched, and settled in a cardboard box filled with paper. Apparently he agreed with the plan, or he would've argued further.

"Come by the cottage for lunch," I said.

Ana eagerly nodded. "Definitely."

The bakery was uncharacteristically full for a mid-weekday morning, but if it hadn't been for the slightly less than full shelves that Maritza was meticulous about, I would've never guessed that anything was amiss.

"How can I help?" I asked Maritza. She was busy stuffing a paper bag with bolillos.

She smiled and audibly sighed. "Thank God you could come. Lupe flaked out on me today. Today of all days. She knows it's Rosa's day off, too. If you could just keep the shelves full and help customers while I man the cash register, that would be great– better than great actually."

"That's easy enough," I agreed and pulled on a paper mask, plastic gloves, and set about restocking all the empty holes in the display cases with the fresh baked goods that Maritza must've whipped up all by herself this morning.

"Thanks for all your help," Maritza said, casually strolling over when it became clear that the rush had petered out significantly. "I think I can handle it from here."

"I can hang out for a while in case things start to get crazy again," I offered.

"Sure, take a beso with you." Maritza held out a paper bag already filled.

"You know me too well, but a beso isn't the same without–"

"Coffee," Maritza reached behind her to a pre-made cup already on the counter.

"Am I that predictable?" I asked.

She shrugged. "Pretty much, yeah, but you're also dependable, so I won't complain."

I laughed and settled on a tiny table in the corner eager to devour my sweet breakfast, made even sweeter by the fact that I was here ready to 'help', so I didn't even need to feel guilty about any of the other duties I could've been doing. But just as I separated the bread to lick the cream, who should walk in but Jessica and Harriet.

I stifled a groan. Were these girls stalking me or what? I scrunched down in my seat hoping they wouldn't see me, and thankfully they didn't, sitting just a few tables away. They were too busy arguing to look or even care about who else was around them.

"I told you to stop it, Jessica, but you never listen to me. You always think you're smarter than everyone else, don't you?" Harriet's pale, freckled face was red with rage.

"Great, and I'll be happy to stop your salary right along with it," Jessica shouted so loudly that all other conversation in the bakery ceased.

"Ha! That's hilarious. I barely get paid as it is, so stop what? You'd never find someone to work as hard as I do."

"There are a lot of people who actually believe in our cause who would love to work with a successful Youtube channel. A LOT OF PEOPLE!"

"Yeah, how long until they figure out who you really are?" Harriet didn't even bother to sit down. She stood over Jessica practically spitting her words.

"I guess we'll have to see, won't we?" Jessica had regained her composure, but her intense expression conveyed the same amount of anger, just in a different form.

"Okay, Vegan B.S. queen, you can take this job and SHOVE IT! But don't say I didn't warn you." Harriet stormed out of the bakery without even a cup of coffee.

Whoa, what a show! I slowly sipped my coffee, wide-eyed, the few other patrons did the same, whispering, and staring around the bakery, probably wondering what these foreign ladies were screaming about in public. Who knew what their frantic tones and screaming, angry voices would be translated to in homes around Santa Rita tonight? There'd probably be several interesting versions making the rounds.

Jessica seemed to have gained full composure and stood to place her order at the counter. Returning, she saw me in the corner and came straight towards me. I wasn't disappointed, though. I had to admit that I was a little bit curious about their fight myself.

"Hi," Jessica demurely tucked a perfect, flaxen strand of hair behind her ear and smiled. "You mind if I sit with you?"

"Sure," I said and pushed the opposite chair out with my foot. I wasn't sure if I should bring up Jessica's fight with Harriet or ignore it entirely.

But Jessica acknowledged it immediately, so I didn't have to worry. "Sorry about that whole *thing* earlier with Harriet." Jessica sighed. "I don't know what's gotten into her lately. She's just–"

"A little moody? Sorry about that. I shouldn't have– I just– That's just been my impression," I finished lamely. I needed to try harder to at least appear professional.

Jessica nodded. "Exactly, don't feel bad. That's how Harriet is. She's sweet as can be one minute. The next she's screaming about something or saying some rude, inappropriate thing. I don't know what to do."

I wasn't sure I'd agree with that, but I understood Jessica's general conclusion, not that she was much better herself. "Didn't Harriet just quit, though? Aren't you even a little bit worried about that?"

Jessica waved her hand dismissively. "Oh that? No, the next time I see her she'll have some new plan for the channel. It's how she is."

"Do you mind me asking what that was even about? It was awfully intense."

"That's the thing. It wasn't that big of a deal." Jessica laughed. "It's stupid when you think about it, really. Harriet isn't happy about how we're handling our content. There's a site that allows you to give access to paying subscribers, you know special videos, livestreams, that kind of thing, and Harriet thinks we're being too old-fashioned about our content over there. I won't bore you with the details, and when I disagreed, she just went crazy. Well you saw her."

"Maybe there's something personal going on," I suggested.

"Maybe. I hadn't thought about it." Jessica shrugged. She seemed to have completely moved on. I wished I had that ability.

"So have you and Harriet been friends long?" I asked, looking to see if Maritza needed my help and hoping she'd flag me over.

"A few years, not as long as Claire and I, obviously, but she's been great. She used to take me to all my chemo appointments."

"Really?" That seemed strange for a new friend to do. Didn't Jessica have family, and what about Claire? I thought they were the best of best friends. Here I was again, trying to overanalyze something out of nothing. I needed to save that for Olga's murder investigation, not petty squabbles.

But Jessica continued. "Harriet was the one who told me to eat whole foods. I was already vegan, but it wasn't all healthy. So

I switched to a raw food diet, and *voilá*, my cancer was cured."

I was pretty sure that's not how medicine or science worked, but I smiled anyway. Who was I to argue? "Well, I'm glad you're healthy now," I said.

"Thank you." Jessica shot her toothpaste commercial smile. She really knew how to turn on the charm. "You know if you'd switch to a vegan diet, it would clear up your skin and help you get rid of those last 20 pounds."

I shifted uncomfortably. What was wrong with my skin, I wondered. And what last 20 pounds was she talking about? I shoved the rest of the piedra in my mouth. How had we gone from cancer to talking about acne and bikini bodies?

"Well, Harriet's not vegan anymore either, so I guess I'm not the only one you should be lecturing." I dug in the bag, happy to find a chocolate donut Maritza had hidden at the bottom and took a big bite.

But Jessica didn't seem to register my passive aggressive ploy. She sighed dramatically. "I know. That's the other thing. Harriet has changed so much. She used to have morals, standards, you know?"

"Uh-hmm," I mumbled around a mouthful of custard. "Well, sorry to run, but I think Maritza needs me. I'll be right there!" I shouted across the bakery in Spanish. Maritza glanced up from the display case, confused.

"Well, talk to you later, Jessica. Have a great day." And I booked it away from the table.

"Oh please keep me away from those Youtubers," I whispered to Maritza.

"You're starting to sound like me. Well, if you'd like to take inventory in the pantry storeroom that would help me out a lot." Maritza handed me a pad and pen.

"What century are you in?" I asked, frowning at her old-fashioned implements.

"Oh, so now you don't know how to use a pen, is that it? All you can do is poke around on your lighted screen."

"It's just that it's a lot easier if you'd use a software that could–"

"Eh, eh, eh," Maritza chided. "Don't get near me with that stuff. All you have to do is check off the boxes, sugar how much, flour how much. I don't think it's gotten to the point of needing a machine for that, at least not yet."

"Okay, okay, you win." I held up my hands in defeat. "I'll do your 19th century inventory for you."

"Thank you." Maritza nodded. "It's all right there on that sheet, organized clearly. I think you might be surprised how simple it is to complete with a flick of the wrist." She demonstrated. "It shouldn't take any more physical exertion than scrolling through your phone, but I can demonstrate how to turn a page if you'd like."

"I think I can handle it, but if I have any questions about the clipboard, I'll be sure to check in with you." I said.

Maritza's thinly suppressed smile broke through, and she offered a pat on the back. "I know you can do it. I believe in you." And her smile gave way to full-bodied laugh.

I was happy to disappear into the back of the bakery for a few minutes, away from any random run-ins, and focus on a mindless task while still being productive.

"That didn't take as long as I thought it would." I handed Maritza back her clipboard with a smile.

"Everything go okay?" she asked.

"Just fine."

"Oh, so you don't think the process needs to be improved. Is that what you're saying?"

"You really are a pain, you know that?" I said.

"Yes, yes, thank you, but a simple, you were correct, Maritza, is enough."

"Not in this lifetime," I said with a smile and exited towards the hotel. Furby was waiting at the front desk and gave an angry protest when he saw me enter.

"He's been waiting for you and berating anyone who walks past," Miguel said. He gave Furby a pat, who tolerated it with appreciative disdain.

"Did you miss me, buddy?" I scratched Furby under the chin. "You know I wouldn't forget you." But Furby eyed me skeptically. I laughed.

"So how has the front desk been overall?" I asked Miguel.

"Pretty uneventful." He shrugged. "No screaming matches. That's always a good day."

"I'll be back at the cottage this afternoon if anyone needs me," I said. "But if they really don't need me, then I'm out for the day." I winked.

"Got it," Miguel nodded and cleared his throat.

Blanca stood awkwardly at the front door. She'd just come in smiling, but her face fell as she shifted weight. I hadn't thought about the fact that maybe Blanca didn't feel comfortable around me either. Maybe she saw me as judgemental or a buzz kill or something.

"Hi," she finally said in English. We often spoke in a strange Spanglish blend, choosing the words that were the most natural to fill the spaces. In Santa Rita it had been strange just picking one language to converse in depending on who else was around. It was also another reminder that we had rarely spoken just the two of us.

"Hi," I said. "I was going back to the cottage for lunch, if you'd like to come." I switched to our more natural Spanglish, and while Blanca smiled and relaxed a little, she still shook her head.

"Sorry, I was just coming by to change. I've got plans for the rest of the day," she said.

"Or tonight, we could have dinner together if you'd like, or maybe tomorrow evening, if you can." Why was I begging her? Even though it felt completely uncomfortable being around each other, it also didn't feel right to send Blanca home having spent zero one-on-one time together, or maybe I should just let it go? Begging wasn't an attractive quality in anyone.

"We'll see," Blanca said, breezing past with a smile and in a tone that meant, *definitely not*. Why was she here if she didn't want to see me, I wondered.

Furby meowed. "Yes, your majesty. Lunch is on the way," I said. "Hopefully, Auntie Ana has picked up something scrumptious, because I don't really feel like cooking." I gave Miguel a wave, scooped up King Furby, ready to finally head home and relax.

"So where were you the night of the murder?" My ears perked up at the phrase in English. It was coming from the downstairs guest hall, and it sounded like Harriet, but I couldn't be sure. I tried to peek around the corner without being seen, and sure enough Harriet had Blanca cornered right outside the stairwell.

"What are you talking about?" Blanca asked, but she seemed to find the question more humorous than irritating.

"I've decided to do an exposé for *my* channel, and what's better publicity than solving a murder? Don't worry. I'm asking everyone. I'm just starting with the English speakers first."

Jessica didn't even think that Harriet had quit, and here she was planning to harass the whole town for some publicity. I held back a sigh.

"I was in my room sleeping all night. Believe me, if I was going to kill someone, it wouldn't have been Olga and definitely not with the hangover I had that day." Blanca laughed.

"Okay, well I'll be verifying that," Harriet shouted up the stairs behind Blanca.

I'd planned on going over the security footage with Ana back at the cottage over lunch, but I hadn't actually thought we'd find anything. Did Harriet know something we didn't, or was she just punching in the dark?

"Miguel," I hissed. "If anyone asks you for any camera footage or wants to go back in the office, and they aren't authorized, including my mother, don't let them."

"Got it." Miguel nodded and didn't seem at all surprised by my request.

I ducked into the office and put the video from the three cameras on the guest hallways side by side and sped through them during the early morning hours to see if there were any odd movements that day. Maybe Harriet had heard something before they'd left that had made her suspicious.

I stared at the screen. It couldn't be, but there it was clear as day, Sara. She was coming out of her room. Surely this had to mean something else, I thought. Frozen. But there she was on camera sneaking down the back stairs and out into the early morning darkness. My phone beeped. It was Ana asking where I was. I scooped up the laptop, my cat, and locked the office door behind me just to be safe. I wasn't sure how Ana was going to react to this, but she deserved to know.

CHAPTER THIRTEEN

"**W**hat took you so long?" Ana asked. She had already let herself in and was setting out Cuban sandwiches and bags of chips.

"Oh, that smells wonderful. I was worried we'd actually have to cook something." I sat down, pushing Furby away. He tried to jump on the table to grab his own piece of meat but relented when I lobbed a tiny piece of ham in his direction and decided to stay on the floor.

"I knew you'd be hungry." Ana smiled. "So what are your leads so far with Olga, anyone new we should add to our suspect list?"

The yummy, greasy goodness turned to cardboard in my mouth. How was I going to tell Ana what I'd found? "Well, uh... actually I was going over some of the security footage from that night, and I found something that you might want to take a look at." I couldn't look Ana directly in the eyes.

She touched my arm. "What is it? What aren't you telling me?"

"Harriet was pestering Blanca about going out that night, and it got me thinking. Well- Just watch it," I said, angling the laptop towards her. Maybe I was making more out of it than I should. After all, there might be a perfectly reasonable explanation that Sara had gone out before dawn on the day of a murder. I just couldn't think of one.

I fast forwarded it until the lower left hand timestamp read exactly 5:02 a.m., and just as before the camera outside Sara's room shows her distinctly leaving her room and instead of exiting through the front door, which would have been closer, more convenient, and what she always did, the video shows her leaving through the back stairway and out the back door towards the parking lot. I switched to the outdoor footage, which captured Sara continuing on across the parking lot, and the last image showed her turning in the direction of the church.

"It doesn't prove anything," I said, trying to sound reasonable. "But–"

"But it certainly doesn't look good, does it?" Ana said. The timing isn't exact, but whoever the killer was might've been laying in wait. The sanctuary is open almost 24-hours. It's locked up for a few hours in the middle of the night, but other than that–"

"It's a free for all," I put in. "Which everyone in town knows, and there are no cameras in or around the church building, at least I don't think so anyway."

Ana shook her head. "None at all, and I had Lía double check when she went down to shame Father Francisco into donating towards Olga's funeral."

"But Sara wouldn't have known that," I said. "Plus, she and Olga argued for just a short time that I saw, which doesn't give her a very strong motive for murder."

"Well," Ana said. "Olga came back in after you left, and she and Sara went back at it. Sara seemed to represent everything Olga hated about the world, and she wasn't reserved about it. It still seems a weak motive for murder, though. But maybe she saw or heard something that morning around the church that could help us. Plus, we still need to be able to rule her out, if we can."

I nodded. *So that's what Olga had gone back in for.* Sara definitely wasn't trying to make any friends in Santa Rita. "But who's going to talk to her? Not me. She hates me and my mom, and after what happened at Olga's wake, I'm going to keep my

Sara interactions to a minimum."

Ana nodded in agreement but didn't answer immediately. She chewed the inside of her nail, still nodding. "It was weird that Sara came to the wake, wasn't it? And her whole behavior–"

"Ana, you don't honestly think–"

"Hear me out." Ana put up a hand to stop me. "What if Sara just happened to take a morning walk, wandered down to the church, saw that it was open, went inside to have a look around, and there was Olga ornery as ever, and after her morning prayers, got in Sara's face yet again. They argued, and bang, bang. Poor Olga's on the floor dead, and Sara runs away."

"I mean it is possible," I admitted. "But this is Carlos's mother we're talking about here, and it's just a theory you made up in your head. Unless we find something more to implicate her, I think it's better if we find out where Sara went that morning before rushing to any conclusions."

Ana nodded glumly. I think part of her wanted Sara to be guilty. What better excuse could there be for not having to see your mother-in-law than her being in prison?

A knock sounded at the front door. "I'll get it," Ana offered.

It was Lía. Ana handed her another sandwich. "I always come prepared with extras," she said.

Lía gratefully accepted it. "Whose idea was it to lock the office door?" she asked. I came by, and everything was closed. Miguel said no one could enter without a key, which I didn't bring. Are we locking everything up now? What's the deal?" Lía dug into her sandwich and glanced between Ana and me waiting for an answer.

"I just don't want anyone poking around." I explained about Harriet questioning Blanca, and that I'd decided to check out the security footage. I didn't mention exactly what I'd found and that a part of me had been terrified that I was going to find Blanca on that footage instead. But Blanca had been pretty drunk that night, and my mother could be a liar, irresponsible, you name it, but she wasn't the murdering type. I looked towards Ana to fill in the rest.

She sighed and explained to Lía everything that we'd seen on the camera footage. If Lía's mouth hadn't been so full of sandwich, it would've fallen open. Ana turned the screen and played the footage for Lía.

Finally Lía spoke. "I hadn't even thought of the cameras. I guess I was just happy the hotel wasn't mixed up in anything."

I nodded. "Me too, and it's entirely possible Sara had nothing to do with it either. After all an argument is hardly motive for murder of a near stranger, but we have to cross her off the list 100%, so we can look more closely at the other suspects."

Lía and I both turned towards Ana. "I'm not questioning her," Ana said. "Carlos can do that."

"So how are you going to broach the subject with Carlos exactly?" Lía asked. "Hello dear, but your mom left her hotel room at an ungodly hour that just about coincides with the time of Olga's murder. Could you double check and make sure she's not a homicidal maniac for me?"

I coughed to hide a laugh, but Ana did not seem amused. "I'll be honest with him," she said. "But I don't think I'll take that blunt of a tactic, if you don't mind."

Lía shrugged. "Just get the information and fast, but my money's on Silvia. I hate her, and I don't think Father Francisco did it, but he knows what happened." Lía narrowed her eyes. "They're both guilty if you ask me."

"Are you just saying that because you guys got into it the

other day?" I asked, but Lía shook her head.

"They have easy access to the sanctuary, and Silvia had plenty of motive. After all, who has Olga's job now?"

"True," Ana agreed. "They're both suspects, but why now? And why would Silvia kill just to get a secretarial job?"

"And according to Father Tomás, Olga hadn't had any serious disagreements with Father Francisco," I put in. "I still think Esteban is the main suspect."

Ana nodded. "He and Lupe had the most to gain, and Lupe called in sick. Maybe she's afraid we're on to her."

I glanced over at the wall clock, shocked at how fast the afternoon had flown by. "I guess we should be heading out. It's the second day of the wake, and we don't want to leave all the work to Beatriz," I said.

We wandered back up towards the hotel lobby where Nico had agreed to pick us up, but Harriet had emerged once again. She'd cornered someone upstairs. I could hear her angry accusation down the stairwell, apparently shouting them into her phone and then playing the automated Spanish translation to whomever she'd managed to corner. I needed to have a serious talk with her. I wasn't sure how it was going to go, but it needed to happen, and I'd still take handling Harriet any day over Sara.

"Give me a sec," I said to Ana and Lía before marching down the hall to find Harriet who stared down at a very confused and exasperated employee. Rosa was exiting the break room and on her way out the door, when she'd apparently been accosted by Harriet.

"What are you doing?" I asked Harriet. I tried to keep the irritation out of my voice.

Harriet wavered for a moment but then gathered herself. "I just wanted to know what others may have seen or heard that night. After all, this hotel has quite the history, doesn't it?"

I knew she was trying to get to me, and it bothered me that it worked. I motioned for Rosa that she could leave and mumbled an apology, thankful that she probably couldn't understand most of what Harriet was saying with the awkward translation app.

"I understand you and Jessica had a falling out this morning, and a real-life murder mystery would be a great start to a new channel." I needed to show some empathy if I was going to get anywhere with Harriet. "Obviously you're free to talk to whomever you wish. I can't stop you as a guest in my hotel." I tried to smile and failed. "But *if* I start getting complaints from other guests or employees that they are being harassed by you in my establishment, *then* I would have to ask you to leave." I kept my tone soft and was proud of myself for not raising my voice.

"Are you saying you're going to kick me out if I start poking around, is that it?" Harriet didn't share by commitment to remaining calm.

"I will ask anyone to leave who is harassing guests or employees, including you. Yes." I looked Harriet straight in the eye. "I would hate to do that, though. We want everyone to have a pleasant stay."

Harriet glowered but didn't respond. At the other end of the hall, Claire stuck her head out of the stairwell. I suppressed an audible sigh. Maybe she could talk some sense into Harriet.

Claire emerged hesitantly. "Hey Hare, you know you can always–"

But Harriet's face transformed into an even angrier mask than it had been before. "You!" She practically spat. "I don't want to hear a word from you, Miss Perfect Claire. I thought you were different, but you're just like Jessica– no, no you're worse. You're her little minion. You pretend to be nice, but it's all fake. Don't even try to '*explain things*' to me. You're going to get it too."

Claire audibly sighed but didn't offer a response.

Harriet pointed her finger in my direction. "I won't ask anyone else questions in your precious hotel, but you don't control the town." And with that she spun around and marched towards the front door, presumably to shove her microphone and automated translator into random pedestrians' faces as they walked down the street.

Once she was safely out of earshot, I turned to Claire. "What was that all about?" I asked.

Claire shook her head sadly. "It's a long story. Do you have a sec?"

I didn't really. We were supposed to be leaving for the wake any minute, but I could meet them later. I wanted to find out what had happened between Harriet and the other two, especially if I might have to kick her out. I needed to know exactly what type of scenario I was dealing with.

I sent a message to Ana explaining that something had come up, and I'd meet them at the wake later and followed Claire into her room. She sat down awkwardly on the end of the bed. I chose one of the desk chairs.

"Sorry about that." Claire looked down and fiddled with one of her bracelets. "I came out to try and help, but it just made everything worse."

"It wasn't your fault," I assured her.

"I don't know how everything got so off course."

"So what exactly happened, with Harriet I mean. Am I going to have to ask her to leave a few days early? Because I really don't want to have to do that."

"I hope not, but she won't speak to me."

I felt bad for Claire and wanted to help her even more than I cared about whatever drama Harriet and Jessica had stirred up between each other.

"I don't even know all the details exactly. Every time I try to ask Harriet or Jessica about it, they tell me different things. But they really got into it at the bakery," Claire said, not looking up.

"Yeah, I was there when it happened. It was quite the production."

"You were? Sorry about that. I know you were hoping that us coming would be good publicity for your business, and it's been the exact opposite."

"Well, I wouldn't go that far," I said.

"So anyway, Harriet quit, and Jessica thought she was just exaggerating, you know blowing off some steam, but she was serious. She said she doesn't want to work with us anymore and wants to sabotage the channel and start her own. As soon as she started making those kinds of threats, I shut off her access to the channel. It doesn't mean that I don't want her. I'd be thrilled if she chose to come back, but we have to protect our brand."

I nodded.

"Oh God, that sounds so awful." Claire visibly cringed. "But it's true. It's how we make our living. Harriet said more than once that she was going to post the truth right on the channel, or her truth anyway. Well, you can see how she sees me now, and since I'm still working with Jessica, I'm the enemy. The whole thing is just ridiculous."

"So what were they arguing about to begin with?" I was curious what had caused everything to blow up so suddenly and severely.

Claire shook her head. "Harriet won't speak to me now that I'm the enemy, and Jessica claims that it was some kind of dispute about pay that got out of hand. Harriet didn't think she was making what she deserved, insults were thrown, end of story."

I nodded. "That sounds like what they were arguing about in the bakery. If they'd just sit down together and put their egos to the side, they could probably work the whole thing out."

"I know," Claire agreed. "But they're both so stubborn, and now Harriet's on this murder mystery kick. She was reading all these articles about the last murder that happened here in the hotel and all the publicity it got, and then she just went off about it. I'm afraid there's no stopping her now."

I was afraid of the same thing. "I didn't know you guys even knew about the murder that happened here last February." It wasn't something I liked to think about. I knew the information was out there, though. One of our guests had been murdered, and while I had helped solve it, the whole thing had been wrapped up, and Olga's murder was completely different. It had nothing to do with the hotel, although it didn't help Santa Rita's reputation much.

Claire shifted nervously again. "Well, it was actually part of the allure in coming here. Jessica's really into ghosts, and she keeps asking if anyone has felt any weird energy." Claire laughed. "I told her all hotels have probably had people die in them, but she doesn't care. That's probably what gave Harriet the idea." Claire shook her head. "I don't know what happened. They used to be so close, and then all this over practically nothing– at least nothing that couldn't have been easily worked out."

"Jessica said Harriet was a big support when she was sick, going above and beyond to take her to chemo appointments," I said.

"She was," Claire agreed. "Jessica didn't even want anyone else except Harriet to go with her. She said we all made her feel uncomfortable and self-conscious, but Harriet made it feel normal and helped Jessica feel normal in the process."

Claire's voice caught. "I've never seen anyone try so hard to put on a brave face. Jessica wanted everyone else to be happy and feel comfortable. And that was when Harriet started helping Jessica with her diet. She went from a regular vegan to everything being 100% natural and raw, green juice, and all that junk."

Claire made a face. "It's disgusting, but Jessica did start getting better and *feeling* so much better. I don't know how much was placebo and how much was a healthier outlook or the diet or a mixture of it all, but her numbers started turning around pretty quickly, and Harriet was always there trying to make her smile, bringing her anything she wanted." Claire shook her head. "I've never seen Harriet this angry before. It's just not like her. They've argued, but never like this."

Claire's whole body started to shake with sobs. I moved to sit next to her and rubbed her back trying to soothe her. Eventually she stopped enough to look up.

"I'm sorry to always bring so much drama." Claire wiped her face, leaving a trail of black mascara behind.

"Don't worry about it. I'm always happy to listen. It's my job to help, after all."

"Oh, and tonight's the second night of the visitation, isn't it?" Claire turned around to look at the bedside clock.

"Don't worry about it," I assured her. "The first and last nights are the main affairs. Tonight will be routine, but I should probably get going. After all, it was my idea for the Gallardo family to host this thing to begin with. I mean if you'll be okay."

Claire nodded. "I'll be fine. Don't worry about me. I'm just going to put on some pajamas and watch an old movie."

"Sounds good. Let me know if there's anything I can bring you." She promised she would, and I left her room. Thankfully, there was no evidence of Harriet in the hallway or in the lobby. Just Furby, who was pacing the reception desk, yowling angrily at anyone who tried to move him. Miguel gave me a look of desperation.

"He just wants his dinner." I went to pick him up, but Furby jumped down and started giving himself an angry bath. "Come on, Furby." I pleaded.

Miguel laughed. "That's one angry cat." But his laugh was cut short when a short, red-faced man entered the lobby. I'd never seen him before. He wore jeans and a checked shirt, and a palm hat that was popular with locals.

"Where's that owner lady, Natalia what's-her-face?" he asked, slightly swaying with each word.

Miguel started to respond, "She's not–"

"That would be me," I said. Probably not the smartest thing to admit to a slightly drunk, angry man that I was the person he was looking for, especially when I wasn't sure why, but I was tired of being scared. If this guy was angry with me, better to just have it out now.

"I wanted to tell you" – he stepped closer. I could smell the alcohol on his breath –"that I don't want you accusing my wife of anything and sending your little spies out to badger us with questions."

Harriet, I thought. She must've happened upon them in the street. Something needed to be done about her.

"You have no right," he continued on, slurring his words.

"My wife's been crying and crying, and she's worked here for years with no problems until you came around."

I was starting to realize who this might be, but I needed to be sure. "Gladly sir, but the only problem is that I have no idea who you are or your wife."

"My wife? You don't know my wife?" He was struggling to stay upright and had to hold onto the desk for balance. "You don't even know your employees' names, huh? Too important, is that it?"

He looked over at Miguel for agreement, but Miguel sat there quietly, probably not wanting to escalate the situation that I had stupidly walked into.

"My wife's name is Lupe. Would you like me to spell it for you?"

This was definitely the infamous Esteban and the number one suspect in Olga's murder, at least on my list. "Oh, your Olga's brother." I knew I shouldn't have tried to antagonize a drunk, angry man, but I couldn't help myself.

"Olga's dead," he hissed.

"Yes sir, I know. I was just on my way to her visitation." What was wrong with me? We did not need Olga's inebriated brother showing up. But thankfully, he didn't seem interested in that.

"Good riddance. Olga always thought she was better than everyone else too, and it finally caught up with her."

Wow, this guy really had no heart. Hopefully, we could get some solid evidence on him and get him locked up, I thought to myself, but on the outside, I just smiled calmly.

"I'm sorry you feel that way, but if you don't mind, I was just–"

"I don't want you telling my wife anything," he continued. "She said you practically accused her of murder in her own home. Lupe would never murder anyone."

"Good to know, sir, but we also can't have you here in the middle of the lobby making a scene, so if you'd please…"

The man blinked like he'd just realized where he was. "Oh yeah, sorry about that."

Furby jumped on the reception desk and hissed in his direction. I'd never seen Furby so aggressive before. Esteban stumbled back a few steps and exited the lobby as quickly and awkwardly as he'd come in.

"Well, that was definitely odd," Miguel said. "I wouldn't recommend introducing yourself when angry, drunk people stumble in, though."

'I know I shouldn't have, but I–" A woman was loudly yelling from the second floor hallway. "Is that Sara?" I asked Miguel.

He nodded dully. "It sure sounds like it."

I groaned. It didn't seem like I was going to make it to the visitation at all at this rate.

"I'll deal with it," I told Miguel before heading towards the stairs. Whatever it was, Sara was clearly not happy about it.

CHAPTER FOURTEEN

I approached the second floor hallway apprehensively, expecting to see blood with all the screaming that was happening, but Sara was upright, and there was no blood in sight.

"What are you talking about? Get away from me," Sara shouted.

"I'm really sorry. I didn't mean to uh–" Harriet stammered her apology to Sara in English. I didn't stop myself from rolling my eyes. What did Harriet think she was doing?

I should just leave and let Sara deal with it. She'd do a better job of scaring Harriet off snooping than I ever could. Even if Harriet couldn't understand the words coming out of Sara's mouth, the tone was terrifying enough. But I approached anyway. After all, the rest of the guests didn't deserve to have to listen to this.

"What seems to be the problem?" I asked in Spanish, ignoring Harriet.

"This girl" – Sara jabbed a finger in Harriet's direction –"she's here with her computer thingy asking me where I was the night of the murder and said someone saw me running away from the scene. Pure lies, all of it!"

I turned to Harriet, more curious than anything else now, and asked in English. "Is that true? Did someone see Sara running away from the murder scene?"

Harriet smirked. "Wouldn't you like to know. I guess you'll have to wait to–"

"I told you to stop harassing guests, Harriet, and now one

guest is definitely complaining about you, so I'd drop this holier than thou act you've got going on right now, or you're going to be spending the night on the first bus out of town."

Harriet had enough sense to look properly contrite before continuing. She shook her head. "No, it's not true. There was no witness. I made it up. It's a trick I heard police use. They make up lies about witnesses to get people to confess."

"So you've been going around town telling everyone that a witness saw them leaving the murder scene?" I asked.

"Well kind of," Harriet admitted. "We were outside in the street when we first started talking, but Sara tried to run away, so I followed her up the back stairs."

"As a general rule, if someone's running away when you're trying to talk to them, it's best to just let them be," I advised. Harriet nodded.

Sara had been standing between us the entire time, her hands on her hips, and her face whipping back and forth like a tennis match, confused and unsure of which team she should be rooting for, if any.

I turned to her. "I'm really sorry, Sara. I told Harriet that if she bothers you again that she'll be asked to leave the hotel." Sara nodded. At least she seemed satisfied with my approach.

Harriet held out her phone once more, and I stiffened, but the automatic voice translated her apologies instead. Sara nodded again, grunted something I couldn't quite hear and entered her room. At least she wasn't still yelling.

I wasn't sure what I should say to Harriet. She did seem sufficiently remorseful. At what point was I just rubbing it in? "No more," was all I said. I hoped it worked this time, and I turned to leave.

"What are *you* doing here?" Harriet asked from behind.

That same angry energy was back in her voice that I'd heard before. I turned around, *not again.*

Surely this was enough for one day. I followed Harriet's gaze and saw Jessica and Claire standing right outside the stairwell. Not this, anything but this. If there hadn't been blood before, there definitely would be now.

"Let's not make a scene, please," I pleaded. "There are other guests in the hotel." Harriet did take a breath and visibly tried to calm herself. Maybe it wouldn't be as bad as I'd feared.

Jessica held up her hands defensively. "I'm not here to make trouble. I just want to talk."

"Talk about what? Now that you know that I–"

"Come on, Harriet." Jessica spoke calmly. "We've been through so much together, both of us. We've both made mistakes. I know I have, but if you bring me down, you're bringing us all down. We're better together."

Harriet grunted in response.

"Let's talk about it tomorrow after we've had some time to sleep on it and can be calmer," Jessica suggested, smiling. I was impressed. I'd never thought of Jessica as the level-headed type, yet here she was.

"That sounds like a great plan," I said. "Talk about it somewhere neutral." I really hoped that the neutral place was not going to be my bakery again. "Your friendship is worth too much to just throw it away like this."

"She's no friend," Harriet muttered, but nodded in agreement anyway.

I locked eyes with Claire, and she smiled. "Thanks, Harriet," Claire said, extending her hand. "We need you."

Harriet glanced over at Claire like she'd just realized she

was there. "I'm sorry about earlier," Harriet whispered.

"Don't worry about it." Claire waved her hand. "We've all been under a lot of stress. I know it's a work trip, but it's still a vacation. I say we start to enjoy ourselves a little bit more. Remember why we do this in the first place. It's a dream job to work with your best friends, after all."

Harriet jerked back like Claire's words had punched her in the face. "You really think of me as a friend?" Harriet asked. Claire nodded. "You're not like Jessica," Harriet said. "You are actually a good person."

I glanced nervously towards Jessica, but she didn't seem hurt or surprised by Harriet's continued vitriol.

"I think sleep is a great idea," I put in. "Everything always looks clearer in the morning." I was relieved to escort the Youtubers back to their rooms and hoped they'd follow through, and there'd be no more yelling for the night.

I glanced at the time. It was too late to make it to the wake. I sent Ana and Lía a quick text of apology, hopefully they'd understand.

Ana was the first to text back. I expect a full report tomorrow. It sounds like it was quite the circus there.

It was and I will. I texted in response. Back at the reception desk, Furby was beside himself. He gave one loud, angry yowl at seeing me while frantically pacing on top of the desk.

"I'm so sorry." I clucked to Furby, but he'd have none of it.

Miguel's shift must have ended, because dim-witted Andrea was back at the helm. She stared at me blankly like we'd never met before.

"I think there's a uh... cat on the desk," she said, not

looking at all bothered or interested in the fact.

"Yes, there is." I refrained from rolling my eyes and scooped up Furby. "He's mine. Sorry, he's just a little upset. It's past dinner time."

She just shrugged and turned back to her phone. "Sure, yeah, okay."

Andrea did realize I was the owner, didn't she? I tapped her on the shoulder. "Excuse me?"

She glanced up. "Yes?"

"You're not allowed to be on your phone while you're working."

"I've seen others do it." She shrugged and put hers down.

How could I explain the difference between surreptitiously checking your phone when business was slow and openly staring at it in front of your boss for minutes on end? But an angry swipe from Furby let me know we didn't have time for that. I'd just have to pick my battles and turned to head back home to satiate Prince Furby.

I couldn't wait for this wedding to be over with and the Youtubers to be on their way as well. I'd give anything to have normal guest complaints like not enough water pressure, more towels, more sheets, lost whatever, but there were still several days to go, and unless I was willing to feign illness, there was no getting away from it. But after all of the day's shenanigans, I really hoped everyone would just take it down a few notches from here on out.

I was beyond thankful that Carlos had had the forethought to have his dad, Luis, stay with him and not at the hotel. I couldn't imagine what would've happened if Luis and Blanca and Sara were all actually staying under the same roof. Blanca spent most of her time with Luis, and I could swear she was avoiding me, but why had she come all this way just to blow me off? It was strange, and she'd seemed so happy with her newest husband. It wasn't like Blanca to cheat. But at least she wasn't the one causing my headaches for once, so I couldn't complain too much.

I awoke the next morning to being headbutted in the face. Apparently, I'd been forgiven for the evening before. "I wish I could lay in bed with you all day," I said, scratching under his chin. But Furby had other plans and directed me towards his dish.

I topped off his bowl and was getting the coffee going when the shrill sound of the landline made me jump. I'd forgotten about my grandma's phone since I never used it. It was probably a wrong number, but I picked it up anyway to stop the ear-splitting noise.

"Please, can you come?" A very flustered Maritza said without preamble. It wasn't like her to sound so overwhelmed.

"Sure, what's wrong?" I asked.

"Lupe didn't show up again. I've been calling your cell all morning, but you didn't answer. I had this old number, and–"

"I'll be right there," I promised, and Maritza offered an obvious sigh of relief.

"See you later, Furby. I won't be long," I promised, but Furby eyed me suspiciously, not believing me in the least.

The bakery was much less chaotic than I'd expected. Maritza was stocking the shelves of bolillo while four or five customers waited by the register. I slipped on a pair of plastic gloves and approached.

"I'll help you with those," I said, lifting the tray of bread.

"You're the best," she said before running back towards

the register.

"I'll remind you of that later," I said as I gingerly lifted the warm, fresh baked bolillos onto the shelves. Every home in Santa Rita bought bolillos daily because no one wanted day old bread, and even at peso a piece, it was always our top selling item.

It was easy to work with Maritza. Her normally prickly personality morphed into patience and friendliness when interacting with customers, and I enjoyed the mindless task of stocking the shelves and answering the occasional question. Once the mid-morning lull set in, Maritza collapsed at one of the small tables, and I sat opposite her.

"What's going on with Lupe?" I asked. "Do you think she's coming back?"

Maritza shrugged. "I don't know, and I'm not sure I care. If I saw her right now, I'd probably fire her anyway."

"But who else are we going to get to replace her? You and Rosa can't handle everything."

Maritza shrugged again. "I'm sorry I bothered you. I just didn't know what else to do. I know it's been nuts for everyone these days, but I wasn't expecting this."

"I'm just sorry I didn't see your calls earlier. Don't worry. I'll talk to Lía, and we'll figure something out."

Lía was in charge of hiring and payroll in both the hotel and bakery. With such a small operation, we all had to wear multiple hats, but that also meant that when things started to fall between the cracks, it was even more of a scramble to pick them back up again.

Nico strolled through the front door of the bakery. I still felt that odd rush of nervous excitement every time I saw him unexpectedly, and when I remembered that he was actually my boyfriend, it felt even stranger.

"Sitting down on the job I see." He tutted, but the smirk on his face betrayed him.

Maritza turned and shot him an irritated look but didn't say anything. "At least we're at work," I chided. "Some people aren't even at their job." I pointed in his direction, but he just grinned wider. Nico had a carpentry shop down the road, and by the looks of his clothing, he'd already been at work.

"I know. I know. I should be working, but I was just going to ask my girlfriend if she'd like to go out for dinner tonight."

"Oh, you two are just too cutesy. I can't stand it." Maritza stood and shuffled towards the kitchen, mumbling as she went.

"What a grump!" But Nico took her seat anyway, still smiling.

"It's been a rough morning," I explained. "So where were you thinking about having dinner?" I asked. "Tacos? Hamburgers?"

Nico shook his head. "It's uh... come to my attention recently that I haven't been the most romantic or generous when it comes to our dates."

He scratched the back of his neck. I smiled, knowing that it was probably Ana who had brought this to her brother's attention. It didn't matter to me where we ate together or how fancy it was, but it was sweet that he cared.

"I was thinking we could go to Monteverde, that fancy Italian place." He shrugged. "Well, fancy by Santa Rita standards anyway."

"Oh." I wasn't sure what to say. My only experience with the place had been on a fake date with a complete jerk for the sake of a murder investigation.

Reading my mind, Nico put up his hands. "I know. I know.

It doesn't hold the best memories, but they have excellent food, and now we can make a positive memory there."

"You're right," I said, nodding. "That sounds great." I leaned over to kiss him just as Maritza exited the kitchen.

"Get a room. You own a hotel for God's sake," she shouted across the bakery. I laughed and kissed Nico again.

"You said I was the best," I reminded Maritza.

"I'm rethinking that statement," she said, before heading back towards the kitchen again.

"I have some projects to finish up, but I could come by afterward. Does that work for you?" He shot another one of his wide grins.

I smiled and nodded. "I'll be ready and waiting at the cottage, " I said and handed him a chocolate donut.

After the door chimed behind Nico, Maritza finally emerged from the back, a cup of coffee in hand.

"You need to find yourself a good guy," I told Maritza, half joking.

She just grunted. "What do I need one of those for?" she finally replied.

"Well, I guess you don't, but at least you should get yourself a cat or a dog."

She nodded. "I might do that. They're much more useful and loyal than a man."

"Well, I'll talk to Lía about the staffing situation, and in the meantime, if you're ever short-handed, just ring the landline again, and I'll be over as fast as I can."

Maritza nodded. The coffee seemed to have worked to calm her grumpiness somewhat. "Will do," she promised. "And

I appreciate you coming at such short notice. You really saved me." She jumped up when a customer came into the bakery.

"You need more help?" I asked after she'd served the customer.

Maritza shook her head. "The afternoon crew should be here soon, so I can bake before heading home. It's the mornings that are tricky."

I nodded. It was hard to find someone who was willing to come into work at what most people considered the middle of the night rather than early morning. It wasn't something I was looking forward to myself, and I hoped Lía could find someone quickly, so I could spend 3:30 in the morning asleep rather than getting up for work.

CHAPTER FIFTEEN

"So what do you think?" I asked Lía, after explaining the staffing issue in the bakery.

She shook her head slowly. "I'm trying to think. Nobody wants to work that shift, obviously. Unless..."

"Unless what?"

"Andrea, the girl who works the front desk here at night. She'd probably agree to do it, at least for the time being."

"Her, but she's..." I couldn't think of a way to finish the sentence that wasn't intensely rude.

Lía laughed. "I know. I know. She's not the brightest star in the sky, but she'll have to do for now."

"Maritza will kill us."

Lía shrugged. "Maritza will probably be happy to have anyone reliable at this point, and if she can't whip Andrea into shape, nobody can."

"That's for sure, but what about the front desk? Who's going to watch it at night?"

"We can rotate that more easily. The hours still stink, but it's a much easier job sitting around all night for a thicker paycheck and doesn't require any training." Lía smiled. "That shouldn't be a problem. We'll reassess after the funeral and wedding and all this." She waved her hand to indicate all the high-maintenance guests currently staying at the hotel. "And we can readjust after that. But for right now, I can't think of adding one more thing to my plate."

I nodded. "Well, hopefully Andrea agrees, and if Maritza

can actually train her, she deserves a medal."

Lía chuckled. "Andrea may not be that bright, but she always shows up on time and hasn't called in sick yet. That's what we need right now."

"What about Lupe? Do you think she's coming back, and do we want her to?" I asked, remembering her husband Esteban's tirade in the lobby.

"I'm not sure. I guess it's between her and Maritza and how everything shakes out with the investigation. Have you gotten anywhere with it yet?"

"Not really," I admitted. Everything had basically stalled. I wasn't sure what to look into next, and it didn't help that I kept getting sidetracked.

That was the question that swam around in my brain the rest of the day. I paced back and forth in the tiny cottage mulling it over, but I still wasn't getting anywhere. "We need more clues. That's all there is to it, but how?" I asked Furby, who was delicately licking his front paw. He glanced up and continued licking.

"Now if someone was going around town stealing cat food, then you'd care," I told him. Furby glanced up again, and this time headbutted my hand. He knew I was upset about something and petting him would surely be the best antidote. I offered him a pat, but there wasn't time for more. I hadn't gotten much accomplished besides going over and over the same facts in my head all day. I couldn't focus on anything.

Nico would be here any moment to take me out. It would be nice to think about something else for a change. Work and a murder investigation weren't exactly the easiest things to surround yourself with 24/7. Maybe I needed another hobby that wasn't my cat.

Monteverde Italian Restaurant was the fanciest Santa Rita had to offer, which wasn't saying a whole lot, but the food was good. I remembered that much at least. My last visit here had been less than pleasant, but that had been because I'd been on a horrible, fake date so I could question a murder suspect and had nothing to do with either the service or the cuisine.

"So what looks good to you?" Nico asked, peeking over the top of his menu.

"Everything," I said. My stomach rumbled in agreement.

Nico smiled. "It feels weird going out for something that's not tacos or pizza. I guess Ana was right. I haven't been the most romantic of boyfriends."

I squeezed his hand under the menu. "I'm really more of a pizza and taco girl anyway, although this is nice too from time to time." I gestured around the restaurant. "Honestly, you don't need to impress me, though. As long as it's not rancid meat or curdled milk, I won't complain."

Nico laughed. "Well, I didn't realize you were *that* snobby. Those are some pretty impossible standards."

The waiter arrived to take our orders. I finally settled on the calamari pasta. I needed something hardy. Nico got a large steak, not exactly Italian. I passed my menu over, ready to tease Nico for his choice when the three vegan Youtubers walked through the front door.

"What's wrong?" Nico asked.

I slid down in my seat, trying to block their line of sight with the drink menu propped in the middle of the table. Why of all places and all nights did they have to come here today? When I'd said they should go somewhere neutral, I didn't mean they should come here. Did Monteverde even have any vegan options, I wondered. Maybe they'd leave. I'd never prayed so hard for every dish on the menu to be coated in meat and cheese in my entire life. What if they made a scene? What if–

"What is wrong with you?" Nico asked again. "You look like you've seen a ghost."

"I wish I had," I whispered. "It would be less upsetting." I leaned forward, careful to remain behind the drink menu. "Over there– don't look," I said as Nico started to turn his head. "The vegan Youtube girls, the ones who almost had a brawl in the middle of my hotel are here, right now, over there."

"Oh no, not now," Nico groaned quietly. "Maybe you should go over there and just say hi. Get it over with."

"Absolutely not! I came here to stuff my face with my boyfriend. I'm not on the clock, and they aren't my guests, at least not at this moment. Let them hash things out, and if they come over, I'll be polite, but there's no way I'm going over there."

"Well, if you're sure." Nico looked doubtful.

"Absolutely."

Thankfully, they either didn't see me, engrossed as they were in their own conversation, or chose to ignore me as well. I glanced over from time to time to see waving hands and animated faces, but nothing was making it to the level of a scene. Maybe they'd been smart coming here. There was something about a place with real tablecloths and classical music that made the child inside of you behave.

"They might work out their issues after all," I said to Nico. "I keep glancing over, and no one has thrown a drink or cutlery or stormed out. That's always a good sign, right?"

"What happened with them?" Nico asked. "You started to explain over the phone, but what were they even arguing about to begin with?"

"Let's talk about it later. It's really not that important. I wouldn't care at all if Harriet, the one with the glasses" – I pointed with my fork – "didn't want to run my business and all of Santa Rita through the mud online. That's the real reason I want them to work things out. Otherwise, I really wouldn't care all that much."

"So you want me to rough her up a little bit. Is that what you're saying?" Nico smiled, his eyes twinkling at his own joke.

But unfortunately he caught me midbite. At first I coughed, and when that didn't work, I grabbed my glass of water. Finally, I was able to breathe again.. My face felt red, but other than that, everything was fine. I glanced around awkwardly wondering who'd noticed.

"You okay?" Nico asked.

I nodded. "A little embarrassing, but–"

"Please!" Jessica was yelling across the restaurant in English. "Somebody help! Please!"

Her cries of desperation didn't need a translator. Within moments everyone in the entire restaurant, including the kitchen staff, had hurried to their little table. Harriet was face down, her glasses askew. She was making a horrible rasping noise like she couldn't breathe, and twitching. I picked her head up, so she wouldn't drown in her pasta sauce.

"Call an ambulance," I shouted to one of the busboys. He jerked out of whatever shock he'd been in and yanked out his cell.

"Find a doctor, anyone who's a doctor, doesn't matter what kind!" I shouted to another waiter. He nodded and disappeared out the front door.

"What should we do?" I asked Nico. "Is she having a

seizure? Do you know CPR?" He shook his head. I didn't either. Why had I never taken those stupid classes at the Y they always offered?

"Let's get her onto the ground," Nico advised. "Maybe there's something lodged in her throat, and we can try and pull it out."

I nodded. We all pulled Harriet to the ground. She wasn't twitching anymore. It had probably only been a minute since we'd first heard Jessica's screams, but everything seemed to be moving in slow motion. Once we got Harriet down, I checked for a pulse or sounds of air, but there was nothing, and nothing seemed to be in her throat either.

"Was she choking?" I asked Claire.

Claire stood stupefied, tears running down her face. She shook her head. "Harriet was just talking normally, then she just started twitching and flopped over and sounded like she couldn't breathe."

"Does she have any medical issues?" I addressed Jessica who, now that she was done screaming, also stood there not moving or speaking.

"Not that I know of, she never mentioned anything," Jessica said in a near whisper, and Claire shook her head in agreement.

A group of people, who I presumed to be paramedics, burst through the front door with a gurney. I stepped back to let them work. The good thing about a small town was that emergencies were few and traffic nonexistent. I hoped they could get Harriet somewhere quickly. Santa Rita had a small public hospital, but its resources were limited.

I stuck around in case they needed a translator, but with Harriet not speaking, and Claire and Jessica ignorant to almost everything, it seemed unnecessary. I relayed the nonexistent information I'd received to one of the paramedics while the other two attended to Harriet. He nodded solemnly.

"Can you help her? What's wrong?" I asked.

He shook his head. "Don't tell her friends yet, but it doesn't look good. There's no heart rate and no breathing. We'll do our best, but unless there's a miracle, she's most likely already gone."

CHAPTER SIXTEEN

"Gone? Are you saying she's already dead?" I asked. *Why couldn't people just speak plainly?*

The paramedic nodded slowly. "I can't say for sure, but it doesn't look good. If you'll excuse us..."

They'd already gotten Harriet on a stretcher and had wheeled her out to the street. "Her friends can meet us at the hospital if they want, but maybe you should warn them not to have too much hope," the paramedic said before turning to leave.

"What is it? What did he say?" Jessica had gotten her power of speech back. "Where are they taking Harriet?"

Now that was a question I could answer easily. "They're taking her to the public hospital here in Santa Rita. Hopefully they can get her stable and send her on to a larger facility, but..." I swallowed. It was true. I shouldn't give them any false hope. "He said it doesn't look good. Does Harriet have any family you could contact? She wasn't breathing, and she had no pulse."

"What does that mean?" Jessica had returned to her hysterics, and now I was the one using morbid euphemisms.

"I think you know what it means." Claire's voice was quiet but free of tears. "Harriet's most likely dead."

I nodded, thankful that someone else had had the nerve to say the words. "We can go by the hospital and wait. Nico can drive us."

Claire nodded. "Let me see if I can contact her family. I know she's an only child, and her parents are both living, but I don't have their number." Claire furiously scrolled through her phone as we walked towards the truck

"We didn't– did we pay?" I asked Nico as we climbed in. Why did I always focus on the stupidest problems?

"I already took care of it," Nico said. "Don't worry."

I hated hospitals, hated the smell of them, the look of them, the harried, irritated nurses, and other patients waiting to be seen. It was a dark reminder of pain that the world usually shut away until patients could emerge free from disease, or at least relatively so. But here we were in the dour waiting room, along with everyone else who had not expected to end up in the emergency room that day. I hated being among them, waiting with dread for news that probably wouldn't be good.

A young woman in blue scrubs, who looked much too young to be a doctor, but apparently was, moved us into a small side room. This was not a good sign. I clutched Nico's hand, and he squeezed it in response.

The doctor looked first at me. "Do they speak any Spanish?" she asked, indicating Claire and Jessica. I shook my head. "Would you mind translating?" she asked. I nodded, hoping my powers of speech, let alone translation, would work. I didn't bother to ask the doctor how she knew I spoke English. In a town like Santa Rita, almost everyone was less than three degrees of separation away from each other.

"What is she saying?" Jessica asked. Her hysterics had now transformed into anger.

"She's asking if I can translate for you." My voice sounded hollow. I hadn't really known Harriet, and it was true she'd irritated me, but I also didn't want to let the doctor say what she was about to, as though stopping the words would stop reality, but there was no stopping it. The doctor was already talking in a low, calm voice that bespoke dread.

"We tried everything we could, but your friend uh…"

The doctor glanced down at the clipboard in front of her and laboriously pronounced "Ha-rri-et, she arrived not breathing and no heart rate." The doctor stopped, giving me room to translate. My brain was on autopilot, and the words came strangely easily. Jessica was already loudly crying, but Claire just stood silently.

The doctor continued. "We tried our best to revive her for over an hour but weren't ever able to get a pulse. Due to her age and healthy appearance, an autopsy will be performed to determine the cause of death, but we can't offer anything definite at this time."

I translated the last bit, which seemed to send Jessica into a tailspin. "What do you mean you don't know? I don't think these people should be doing any type of autopsy on our Harriet. Her family isn't even here yet. Don't they have a say?"

After I translated, the doctor simply shrugged, uninterested in Jessica's dramatics and probably used to grieving friends and family acting in all kinds of crazy ways. "It's a legal matter," she said. "We will contact the US embassy, and if the government or the family would prefer to have the autopsy done somewhere else, then we would comply with that, but it needs to be a relative of the deceased. Have you contacted them yet?"

I translated and looked towards Claire. She shook her head. Tears glistened but so far she was composing herself better than I'd expected. "I haven't been able to locate them on social media, but I'm working on it."

"I think I have their number," Jessica said, more composed than before. "I'll go through everything at the hotel and contact them. If we have to, we can go through Harriet's computer. I'm sure there's something there."

The doctor nodded and asked for more information about Harriet to put on her chart. Sadly, there wasn't much to add.

Some of it Jessica and Claire knew, most they didn't. It was all so sterile, so final, and then we were done. Claire and Jessica wanted to go back and say their good-byes. I didn't want to intrude on their grief, but mostly I wanted out of the stuffy confines of the building. So Nico and I stepped back out to the parking lot to wait. It felt good to breathe fresh air away from the antiseptic smell of the hospital.

"Well, I'm never going to Monteverde again," I told Nico. "I don't care how good their food is."

He smiled weakly. "Yeah, not the best of luck. Sorry about that. I just wanted you to have a nice night out."

"Well, it's not like you could've anticipated that someone was going to drop dead." People who poo-pooed gallows humor had obviously never needed it before. It wasn't appropriate, but it sure felt good to laugh a little.

"Ana wants to know if she should meet us at the hospital?" Nico asked, looking down at his phone. "She said everyone's talking about what just happened with uh... Harriet, and Blanca and Carlos's parents want to come as well."

I shook my head. "There's no reason for them to come here. Tell her we're heading back to the hotel if she wants to meet us there."

When Claire and Jessica emerged, we all piled back into the truck for a silent ride back to the hotel.

"I think I'm just going to crawl into bed," Claire said as we entered the lobby.

"Me too," Jessica agreed. "And I need to try to find Harriet's parents' information. I hope I have it somewhere."

"Of course, let me know if you need anything," I said, glad that they'd chosen to excuse themselves before the rest of the curious mob descended.

All I wanted was to head back to the cottage with Nico, but I knew Ana and Blanca were coming and probably Carlos and his parents as well. I did not want to bring both Blanca and Sara back to the cottage where they'd be sure to follow me, and I'd be left with no escape. So Nico and I lounged in the lobby, waiting.

"What do you think happened to her?" Nico asked. "Do you think it was natural, or..."

The thought that this could be tied to Olga's murder hadn't occurred to me, but who would want to take out Harriet here in Santa Rita, and what connection could Harriet and Olga have had? They hadn't even met that I knew of. But Harriet had been poking around. She'd harassed God knows how many people on the street trying to dig up information. What if she'd poked around the wrong person, and they got spooked?

I shook my head. "We can't rush to judgment yet. We don't even know her cause of death. Maybe Harriet did have some medical issue we're not aware of."

"That's true," Nico agreed. "I guess we'll have to wait and see." We fell into companionable silence until Ana and Carlos entered followed by Sara, Luis, and a moment later, Blanca. Had they all been hanging out together or something?

"We were at Olga's visitation when we heard the news," Ana said, as way of explanation.

Of course the visitation. What day number was it? I couldn't even remember the day of the week, and I'd missed it yet again. Nico and I had planned to go over after our dinner, but I hadn't expected one of the guests to keel over and end the evening at the hospital.

Everyone sat and stood in awkward silence. I had no desire to play the genial hostess for the sake of their morbid curiosity. Why had they all come anyway? Everything felt strange, and maybe it was just the awkward state of affairs, but there seemed to be an added layer of tension around Blanca and Luis, or at least around Blanca. She was angry about something.

Finally Ana cut the tension. "So how are you guys doing? I know it must have been awful."

I glanced over at Nico, and thankfully he took over explaining step by step what had happened during dinner and right afterward.

"Poor girl, just goes to show that you need to savor every day. One moment we're here, and the next we're not." Sara spoke in a slow, overly dramatic way.

Why was Sara even here, I wondered. She had just been screaming at Harriet the other day in the hallway, and here she was pontificating like a sage. And why had she wanted to go to the visitation yet again? Was she that lonely, or did she want to supervise Blanca around her ex-husband, Luis? Either way she was being extremely irritating, and I had to keep reminding myself that she was Carlos's mother in order to control myself.

"I don't know who you think you're fooling with this whole act, Sara." Blanca's voice had the quiet harshness that had struck fear into me as a child. I snapped my head towards her in a panic. Her eyes were slits of anger. All I wanted was to run back to the cottage and cuddle my cat. Why wouldn't these people just go away? They obviously hated each other. Why did they want to hang out together?

I turned to Ana, ignoring the unfolding argument. "How's Lía? Is she planning on coming by too?" I knew it was a lame attempt to change the conversation and probably rude to ignore Blanca's comment, but I was desperate to avoid a confrontation in the lobby.

Ana smiled, knowing my plan all too well. "Lía's still helping with the visitation. She sends her love and asked if we could have lunch tomorrow."

I opened my mouth to respond when Luis, of all people, stepped in. "Why can't someone be sad about hearing about a death? Do you have to be related or best friends to offer your condolences? Is that what you're trying to say?"

"Thank you, Luis," Sara said quietly, dabbing at her dry cheek with a tissue. Well, apparently it had worked. Sara's latent love for her ex-husband had driven a wedge between Blanca and Luis's friendship, or whatever the heck was going on between them.

"Who exactly was she offering condolences to? She was just disingenuously blathering on. Be compassionate all you want, but don't be fake. Everyone can see through it." Blanca ignored Sara, speaking directly to Luis, until the last word and then turned to look Sara dead in the eye. Even I shivered.

Ana's panicked eyes darted around, sending a pleading look towards Carlos. He suddenly snapped to attention. "Hey dad, it's getting late. How about we head back to the apartment? It's been a rough day."

"Great idea," Luis said. His words were kind, but his tone wasn't. He did, however, nod politely towards Nico, Ana, and me before turning to leave with Carlos.

Carlos bent over to kiss Ana and sent out an apologetic smile around the lobby before turning to leave as well. I'd never considered the advantage before of not having a father. At least I only had to manage Blanca.

Sara stayed right where she was. Apparently Luis and Sara hadn't reconciled that much. She remained there awkwardly for several moments before mumbling an excuse and stomping away. Blanca sank down in the chair next to me and put her head in her hands. I'd never seen her so defeated before. Normally she'd just brush it off and soldier on. Sometimes she'd hide in the bathroom and cry quietly, but she never let anyone see her suffer.

"What happened?" I asked her in English in case Sara was lurking around the corner listening.

"It's nothing, really." Blanca tried to smile, but she just looked sadder.

"Obviously, it's something," I pressed.

"It's been a hard night for everyone. I should just get some sleep." Blanca started to stand, but I touched her arm.

"You can come by the cottage if you'd like to talk about anything," I offered.

But Blanca stiffened and shook her head vigorously. "No, not there. I mean…" She back-pedaled her words. "Sorry, I didn't mean to sound so abrupt. I just need to sleep. We can talk about it later." She offered another sad smile and headed towards her room.

"Do you two want to come back to the cottage for a cup of coffee?" I asked Ana and Nico.

Ana hesitated. "I'd like to, but I don't want to interfere with your romantic evening."

Nico laughed. "I'm sure Natalia is curious about that little love-triangle spat we just witnessed, and I know you're dying to know all the details about tonight."

"Nico!" Ana's face was so stricken I had to swallow a laugh. "That's a horrible choice of words."

"Sorry," Nico mumbled. "I didn't mean it like that."

"Let's go get some coffee, and I'm sure Furby's hungry." I stood to leave, and Nico and Ana followed.

"So what happened with Blanca and Luis. The tension

was thick between those two." I strode over to the coffee maker. I knew Ana was interested in hearing more about what had happened to Harriet, but I didn't want to dissect it quite yet and wanted to focus on some pointless drama for just a few more minutes.

Ana shrugged. "I didn't see everything, but from what I gathered, apparently Luis was under the impression that Blanca was interested in having more than just a friendship, if you know what I mean."

"The cat knows what you mean, Ana." Nico had given up trying to push Furby away and scratched his chin instead. I smiled. Furby had a way of worming his way into even the most devoted non-cat-people's hearts.

Ana rolled her eyes. "Well anyway, Blanca was apparently offended by that assumption, seeing as she's married and all, and then it really escalated. Luis started bringing up the past, insulting her character, which was when I overheard them yelling, and once Sara realized what was happening, she was more than happy to join in with Luis."

I shook my head. "I can imagine, but why did they all come to a visitation just to make a scene yet again?"

"I'm not sure. Sara has come every day for Olga's wake. I have no idea why, but Carlos said he's banned them. They can come for the final mass if they promise to behave but nothing else."

"Your poor mother," I said. "I'm sure Beatriz didn't want to step in between your future in-laws."

"Oh, mom has a PhD in diffusing arguments." Ana laughed. "Thankfully, mom and dad and Carlos were able to separate the three of them. I felt really bad for Blanca. They were just piling on her and saying all kinds of rude things. I mean I know Blanca's not perfect but..." Ana glanced towards me quickly. "She's your mom, I know. I'm sorry I didn't mean to–"

"Don't worry about it." I waved my hand. "I know every rumor, or a version of every rumor about my mom, and she can be just as obnoxious when she chooses to be. At least she seems a little better now, though, and she's happy in her marriage. I don't know." I shrugged. "Of course her and Luis seemed pretty cozy there, but Blanca's not a cheater. She loves to flirt, but she wouldn't have been married five times if she were willing to cheat. That's not her style."

Ana nodded. "Carlos was pretty angry, and if it hadn't been in the middle of a wake…" Ana's eyes went wide.

"Poor guy," Nico put in. "He certainly didn't win the familial lottery."

"No, but he's marrying into it," Ana joked. "I felt bad for him, but I was happy to see him finally stand up to them. I just wish it hadn't taken him so long. Oh well, it's over for now at least. The wedding's in a few days. Carlos and I will be on our honeymoon in Sayulita, and the hotel will be filled with, hopefully, more normal guests."

Ana clapped her hand over her mouth. "Oh dear, I didn't mean that. I forgot all about… You guys have to tell me exactly what happened. I still can't believe it. Between Olga's funeral, the wedding being postponed, and now this, I had no idea Harriet even had any health problems. What did she die of? You never told me."

Ana looked expectantly between Nico and me. I expanded on Nico's bare-bones information from earlier and explained step by step everything that had transpired from beginning to end.

"They don't really know why she died then, so it could've been not natural after all?" Ana asked.

"As in murder? It's still a possibility, but we don't know yet," I said.

"Oh, I have goosebumps." Ana held up her arm to show us. "It has to be. Harriet kept poking her nose into things, harassing people on the street. I'm sure she didn't know anything, but someone must've thought she did, and– Dear Lord!"

"Calm down, Ana. We don't know anything yet. Let's just wait for the autopsy to get back. That's all we can do." But Nico's attempt to calm his sister down fell on deaf ears.

Ana sighed, exasperated with her brother. "Nico, don't be ridiculous. Yes, we can wait for the autopsy, but it's obvious, to me at least, that Harriet was murdered."

CHAPTER SEVENTEEN

I'd offered to meet Claire and Jessica in the bakery to help with navigating any language and legal issues involved with Harriet's untimely death, not that I was any expert. Apart from translation, I was as completely out of my depth as they were.

"It still doesn't feel real. I keep thinking we should ask Harriet what she wants to do." Claire's puffy, red eyes betrayed the effects of yesterday.

'I know." Jessica nodded. "I keep thinking how stupid our argument was. Promise we'll never argue like that, Claire." Jessica looked pleadingly over at her friend.

"Jessica, this isn't high school. You're acting like a teenager." Claire's uncharacteristic irritation surprised me. "I'm sorry. I'm just tired," she apologized quickly.

Jessica nodded. "I know. Everything is so strange. But what about the channel? We haven't put anything up in a few days, and without Harriet to manage the social media... People are starting to ask a bunch of questions. Should we make a statement about Harriet?"

Claire shook her head. "How can you even think about the channel now? And if we announce it, it's going to be all over the internet, and everybody's going to be speculating. We should wait until we have more information."

"Well excuse me, Miss Goody Two-shoes, but this 'channel' that you're so dismissive of is how we actually pay for everything, including your bills, and this vacation, I might add. It's all well and good to pretend like you don't care about the money, until it stops, and that's what's about to happen, if we don't manage things properly. And if this gets out, we'll have no control over the narrative. We need to decide what we're going to do. That's all I was saying."

I did not relish getting in between these two in yet another installment of *Bickering with the Vegans*. "I forget, when did they say the results of the autopsy would be ready?" I asked.

Claire shook her head. "They said anywhere from a few days to several weeks. Basically, they don't want to agree to anything."

I nodded. I knew the answer, but I was trying to get them to return to the facts and away from the emotional back and forth that was about to take over the bakery that was already crowded with nosey locals, straining to pick up any English words they might be able to decipher.

Another death of an otherwise healthy woman in Santa Rita had caused the rumor mill to go into hyper speed, and with few details or facts at the ready, it was easy to speculate and throw theories around. I was grateful for the language barrier between most of the residents and the Youtubers. Jessica and Claire sat mired in their own grief, oblivious to the rubberneckers stationed throughout the bakery, nursing long cold coffee in the hopes of seeing or overhearing something to satisfy their curiosity.

"Have you contacted Harriet's parents yet?" I asked.

Jessica nodded. "They said they'd be coming as soon as they could. Of course, they seemed in quite a bit of shock when we spoke late last night."

I hadn't known Harriet very well, let alone her parents, so I wasn't sure how much blame they'd put on Santa Rita in general, the hotel, or me personally. If they were anything like Harriet, I wasn't hopeful, but neither Claire nor Jessica appeared nervous about it, though, so why should I be?

We sat for a few moments in silence, long enough for most of the patrons to get bored of waiting for some juicy gossip and slowly wander off. I was searching for an acceptable excuse to head out myself, seeing as they were both on edge, and there was nothing for me to help with.

Thankfully, Father Tomás entered the bakery and headed straight for our table, easing the tension, and hopefully giving me an easy out. He knew enough English to greet the two Youtubers and offer his condolences.

Jessica was visibly uncomfortable by the priest's presence and leaned over to whisper. "I've seen way too many horror movies. Guys in collars make me nervous. If you'll excuse me," she said louder before hurrying away.

He and Claire had already met on the fateful day that Olga's body had been discovered. Father Tomás's English vocabulary was limited, and Claire's Spanish even more so, but they made the most of it with wide smiles and broad hand gestures. I helped to fill in the gaps between the two when a look of confusion would cross their face or the ubiquitous, "How would you say…"

"I really am sorry," he said to both of us, and then to Claire. "This has been such a horrible vacation for you, losing your friend and… Well, I am here. I know it can be hard to uh.. explain your feelings, and priests are here to listen and not judge. It doesn't have to be a confession. If you just want to talk, my door is always open."

Anyone could have said those words and come across as insincere, just hungry for gossip, but Father Tomás had a way of making everything feel like it could be solved with a simple conversation. We chatted for a few more minutes before Claire excused herself as well.

After she left, Father Tomás turned to me and switched

back to Spanish. "I haven't forgotten what you said, Natalia," he said.

Wait, what had I said? My brain raced. Was he angry with me, but he didn't look it.

He continued, "I have been praying about what to do about the Father Francisco and Silvia situation. I don't agree with it, but I want to approach everything the right way. You convicted my conscience."

"Well, I guess that's good." *Was that good?* I wasn't sure. "I didn't think you really meant it when you said you'd pray about it."

"Oh no," he shook his head. "I would never lie about something as serious as praying. I didn't want you to think I'd forgotten," he repeated.

I shook my head. "Of course not. Well, you should do what you think is right. After all, you're the one who has to work with them."

"Well, I will continue to pray. Yes, and my door is always open. I mean that too, and you don't have to pay to talk." He laughed, and I joined him. Father Francisco didn't even counsel a parishioner without asking for a *donation* in return.

I thanked him again, and Father Tomás left, but not without first purchasing some bolillos and a large chocolate muffin.

The mid-morning lull had hit the bakery, so I headed in the back where I knew Maritza liked to hang out during her downtime to see how things were working out with Andrea, the bakery newbie.

I found Maritza with her hands around a cup of coffee, looking just as tired as everyone else had this morning.

"Do I dare ask?" I hesitated, knowing the answer wouldn't be good.

She slowly looked up and shook her head.

"That bad?" Surely Maritza was exaggerating.

"It was worse than you're even imagining," she said, looking around to see if anyone could overhear our conversation. "Shut that door," she instructed. "I know I can be unprofessional, but I'm not that bad, yet." She gave a dry laugh.

I closed the door before crossing back over and sitting next to Maritza at the tiny table she'd moved into the storeroom. Around us were bags of sugar, flour, chocolate, canisters of sprinkles, everything a baker might need, along with two large refrigerators that held everything else.

'I've trained 16-year-olds who don't even know how to make a tortilla," Maritza said. "I enjoy the challenge, actually, but this girl, Andrea." She shook her head. "I've never seen anything like it. She's beyond dense. She's completely opaque, wrapped in a layer of concrete."

I remembered my first interaction with Andrea introducing the foreign Youtubers, and I could only imagine how exasperating she'd be in the kitchen. I felt sorry for Maritza but stifled a smile, imagining the interchanges.

"Do you want me to tell Lía to put her back at the front desk, so you can hire someone else?" I asked.

Maritza shook her head. "Not yet, let's wait till after the wedding. Maybe things will improve," but she looked doubtful.

A tentative knock at the storeroom sounded. "Who could that be?" I asked. Maritza just shrugged.

I crossed the small, crowded space and opened the door. Of everyone I imagined it could be, I was shocked to see a very humble and distraught Lupe on the other side, and she seemed just as surprised to see me standing there instead of Maritza. I probably was not her favorite person right about now, but she came in anyway. I offered her the chair I'd been sitting in.

Even though it was technically my bakery, or at least mostly mine, Lía and Ana were part-owners as well, I felt awkward standing over their conversation. I wanted to know why she was there, though. Maritza met my eye and nodded, indicating I should stay.

Maritza remained silent, and I followed her lead, leaving Lupe to shift awkwardly in the chair before she finally got the nerve to explain her sudden arrival after such erratic behavior.

"I guess you're wondering why I'm here," she said in a voice so low, Maritza and I had to lean in to hear.

Maritza nodded stoically and flipped her long, tight braid over her shoulder. "Yeah, it is a little odd."

"Well, I know we didn't leave on the best terms. I wanted to apologize," Lupe said, finally looking up. "And I wanted to know if there's any way I could have my job back, even if it's just part-time, or if not the bakery, I could clean rooms, just something." She looked towards me now, desperate.

Maritza asked the question I was thinking. "What's changed? Why are you suddenly so eager for work?"

Lupe looked down and shifted nervously again. "It's my husband, Esteban."

"What about him?" Maritza pressed.

"He's gotten into a bit of trouble, nothing huge, but money's tight. He likes a good card game and drinks from time to time with his friends, but the two aren't the best combination." She chuckled dryly. "He's able to pay most of it back, but we need something to live on."

Maritza looked at me. "Well, it's up to Natalia. It's her bakery after all. I'm just a worker." Her eyes twinkled.

Funny how Maritza was *just a worker* when awkward choices had to be made. I appreciated Lupe's honesty. She did seem sincere, and with Maritza's exasperation with Andrea and the wedding coming up, it didn't seem like we had much of a choice.

"Well, I'm open to having you back on a probationary basis, if Maritza's okay with it, and if I can talk to Lía, and she's okay with moving Andrea back to the front desk." Lía had always handled staffing, and I did not want to step on any toes.

Maritza nodded. "Well, it's okay with me as long as Lía gives the go ahead."

"I'll go speak with her, and either she or Maritza will get in touch with you."

Lupe looked visibly relieved, and something told me that while she'd been honest, she'd also downplayed the severity of the situation. She smiled, let out a sigh, and after thanking Maritza and me numerous times, finally left the storeroom.

"So what did you make of that?" I asked Maritza.

"It was definitely odd," Maritza admitted. She spun her mug around between her hands and glanced thoughtfully around the storeroom.

"Do you think she was being honest?" I asked.

Maritza shook her head. "Partly but not completely."

"That's the sense I got too," I said. "Hey, maybe now you could get some more info out of Lupe and report back to me if you find anything interesting." I wiggled my eyebrows.

"Are you roping me into this little investigation of yours?"

she asked.

I nodded. "Olga was murdered, and now we have evidence that Esteban might've had an even bigger motive than we first suspected with these serious money troubles, and when he came in the lobby all drunk and yelling, he said Harriet had been harassing him on the street. Find out as much as you can, but be careful, and don't be alone with Lupe. Who knows how much she knows or participated in."

"I'm a big girl. I can take care of myself, especially against Lupe." Maritza smiled. It was true. Physically Lupe was no match for Maritza, but Harriet hadn't been physically attacked, and she was still dead.

"*If* Harriet was murdered, it wasn't a direct attack. Watch what Lupe puts into the food, and don't eat or drink anything she gives you." I really hoped I hadn't just contributed to another possible murder, and this time in my own bakery. I was starting to have second thoughts about the whole thing. Andrea might be dense as a brick, but Lupe was an unknown quantity, possibly a murderous one. Maritza didn't seem afraid, though.

"You worry too much. I grew up in an orphanage, remember? I can take on the likes of Lupe. You see me as sweet now, but I can be scrappy."

I smiled. Maritza was a friend, and she was sharp and generous, but I'd never use the word *sweet* to describe her. That's for sure, but I nodded anyway.

"Let me go check with Lía about the staffing situation, but I can't foresee there being any problems," I said.

I found Lía in the hotel office, hunched over the desktop. Furby stood, stretched, and attempted to walk across the keyboard, but Lía batted him away. So he simply laid down on top of it. Lía let out an exasperated sigh. I couldn't help but giggle at the spectacle and picked up Furby to cuddle him, but he squirmed away, hopped to the floor, glared at me for the indignity of being cuddled in public, and promptly bathed himself on the office floor.

"That cat is one of a kind." Lía shook her head.

"If he's bothering you too much, I can put him back in the cottage," I offered. Furby stopped bathing and glared in my direction even harder.

Lía shook her head. "He's the grumpy manager. I can't manage without him." Furby had hopped back up on the desk and accepted the praise and pat from Lía with a dignified purr. I shook my head. Who were we kidding? Furby was the owner of this hotel, not me.

"Lía, you'll never guess what happened," I started.

"I have some big news too," Lía said, "but you go first."

So I explained everything that had just transpired with Lupe and Maritza, including Maritza's exasperation with training Andrea.

"So do you think Andrea would be offended or upset if you put her back at the front desk?" I asked.

Lía shook her head. "She was in here complaining to me this morning. She's not very fond of baking, apparently. I assured her it was temporary. She'll be thrilled to know just how temporary."

"What do you think about Lupe's story?" I asked. "She seemed quite desperate."

"I'm not surprised," Lía said. "Esteban has quite the reputation for gambling. I just hope he hasn't gotten himself and Lupe wrapped up in anything really dangerous. Now are you ready for my news?" she asked. "It's juicy but not good, I'm afraid."

I sat across from Lía. Furby had apparently forgiven me because he jumped into my lap and allowed me to scratch him behind the ears.

"Well my husband, Eduardo, his brother works in the medical examiner's office as a porter," Lía said.

"Really?" I didn't know Eduardo very well, and I had no idea he had any ties to such a macabre place. "What a creepy place to work at."

Lía nodded. "Well, I told Eduardo to contact him, and if he heard anything about Harriet's autopsy, to let us know."

"And?" I stopped petting Furby. He swiped at me to let me know I wasn't finished yet, so I continued.

"And Ana was right, she'll be thrilled to know. Well maybe not in this instance, but Harriet was poisoned."

"Poisoned? With what?" I asked. Had it been in the restaurant or before, I wondered. We needed to know what poison it was and how quickly it would've acted in order to narrow down our suspects.

Lía shook her head. "He wasn't sure. They haven't gotten the official results back yet, but she was definitely poisoned. He knew that much. It wasn't natural."

"Are you sure?" I asked. "Or is this just more gossip?"

"I'm certain," Lía assured me. "Eduardo's brother is a very stoic kind of guy. It took quite a lot to convince him to talk about it."

I tried to imagine the personality of a porter at Santa Rita's medical examiner's office. Lía's story appeared reliable. Plus, it was the only thing we had to go on so far.

"Have you told Ana and Nico yet?" I asked. Lía shook her

head.

"Have you told Ana and Nico what yet?" Ana asked, pushing through the partly closed office door.

Lía filled Ana in on the particulars, and Ana lost no time in getting right down to business.

"So what's the connection between Olga and Harriet?" she asked. "It had to have been one of the people she questioned about the murder. Which of our suspects do we know for sure she questioned?"

"She probably questioned about half the town on the corner," Lía said, "although I'm not sure how many people understood her odd Google translate confrontation."

"Well, she for sure questioned Esteban, Lupe's husband. He mentioned it when he stormed into the lobby, although he doesn't really strike me as the poisoning type, but who knows. She and Sara also had a pretty intense run-in that same day," I said.

"Really?" Ana was intrigued.

"Did you ever find out from Carlos a reasonable explanation why his mom was sneaking out the back of the hotel in the middle of the night right before the murder?" Lía asked.

Ana shook her head. "I asked him about it, but he just blew me off, and I think I might've offended him."

"Imagine, accusing his mother of murder, and he had the gall to be offended," Lía joked.

"Sara is an interesting suspect," I said. "She argued with both victims just prior to their death but has very little motive otherwise, and she's the easiest to investigate."

"But Sara has argued with most of the town since she's

been here," Lía put in. "No offense, Ana."

"None taken," Ana said. "Natalia's right. She's the easiest to investigate and either get more evidence or rule her out completely."

"And what do you have in mind?" I asked, not sure I wanted to hear the answer.

"All we have to do is get her out of the hotel for a while, so we can search her room. We have the key after all, and it's our hotel. It wouldn't even be breaking and entering."

Ana made it sound so easy and harmless. "It may be our hotel, but we don't own Sara's things. I don't know if it's right to go through them even under the circumstances."

"This is a murderer we're talking about here," Ana pointed out. "If someone else is murdered, and we could've stopped it, do you really want that on your conscience?"

"You're right," I agreed. "Find a way to get Sara out of the hotel for a while, and we'll go through her room tomorrow. If we find something, Carlos will have to agree to question his mother."

"And if not?" Lía asked.

"If not, we'll just keep an eye on her and move onto our next suspect," I said.

"Do you really think Sara murdered two people because of a stupid argument?" Lía asked.

"Who knows?" I said. "But I guess we'll find out."

CHAPTER EIGHTEEN

I was just waking up when the landline started loudly ringing in the corner. I really needed to adjust the volume on that thing. I groaned slowly moving toward it. *Don't tell me Lupe flaked out again after all that drama yesterday.*

"Hello," I said groggily into the receiver.

"Yes, this is Veronica from *Social Tea*. Are you the owner of Hotel Leticia in Santa Rita?" a perky voice asked in English.

"Yes," I said, confused. "Why? What is this about? How did you get this number?" Why would some social media gossip site be contacting me, I wondered.

The perky voice on the other end ignored my questions. "I was just wondering if you could offer a statement for us."

"A statement about what?" I asked. My head was starting to clear, but I was still confused.

"About the recent death of a popular Youtuber who was staying in your hotel. Was it true she died after eating a cheese dish?"

Oh no, that angle hadn't even occurred to me. "I hardly think the most pertinent issue is that Harriet was eating cheese," I said.

"So is that your statement?" she asked, giddy at the prospect.

"What? No, of course not." I had finally recovered all my faculties, and now that the reason for the call was clear, panic set in. "I have no statement. No statement at this time!" I shouted louder just for clarity and slammed down the receiver. That was the nice thing about a landline, you could slam it back into the cradle without cracking it, quite satisfying.

How had the news of Harriet's death gotten out so quickly, I wondered, and where had they found out about her hotel? Oh, obviously the Youtube videos. Stupid me, I'd plastered myself and the hotel and bakery all over their channel, encouraged the publicity, and now it had backfired.

Did we need to do any damage control? After all, nothing had happened to Harriet at the hotel, and while it wasn't a good look for the town of Santa Rita, the cause of death still hadn't been revealed yet. My heart sank. Once it was, things were only going to get worse.

I needed to kick the investigation into high gear and fast. Once the culprit was identified, a lot of the energy and speculation would evaporate, and people would move onto the next thing, or at least I hoped so.

I had to get to the front desk. If a reporter was calling on my personal, rarely used landline, there must've been a dozen who had called the hotel directly. Surely Miguel would be smart enough not to reveal too much information. I glanced at the clock, and my heart sank. It wasn't Miguel at the front desk right now. It was Andrea.

"Oh my God, Furby. This is a disaster." Furby blinked up at me and then turned to yowl at his food. He had his own disaster to worry about, being able to see the bottom of his food dish.

I raced across the patio and arrived at the front desk out of breath. I stood gasping for several moments before I was even able to speak. Andrea just stared at me.

"Have you... Sorry I was running," I said, sucking in air. "Has anyone called the front desk?" I was finally able to gasp out.

Andrea nodded. *Oh, not this again.*

"Who... who called?" I needed water. Maybe I should cut

back on the pastries.

"Some people, but most of them were speaking English, and a few were asking weird questions and didn't want a room, so I just hung up." Andrea shrugged.

I had never been so grateful for Andrea's dense lack of professionalism before. I didn't even care if she'd scared away potential guests. Hopefully Harriet's parents hadn't been one of the English speakers Andrea had hung up on, but other than that, I was thrilled.

"That's great! You did really good." I knew I was grinning like an idiot, but I didn't care. Andrea raised an eyebrow, probably not expecting praise.

"If any English speaker calls, forward them to me in the office. If they're a reporter, they're not staying here." I was all for freedom of the press, but my hotel was full of nutjobs and a possible murderer, I didn't need anyone reporting on that. It was bad enough that we had the Youtubers.

Andrea nodded mutely.

"And if anyone calls, especially from Social Tea, don't speak to them, and if anyone… *anyone* asks about Harriet or the Youtubers, just say 'no comment'. You got it?"

Andrea nodded. "Can I just hang up?" she asked.

"Well, that's probably not the best plan because they'll call back," I pointed out.

"Oh, I just left the phone off the hook," Andrea said, pointing to the black receiver hanging over the side of the desk.

"But what if the guests need something?"

She shrugged again. "The hotel's not that big. I guess they can walk down here, right?"

"Well, let's try to answer the phone," I said calmly. After all that was literally the only thing that we had Andrea at the front desk for all night. "And if they ask for a statement or about Harriet or the Youtubers, it's better if you say 'no comment', but if you have to, you have my permission to hang up on reporters."

Andrea smiled for the first time since I'd met her. "Really?"

"It's better if you say no comment," I reminded her.

"Okay," she nodded eagerly. Being given tacit approval to hang up on people was probably the best thing that had happened to Andrea since she started working here.

I hung around in the back office with Furby for the rest of the morning to keep an eye on things, but they were pretty calm. I'd probably blown the whole thing out of proportion, and it'd just been an overanxious journalist who'd gone above and beyond for a story. After all, Harriet only appeared in some of the videos. And how popular could vegan Youtubers actually be?

Ana burst into the office just as out of breath as I had been earlier. Her normally perfectly-styled, curly hair had been haphazardly pulled back, and she was wearing sweats. This was not a good sign.

"Why didn't you answer your phone?" she managed to gasp out.

I glanced down at my cell next to me on the desk. "It must be on silent. I'm not really used to people calling me so early. Why didn't you call the front desk?"

"I tried, but Andrea just said 'no comment' and hung up when I asked for you." I smiled, at least Andrea had listened, although there might be more than a few confused, potential guests.

"What's wrong?" I asked, but I was afraid to hear the

answer.

"There have been reporters contacting every business they can in Santa Rita, trying to get info. I guess the story leaked late last night. They even called the police station. Santiago called Nico, demanding to know what was going on, but of course, he had no idea."

"Did Santiago say what he's going to do about the murders?" I asked Ana. "Or is he still denying that there ever were any?"

"He said he's going to make a statement this morning," Ana said. "I'm sure he's consulting with every politician he owes his job to, including his dad."

I wished I'd had the chance to be happier about Santiago's predicament, but we had one of our own, and it was probably better for everyone in Santa Rita if this thing didn't blow up in the news.

Ana and I tried to think up a strategy, but it was difficult. It all depended on Santiago's statement.

"Do you think he'll admit that they know Harriet was poisoned?" I asked.

Ana shrugged. "Probably not. Whenever they get a chance to buy time, they take it. Announcing that will just turn this into a full-on tornado. He's supposed to make his statement at 10:00 this morning," Ana said.

I nodded. "Okay, we've got about three hours. Have Lía and Nico come by the cottage. We can go down together."

At quarter to ten, Nico, Ana, Lía, and I headed across the street to the main square. I knew it would be crowded, but there were even more people than I'd expected. They were packed in every corner of the square. Small topiaries and paths zig-zagged around the stone gazebo where Santiago stood flanked by his father, the mayor, and I assumed other key people in town whom I'd never met before. Every eye was glued to the platform, a few darted in our direction, but not for long.

Finally, Santiago's father, Rubén, took the microphone. He wasn't that old, maybe mid-60's, but police officer years were probably longer than normal civilian ones. Technically, his father was head of police, but he wasn't active anymore. He collected the salary, but Santiago was running the show.

Rubén was round in the middle with a thick mustache over his lip. He didn't even bother with the charade of a uniform, although he did try to pander with a palm hat popular with the locals, even though the Gucci jacket he wore was worth more than most people made in Santa Rita in a whole year.

After introducing himself and saying a lot of politician-esque things about the beauty and innocence of Santa Rita, he passed the microphone to his son and let him do the difficult bit. I could see now why the father was in charge. Santiago would get all the blame, while his father just sat back and got paid a fat check from the government.

Santiago accepted the mic. Even from the corner by the fountain, I could see that he was sweating profusely through his uniform. He started off mumbling so badly that people in the crowd had to yell for him to speak louder even with the microphone.

He cleared his throat and continued. "I am Santiago Sanchez-López, the..." He looked over at his father. Surely, they should have already researched his title. "I work on the police force," he finally answered. He pulled out a piece of paper to read the statement that had obviously been written for him.

"There has been an unfortunate death of a tourist recently in our town. She had a medical issue at a very popular restaurant and was pronounced dead at the hospital. We are waiting for

175

more information and the results of the autopsy before we can say anything else about this at this time. Thank you."

Santiago stepped down amid discontented murmurs."What kind of a non-statement was that?" Ana asked.

"That was ridiculous," Lía agreed.

Even pragmatic Nico was disappointed. He shook his head. "Well, that was a waste of a perfectly good morning." We started to make our way through the crowd and back to the main road.

"If Santiago wants to be taken seriously, he needs to take a public speaking course. That was painful even if he'd had anything interesting to say," I said. But when both Ana and Lía just stared vacantly back at me, I wondered if *they* were okay.

Thankfully Nico prevented me from embarrassing myself further. He wrapped his arm around my shoulders and turned us slightly to face a very red Santiago.

"Hi, Santi, how's it going?" He reached out to shake Santiago's hand, which he tepidly accepted.

"Your girlfriend's quite opinionated, isn't she?" Santiago's voice was low, and I felt Nico's arm tighten protectively around me.

"Let's not get personal here, Santi. You're a big boy with thick skin. I'm sure you've heard a whole lot worse. She didn't mean any harm by it."

Santiago wasn't physically intimidating but the authority he could wield in a little town like Santa Rita definitely was. I'd never seen someone glower before, but he definitely glowered at me before putting on his sunglasses.

"Out of respect for you, Nicolás, I'll keep my mouth shut," he said. "And I'd advise you to do the same, Natalia. Ever since you've come here, you've been nothing but trouble."

I shivered, and Santiago excused himself before continuing on. "Why didn't you warn me?" I hissed at Ana as soon as Santiago was out of earshot.

"He just came up suddenly. I didn't know he was there until right before you did," she said.

"That's true," Lía agreed.

"I'm sorry I messed up things between you and your friend," I said to Nico, and I *was* genuinely sorry. Although they weren't close now, Nico and Santiago had gone to school together, and having an in with the police had been priceless, but I'd sure burned that bridge.

"Oh, you just injured his pride a little bit. That's all. He'll get over it." Nico's voice sounded confident, but his eyes looked doubtful.

"He's just jealous that you're a better detective than he is," Ana put in.

"I didn't realize he hated me so much." Every other personal encounter with him has been cordial enough. Maybe he was still angry that I'd found the killer before he had last February.

"He doesn't hate you. He can be moody sometimes. I'd just try to stay out of his way for a while," Nico advised. "He'll forget about it soon enough."

I nodded. I hadn't expected any type of support from the police before, but I'd certainly slammed that door closed now. Whatever needed to be done to find the killer, I'd have to do it myself. The police were evidently going to just sit on their hands, make a bunch of PR statements, and hide any evidence that came to light.

CHAPTER NINETEEN

"What excuse are you going to use to get Sara out of the way?" I asked once we were back at the hotel.

Ana bit her lip. "I told Carlos about our plan, and he agreed to take his mother out to lunch."

"Really? He wasn't angry that we want to go through his mom's things?" I asked.

"Well, he wasn't thrilled about it, but he said if we don't find anything, then we need to just drop her as a suspect."

I shrugged. "Well, if we don't find anything, there's not much else we can do, but until she gives us a legitimate alibi…"

Ana nodded. "That's what I told Carlos too. He agreed to talk to his mom about it when the time is right."

"That's good." I sighed. Tomorrow was the last mass to honor Olga, and with a luncheon at the hotel afterwards, I needed to know if Sara was an imminent threat, especially for Blanca's sake.

I settled in for a day of tedious paperwork with Lia while Furby oversaw the whole operation through squinted eyes from his filing cabinet throne.

Ana poked her head in the hotel office two hours later. "Let's go," she said. "Carlos just left with his mother, so we have at least an hour."

I hopped up, but Lía rolled her eyes. "What exactly do you want me to do?" she asked.

"Just stand in the hallway and be a lookout," Ana said.

"Carlos is supposed to text when they leave the restaurant, but just in case, you need to stall her if she arrives suddenly. If Sara is anything, she's unpredictable."

"Unpredictable? That's not the first word that comes to mind with Sara, but I guess it's one of them." Lía laughed at her own joke. "Okay, but you guys need to make this fast. I've got a lot of work to get to. I don't know what you're expecting to find, a diary that says '*I murdered Olga and Harriet*'?"

"That would be nice, if it's true," I said, smiling. Lía just rolled her eyes.

We started up the back stairwell to the second floor. Even though we weren't doing anything technically illegal, I couldn't help but feel a little bit guilty, but just a little bit.

Ana opened the door with the key card, and we stepped inside. The room was relatively neat. Sara had even packed her clothes away in the dresser and closet nearby.

"So what do we do first?" I asked.

"You start with her clothes. I'll go through this paperwork." Ana pointed to a large stack of binders and papers at the side of the bed.

I nodded. "Remember to leave everything exactly how you found it."

"Of course," Ana said. "Do you think I'm an amateur here? I have an older sister *and* brother. I've been doing this since I was five."

I went through the dresser drawers first and poked in, around, and under all the clothing trying not to disturb it.

"Check underneath the mattress too," I called to Ana.

She nodded. "Good idea."

Next I went through two suitcases zipped up and lying on the floor, but all I found were dirty clothes and a few romance novels. I smiled. *Why would Sara be embarrassed of that?*

"This is a waste of time, Ana. I can't find anything. Maybe this wasn't such a good idea."

"Just look in the bathroom, and if you don't find anything there, we'll stop. All this paperwork seems to be work-related, nothing interesting."

"Okay," I said. The idea of snooping through Sara's room had been much more intriguing in theory than the reality was proving to be.

I glanced around the small bathroom, nothing that I could see except a few tubes and jars of skin cream and makeup laid out. I opened the top drawer of the vanity; some aspirin, stomach medicine, cough syrup. *Wow, this lady packed for everything.*

I pushed my hand to the back of the drawer and pulled out another medication. I'd never heard the name before, so I snapped a picture of it just in case.

I shrugged. "Ana, let's get out of here."

"Shh," Ana hissed from the bedroom. "Listen."

And sure enough, I could hear Lía speaking quite loudly down the hall.

"Of course, Sara, I understand, but I actually have a phone call for you downstairs. – I'm not sure why they called there, but it's urgent."

"Oh my God, what do we do?" Ana's face looked as panic stricken as mine probably did.

Think, think. "Look out the door. I think they left. We

have time to sneak out and go down the back way towards the employee break room," I said.

"I'm not looking. You look!" Ana whispered.

Ever so slowly, I eased the door open. The hallway was silent. Sara must have followed Lía downstairs.

"We got it. Let's go," I said to Ana, seeing no one within view. We both edged out, clicked the door closed behind us, and walked as quickly as we could down to the break room.

"I'm going to kill Carlos," Ana said. "He didn't even text me. Can you imagine if Sara…" Ana shivered, not finishing the thought.

"I can, but I don't want to." I sighed and sank down on the faux-leather couch.

After several minutes we made our way back to the office, anxious to hear what had happened, where we found a not very enthusiastic looking Lía.

"I am never doing that again," she said. "Close that door, Ana. I don't want anyone overhearing."

Ana lightly closed the office door before smiling. "So what did you tell her? What happened?"

"Apparently she forgot her sunglasses and wanted to pop back in to get them," Lía said. "I couldn't think of what to say, so I told her she had an urgent call downstairs. She was super confused, and when we obviously found a dead line, I told her they must've hung up. She was irritated and suspicious but didn't push it, thankfully. Ugh! You better have found something useful."

Ana shrugged. "Unfortunately, I don't think we did."

They both looked over at me. "I found a strange medication I've never heard of, so I snapped a picture of it, but that's it."

"What was it called?" Lía was intrigued.

I messaged the picture I'd taken, and Lía promptly started googling the name. I didn't expect it to be anything, but she audibly gasped.

"Does Carlos's mother have seizures?" she asked Ana.

"No, I don't think so, why?"

"Well, she has medication for it," Lía said. "Why would she have medication for a condition that she doesn't have?"

"Let me see that," Ana said, pushing her way over to the computer screen. "Wow, does it have any other uses?"

"None that I can see listed," Lía said. "But I'm not a doctor or anything."

"Has Carlos mentioned his mother being ill before?"

Ana shook her head. "I think he would've mentioned that but maybe not, who knows? Do you think he would?"

"Maybe... I don't know," Lía admitted. "I think you should go talk to him, though."

Ana agreed. "I also want to give him an earful about not warning me that his mother was marching right back in the hotel. That could've been a disaster."

I nodded. "We shouldn't rush to judgment," I said. "Does it say anything about an overdose? Maybe the effects don't match what happened to Harriet."

"That's what I'm looking for," Lía said, engrossed in the screen. "Here it says overdose effects are not entirely known, but they could contain rapid heart rate and possible asphyxiation."

"That's exactly what happened to Harriet, or at least it

looked that way. Even if it is her medication, do you think it's possible that she gave some to Harriet?"

Lía nodded slowly, and Ana's face had turned an odd color.

"Sara just went from a possible suspect to the number one spot. She had the motive and the means to kill Harriet," I said.

"Well, she only had a motive to kill Harriet," Lía put in, "if she had already murdered Olga, and she didn't want anyone to find out."

"Carlos isn't answering his cell," Ana said. "And his Whatsapp hasn't been looked at. His phone must be dead. That's why he didn't warn me. I'm going to do it the old-fashioned way and call up the restaurant and ask for him."

"Really?" Lía said. "Are you going to say it's you?"

"Of course not, I'll say it's from work."

Lía shook her head. "How are we related?"

I was thankful Ana was taking such a proactive approach. We needed to know if Sara had any legitimate reason to have this medication, and if not, then I needed to warn Blanca after all the dust-ups the two of them had recently had.

Ana used her most businesslike tone to ask for one of the diners, gave Carlos's name, and said it was an urgent work issue. After a minute or two of waiting, Carlos must have answered.

"Carlos, it's me, Ana. – Yes I know I shouldn't have lied, but what's up with your phone? – I told you to carry a charger. – Well, it is urgent. I didn't lie about that – Does your mom have seizures? – No, I'm not crazy. – Because she has medication for it in her room. – No, I won't say anything to her, but you should – Okay, we'll talk later."

"So?" Lía asked.

Ana shook her head. "Carlos said his mom doesn't have any health issues that he knows of. She just had her yearly physical and said everything was great."

"It is odd," Lía admitted. "But she got into arguments with Olga and Harriet *after* she arrived. Why would she have brought the medicine here?"

Ana shrugged.

"Maybe she was planning to murder someone else but hasn't gotten around to it yet," I said. "What if Harriet was just practice? You said yourself that the effects of an overdose are unknown. Maybe she just wanted to see what would happen and how much she'd need."

"And…" Ana said, looking confused. "I don't get it."

"And now she knows exactly what to do, which means someone else could be in grave danger."

"But who?" Lía asked.

"I'm not sure yet, but I need to warn Blanca," I said, before darting out of the office. I hoped she was in her room. Since she and Luis had had their falling out, she'd spent a lot more time there, even though I'd invited her multiple times to hang out with me at the cottage. She always turned me down, so I'd stopped offering. I knocked hesitantly at her door and waited. Slowly she pulled it open.

"Blanca, we need to talk. It's really important. I know you don't want to, but please come back to the cottage. It's the safest place." She opened her mouth to refuse. "Please!" I pleaded.

She must've sensed something in my voice because she nodded slowly. "Okay, let me just put on something. I'm here in my pajamas."

I nodded. "I'll wait."

Blanca changed in record time, and we headed back to the cottage, followed by Furby, always interested in overseeing whoever entered his domain. He would've preferred to hang out in the house all day, but he always chose company over comfort.

"So what is this about?" Blanca asked. Her eyes darted nervously around the room, and she shifted in the chair. "Nothing has changed has it? It's creepy. I almost expect mama to…" She didn't finish her thought and was so visibly uncomfortable that I regretted asking her to come here.

I decided to just get down to business. "I need to tell you something. It's *extremely* confidential, but you need to know for your own safety."

"Whoa, that sounds pretty dramatic," Blanca said, laughing nervously.

I took a deep breath before explaining everything I knew. I told her about the footage we had of Sara leaving the hotel out the back just a couple of hours before the murder and the run-ins she'd had with Harriet questioning her, how Harriet had died, what we knew, what we didn't know. All the arguments she'd had with both victims and about the medication we'd just discovered in her hotel room that, from what we could tell, she didn't have a legitimate use for."

"But you can't tell anyone, not even Luis. Literally, Mom, no one."

Blanca flinched at being called mom, and I instantly regretted it. "Sorry, I meant Blanca."

"That's okay." She waved off the apology. "But what if Luis is the one she was planning to kill all along?" Blanca pointed out. "He's the only one, besides Carlos and Ana, who she already knew before arriving. She didn't even know I existed until she saw me at the rehearsal dinner."

"That's true," I said slowly. Blanca was right. "But she's been all sweet with Luis, jealous of anyone who gets close. I can't imagine her wanting to–"

"What a great cover-up to get close to him, and with me around she never could," Blanca said.

Blanca did make a lot of sense. "Well, don't tell him anyway, and you need to be careful. You haven't exactly made friends with Sara, and if she is the murderer, she hasn't been afraid to kill people she's barely met who looked at her wrong."

"I'll be careful," Blanca said, "if you also promise not to confront Sara yourself. You should let Carlos handle it. She's his mother, after all. You never know, there could be a perfectly good explanation for everything. Maybe she picked up a friend's medication by mistake, or maybe she's using it for something else. Doctor Google isn't always reliable. Or maybe she just doesn't want to tell everyone her medical history."

I smiled. "Okay, it does seem odd that she would've bashed Olga over the head so violently if this was her plan all along, but it would make sense why she's been so interested in attending all of the funeral and visitation events."

Blanca nodded. "We don't know, but you're right, better safe than sorry."

"Do you want to have something to eat, or does this place make you too uncomfortable?" I offered.

Blanca started to shake her head, but nodded instead. "That would be nice. Am I that obvious?" she asked.

"Kind of. At first I thought you didn't want to be around me, but then I realized it was the cottage you were avoiding." I stood to reheat some tlacoyos I'd made the day before.

She nodded. "There's a lot of memories here, and I felt like if I didn't actually come in that maybe it wasn't real that mama wasn't really gone, but here, without her, it's just too real. I don't deal very well with real." *Boy did I know that was true.*

Blanca continued. "But she's gone, and I never got to change her opinion of me as the embarrassing, selfish daughter she wanted to hide away."

I shook my head. "Grandma never talked about you like that. You didn't always get along, but she loved you."

There were actually tears in Blanca's eyes. Growing up, I thought this woman was made of steel, and here she was crying again for a sentimental reason. She dabbed at her eyes before continuing.

"I know I wasn't the best. That's why I came. I thought maybe we could patch things up, even if I couldn't with my mother, maybe I could with my daughter. Maybe it's been too long, though. I know I asked a lot of you growing up, and you felt like I abandoned you for a couple years here in Santa Rita. "

I nodded. "Sometimes I did," I admitted. "But I also have some of my best memories during that time of husband number three when I lived here for middle school with grandma, so maybe it was for the best."

Blanca smiled. "It wasn't easy being 18 pregnant and then crossing the border as a teenager. It was really different back then, but it was still hard."

I hadn't thought a lot about Blanca's story, only where it intertwined with my own. All I really knew was that she'd run away to the US when she'd found out she was pregnant, to this day hadn't revealed who my father was, had worked odd jobs, including as an exotic dancer, for a short time before working her way up the ladder of successful husbands. Our life had been chaotic, but I'd never gone hungry, and I'd always been comfortable. Maybe she'd done the best she could. She just didn't have a lot to give.

"When I was your age, you were 11," Blanca said. "And I'd just married husband number three." Neither of us ever referred to him by name.

"Really?" It was hard to believe, but the math worked.

"I know I was a selfish you-know-what all these years, but I always loved you, even if I didn't always know how to show it."

"I think that's exactly how grandma felt too," I said.

Blanca nodded sadly. I knew there were plenty of stories that contributed to the hard shell that Blanca carried, most of which she'd never reveal. I felt angry at her and sorry for her and love for her all at the same time.

"Maybe you should stay in the cottage with me," I said without thinking. "With Sara running around, it might be safer, at least until we know more."

"Oh, we'd just kill each other bumping around in this little space." She laughed. "Don't worry, I can handle Sara. I've dealt with way worse than her."

But if it was true what we'd theorized, I wasn't so sure about that.

"Really, Blanca, how many serial killers have you been around?" I teased her.

"Who knows? They don't usually introduce themselves that way, but I've handled myself so far."

Well, I hope you can keep it up, I thought to myself but just smiled and agreed. There was no use trying to convince Blanca to do anything that she didn't want to do, like telling me who my father was. Blanca had never felt like I deserved or needed to know, and for the most part, I hadn't cared. But since moving to Santa Rita, I'd thought about it a lot more. What if I was passing him every day and didn't know?

"Blanca?" I asked tentatively. Every time I'd brought this up before, she'd shut me down immediately.

She nodded, but I could tell her guard was up.

"Do you think you could tell me... I mean I think I deserve to know who my fa–" How was I fumbling this so badly already?

Blanca put up her hand, guessing where this was going. "I'm not going to tell you, Natalia. It's better if you don't know, okay? Just take my word for it. I'd tell you if you needed to know, you can trust me there."

Blanca pulled out her compact mirror to check her makeup and put her large, expensive sunglasses on top of her head, ready to go. Her smug attitude and irritated words made me want to yell and throw every insult I could, but I knew that would only make things worse.

"Well, I think you're being selfish," I said quietly. "But since I can't force every male in Santa Rita over the age of 45 to take a DNA test, I'll just have to let it go *again*." I tried to give her the most pointed look in hopes of shaming her into at least offering something.

Blanca had never been sensitive to shame, though. "It's okay if you're mad at me. You wouldn't be the first." Blanca shrugged like the entire conversation was boring her.

"Well, I'm sure you have some things to get back to," I said through gritted teeth. I needed to get away from Blanca before my self-control grew too thin to handle. She nodded gratefully and breezed out of the cottage. I showed her out before punching a couch cushion and dissolving into tears.

Furby tapped my arm with a soft paw. "I'm glad she didn't want to stay with us," I said to Furby, picking him up to cuddle and flipped on the TV, quickly absorbed into an overly dramatic but highly entertaining telenovela. Furby purred contentedly, kneading the couch cushion on my lap.

"I think cats might be superior to humans," I said to Furby, gesturing to the screen as a man fought with his evil twin after waking from a coma. Furby squinted his eyes in agreement.

CHAPTER TWENTY

Today was finally the last day of Olga's funeral festivities. I normally appreciated the long, drawn out burial and mourning process that Mexico had versus the US, but in this case, I would've appreciated a simple visitation and funeral, that's it. I'd offered Beatriz that option. After all, a lot of Mexican families were starting to forgo the old way of doing things, but Beatriz had been adamant. If she was going to adopt a dead person into her family to honor, which was how she saw it, she was going to do it right.

So after the first couple days, there'd been the funeral mass and burial, and then after the nine days of nightly prayers and songs, there was another funeral mass. After seven years, Beatriz would probably want to do another mass, not to mention keeping Olga's picture on her family's altar every year on the day of the dead.

"If I'd thought through how much work this was going to be for your mom, I never would've asked her to do it," I said to Nico as we strolled towards the church.

Nico was out of his usual work or casual clothes and in an actual suit, clean-shaven, with his dimples on full display, and his black hair slicked back. "Mom, has always been a sucker for anyone ostracized by their family that she can take under her wing."

"Like me?" I joked.

"Exactly, but it's not a burden. We all love you." Nico turned to plant a kiss on my cheek.

"Well, I hope *you* do." I playfully elbowed Nico in the ribs. "But Olga?"

"Olga is a lot easier to adopt after she's passed on than when she was with us." Nico laughed. "And my mother was hardly going to let her be put in a pauper's grave without all the preparations. If you hadn't asked her, she would've done it anyway."

We stepped up the stone steps into the cool, dark interior of the extremely tall sanctuary. I made sure to soften my expression and erase the smile. I didn't want to appear disrespectful, considering the occasion. I watched Nico genuflect, dipping his fingers in the small stone container of holy water. I tried to copy him, but I had no idea what to do. Grandma had shown me a million years ago, but I hadn't bothered to care. It would've been nice to know now, though, just to make sure I wasn't committing some giant faux pas.

Father Francisco conducted the service. I was surprised that he'd agreed to do it for free until he got to the part where he commented that since no one in Olga's family had been willing to pay, the church had donated its resources and would be taking up a collection for the rest of the funeral expenses.

Obviously, Father Tomás had been unwilling to commit such a vagrant display of greed, especially when we all knew that Lía and Beatriz had raised the rest of the money already, and if anyone wanted to donate, they should give it to them directly. None of what Father Francisco gathered would actually go towards Olga's burial expenses. When the young nun came around with the donation basket, I simply shook my head and didn't care what she or anyone else thought.

The rest of the mass droned on. I started to wonder if the priest's goal was to actually put everyone to sleep, so they wouldn't remember just how awful the eulogy was.

I glanced around the sanctuary. There was a bigger turnout than I'd expected, especially for the mass. Everyone else seemed as lulled by the monotonous, echoing words as I was and were struggling to stay awake. The hard, unforgiving pew was the only thing keeping me conscious.

We were sitting about halfway up the long church, so I glanced behind as well. Sitting all by herself in the last pew, I was stunned to see a quietly weeping Lupe. My first instinct was to pass over and comfort her, but I stopped myself.

Why was Lupe crying? Was it really because she missed her sister-in-law and regretted their years of feuding, or was it because she knew something or *had done* something that she now regretted?

I glanced away quickly. Esteban still hadn't shown up for anything honoring his sister, at least Lupe had, and while it made sense that she might be ashamed and want to keep her distance even if she was innocent, her behavior was still suspicious.

After the service, everyone solemnly filed out down the street towards the hotel and up to the multipurpose room where the lunch had been laid out. After that endless blathering that Father Francisco had given us in lieu of a decent eulogy, I was starving. The conversations around the room grew livelier as people piled their plates. I scanned the room for Lupe but didn't see her anywhere. Had anyone else seen her crying in the back?

"You've been awfully quiet," Nico said, handing me a plate piled with carnitas.

"Sorry, I've just been thinking." I looked down at the food. "I can't eat all this."

"Whatever you can't finish, just pass over to me." He winked.

I shook my head and smiled. "Have you seen Ana around anywhere?"

"Why? What hijinks are you two up to today, breaking into the coroner's office?"

"Not yet, but that's actually not a bad idea," I teased. Nico rolled his eyes.

"Did you see Lupe in the back of the church crying during the service?"

Nico shook his head. "Is that suspicious behavior now? Olga *was* her sister-in-law for quite a while. It's only natural for her to be sad."

"I know, I know." *Where was Ana?* She was a much better sleuthing buddy.

"I'm boring you, aren't I?" he asked.

"Kind of, you're just too practical about everything. Even Lía will sometimes indulge our potential theories."

"Okay, okay, I'll try to be practical but not a wet blanket, if you'll at least *consider* some of my practical observations."

"Deal. Oh look, there's Ana and Carlos," I said, waving them over.

Nico frowned. "I'm not sure if it's even worth it to try with you two."

I ignored his complaints, eager to finally talk to Carlos face to face. He was a reasonable person. I really hoped I could convince him that we weren't accusing his mother of anything but just wanted to rule her out as a suspect.

We chit-chatted for a while about the delayed upcoming wedding and the quality of the food. But I could see Carlos was on edge, probably anticipating the upcoming mode of questioning. This might be harder than I'd thought. I decided to bring up Lupe, a possible and more likely suspect than his mother.

"Did you see Lupe during the service?" I asked.

Ana shook her head. "No, is she here now?"

"I haven't seen her, but she was at the mass. She sat in the very back of the chapel, and she was quietly crying the entire time."

"Well, Olga was her sister-in-law, and she knows people suspect her," Carlos said defensively, but Ana just rolled her eyes.

"Ignore him," Ana said. "He doesn't like the fact that we're conducting our own investigation again. He says it's too dangerous, but it worked last time, didn't it?"

Carlos snorted. "Just barely."

"Barely counts, and we've learned from our mistakes, which brings up the fact; have you talked to your mother yet about that medication we found?" Ana had read my mind.

Carlos shifted uncomfortably and tugged at the cuffs of his dress shirt. "What am I supposed to say, 'Ma, while my girlfriend was going through your stuff, she found a medication in your suitcase that we'd like you to explain because we think you might've murdered at least one person'?"

I glanced toward Nico for help. He shook his head. "The guy makes a good point."

"Thank you," Carlos said. "I know you two love playing detective, but this is my mom we're talking about here. Unless you have something more solid, I'm not going to insinuate to her that I think she might be a murderer."

My heart sank. This was not going at all how I'd planned. Ana looked panic-stricken, probably fearing I was going to rope her into doing something that would put her on her future mother-in-law's bad side for the rest of eternity.

"Don't worry, Ana," I said. "I know it's going to be hard enough to be Sara's daughter-in-law without asking you to confront her about a murder. Oh sorry, Carlos. I didn't mean that. Your mother is… lovely," I stammered, realizing what I'd just implied and impotently trying to backpedal. Nico chuckled at my misstep.

"What about this?" I said, taking a deep breath. "What if I delicately approach the subject with Sara since I'm not, nor will I ever be, related to her." *Thank God!* "Can I at least have your unofficial blessing for that?"

Carlos looked thoughtful. "Okay, but if she asks me about it, I didn't agree to anything, nor did I know about any of this ahead of time."

"I can go with that," I said and turned to look for Sara. I saw Blanca already drinking and having a fabulous time with a small crowd gathered around her watching her performance. I bristled. I had told her to watch out for herself. Getting tipsy at a large event with food and drinks and Sara was not my idea of a smart move. I needed to find Sara and fast, if only to keep an eye on her and away from Blanca.

I felt Ana touch my arm. "Are you really going to do this now?"

I nodded. "Why not?"

Ana bit her lip. "Well, just be careful."

"Of course, I can handle myself," I said. I hated that I sounded just like Blanca.

I spotted Sara sitting at a table in the far corner of the room, an empty chair right next to her. I made a beeline in her direction before I could second guess myself.

"Hello, mind if I sit here?" I asked. Not waiting for a

response, I sat.

Sara stared at me, and I stared back. I hadn't thought this through enough, apparently. I wasn't sure how to broach the subject, what angle to take. Maybe Carlos was right, but it was too late to admit defeat. I was just going to have to get it over with.

"Sara, I was just wondering if you saw Olga the morning she was killed?" I asked. Well, nothing like just jumping right in there, but I never was any good at beating around the bush.

"What?" Sara was flustered, good.

"Well, we were checking the security footage, and we saw you leaving extremely early through the back and walking towards the church. I was just wondering if you happened to see anything."

But Sara was too smart for that. She squared her shoulders and replied defensively. "Yes, well did you check to see that I go out at the same time *every* morning. It's good for my health, and I prefer walking the side streets while it's still dark and everything's quiet."

Oh, another good opening. I was already in this thing knee deep, may as well drown myself while I was at it. "Do you have any health concerns then?" I asked the baited question and waited.

"What do you mean by that?" She eyed me suspiciously.

"Just what I asked. Are you healthy? Do you have to take any type of medication?"

"I don't know what you're implying, and I'm not sure I want to know. I may not have *liked* Olga, but I certainly never murdered her."

"Then why have you been to every single event honoring

her, if you didn't even like her? Doesn't that seem a little odd?" Okay, now I was losing it. I told myself to stop, but I couldn't help it.

"Because I felt bad about how we had argued the night before she died and that she didn't have any family who cared about her, *and* because there's nothing else to do in this godforsaken town. But if you'll excuse me, I've lost my appetite. I think I'll go back to my room and lie down." Sara was practically in tears, and she was speaking loud enough that most of the room had turned in our direction.

How had I become the villain? I was on the side of justice. We were doing the right thing, weren't we?

Nico shook his head when I returned. "Did anyone ever teach you about subtlety?" he asked.

"Maybe I was a little too heavy-handed. I'm sorry, Carlos. I didn't mean to offend your mother like that. I'll apologize later."

"It's okay. I know you meant well," he said. "But maybe wait a little, give her time to cool off."

I nodded. How had I just managed to mess everything up in one fell swoop and was still no closer to figuring out who might've murdered Olga and Harriet?

CHAPTER TWENTY-ONE

The room suddenly felt too small, and my face was growing hotter by the second.

"I promised Miguel that I'd cover the desk while he came up to eat," I mumbled in Ana's general direction.

"Come on, Natalia. It's not that big of a deal," she said, but I just nodded, gave a weak smile, and hurried out as quickly as I could. The farther I got away from Sara and everybody else who'd heard our argument, the better.

"Hi Miguel, you're welcome to pop upstairs and get a free lunch. I'll watch the desk for you," I offered.

Not questioning the offer of free food, Miguel gave a grateful thank you and hurried upstairs. I sunk into the chair behind the desk with a sigh. I'd painted myself as the villain and had an argument with Sara in the middle of a funeral lunch, but I still had no idea what that medication was for or if it had played any part in Harriet's death, but at least now I'd get a half hour of silence to mull it all over.

Unfortunately my silence was short-lived. Claire poked her head around the corner. "Oh, it's you. I'm glad I caught you," she said. "Have you seen Harriet's parents around anywhere?"

I shook my head. "When are they supposed to be getting in?"

"I'm not sure, any day now, I guess. I just wanted to keep an eye out for them, just in case." Her voice was soft and hesitant.

"How are you doing?" I asked. "We haven't gotten any more calls asking about Harriet. That's a good thing. Maybe the story won't be huge after all." Then, realizing, I might've sounded a bit too cold and selfish, I added. "I mean for you, it's hard enough to grieve without reporters breathing down your neck."

Claire nodded sadly. "Yeah, it's awful, but at least there were just a few blog posts and some stories here and there. Jessica did an interview with another channel and explained that the cause of death still wasn't confirmed and could've been natural. They're all just sharks looking for content. When they don't see any immediate blood in the water, they move on to the next thing."

I smiled at Claire's analogy. "That's good, especially for Harriet's family. I was wondering for a little while there if we were going to get descended on by the media."

Claire shook her head. "Just a few internet sleuths. They're not about to get on a plane."

Claire twisted one of her many brightly colored, beaded bracelets over and over between her fingers.

"Is there anything else you wanted?" I asked, sensing that there was.

Claire opened her mouth to speak but shook her head. "No, I just came down to make sure you weren't being harassed by some internet troll or something. People can be crazy." She gave an awkward laugh.

"No, I don't think so. I haven't been online too much these days, what with all the uh... stuff. So if they're trying to harass me, there's no one online to notice."

"Good, that's good." Claire stood, still twirling her bracelets.

"You're welcome to go up and have some lunch. Don't feel bad about it. You and Jessica both. But you better hurry."

"Really?" Claire smiled. "Anything vegan?"

"Well, there's tortillas, nopales, and potatoes, I think, but other than that, I don't think so. Maritza might've brought some vegan desserts, though."

"Thanks, I'll go check. You sure it's okay?"

I waved my hand. "Please do. I don't want to have to worry about leftovers with a wedding at hand. We'll probably just send food home with people if it doesn't get eaten."

"Thanks," Claire said again, and exited the way she'd come.

Furby sauntered up from the office, waking up from his seventh nap of the day.

"I didn't know you were here, bud," I said, patting him on the head. He arched his back in appreciation.

But he stiffened at the sound of approaching steps. Furby was a social cat. He enjoyed attention from everyone, including strangers. Everybody was a potential subject he could induce into his orbit, but very rarely, there were people he didn't like, and I trusted his judgment.

The last person Furby hadn't taken a liking to had been Sara. Not wanting to have another battle in the middle of the lobby, I swiftly exited towards the office, leaving the door open because I'm nosy. *Hey, at least I'm honest about it.* Furby padded slowly after me.

"Yeah, you should come by. The spread isn't bad. There's plenty of food."

Someone was talking by phone, but I couldn't quite place the voice.

"Oh, don't worry about it. Nobody's mourning that

zealot." The woman gave a throaty laugh, and I knew who it was. Silvia. I froze. I'd never heard her voice so icy before. It was always subdued, soft, with a hint of irritation or apathy but nothing more. This was like a completely different person.

"Everyone would be happy to see you. Don't worry, even that sanctimonious Gallardo family would fawn all over you if you came. *'Oh Father, so kind of you to come,"* she mimicked. "I'm telling you that's how these people are, simple."

"Okay, well if you don't want to, I'll bring you home a plate of cake. You want carnitas too? – I told you, these people pulled out all the stops, for what? Stupid, that's what it is. That's why they stay poor. They give it all away." Silvia laughed again, and I heard her heels echoing down the tile hallway as she turned back around.

I unclenched my fists that were balled up at my side. Furby had just saved me from engaging in an altercation that would've made my argument with Sara look like a makeout session. The crass disrespect on so many levels that Silvia had just engaged in, and I couldn't tell for sure just by listening to her side of the conversation, but from what I heard, her priest consort was just as guilty.

If I'd followed my instincts, I would've marched right back upstairs and kicked Silvia out in a truly dramatic fashion after she'd just maligned my friends in my own lobby. But seeing as Silvia did have some power, and I didn't want to delay Ana's wedding yet again, I decided against it. But she had just placed herself squarely in my focus as my number one suspect.

Even though Silvia hadn't said anything legally damning, she'd insulted my friends and made me angry, and since she was a suspect along with Father Francisco, anything I found… *anything*, even if it was just morally incriminating and not connected to the murder, I'd leak it in a heartbeat. My mind started to race with all the horrible ways I could ruin Silvia's life, knowing full-well I'd never actually go through with any of them, but I enjoyed imagining it and cursed her under my breath.

"Who are you mad at?" Maritza poked her head around the office door.

I jumped. "You shouldn't sneak up on me like that. What do you mean? I was just making a note to myself."

Maritza grinned. "I may not speak English, but I've watched enough movies to understand *that word*, and it was no note."

"I was just thinking about something," I said. I'd tell Maritza eventually, but I was too angry right now to focus on Silvia and was grateful for the distraction. "So what's up? Everything okay?"

"Well, I'm not sure, but I don't think so. Do you mind if we talk privately? I don't want anyone to overhear."

"Yeah, okay, sure," I said, ushering Furby back inside the office as he frantically weaved his wave between mine and Maritza's legs.

Maritza and I both settled into chairs opposite one another, and instead of choosing a lap, Furby opted for the desk and paced back and forth, allowing us to take turns scratching his cheek.

"I'm not exactly sure how to say this, but it has to be said." Maritza took a deep breath, and my anxiety ratcheted up even more.

"Just spit it out. You're killing me," I said.

"Well, we started missing some things in the bakery," she said.

"Things? What things?" I asked.

"Things from the stockroom," she clarified. "We've always been generous about giving everybody day-old pastries or bread that's not perfect to take home with them, but the stockroom was off limits. It's one of the first things I explain to anyone new when they come onto the team."

I nodded. That's exactly how grandma had been, generous but strict.

"At first I just thought maybe I'd miscounted," Maritza continued. "But then it became obvious there was a thief. It wasn't anything huge, and I didn't want to make more of it than it was. So I just mentioned to everyone that the stockroom was off limits, and I hoped that would be the end of it."

"But it wasn't?" I asked.

Maritza shook her head. "Well, it was, sort of, but then we started missing money from the cash register. Every day we came up short. Sometimes it was just 20 or 30 pesos. I thought it could've been an honest mistake, but yesterday, we were short by almost 1000 pesos."

I gasped, in tiny Santa Rita that was almost a week's salary, nothing to be sneezed at.

"Did you notice any coincidence about the missing items or money?" I asked. Maybe Andrea wasn't as ditzy as she appeared. "Could it have been Andrea? She was new to the bakery after all."

Maritza shook her head. "Nothing went missing while she was there. In fact, when Lupe was gone, nothing at all, not even a stick of butter came up short. But as soon as she came back, that's when the money started disappearing."

"Do you have any other proof, besides circumstantial?" I asked.

"Not really," Maritza said. "I'm not sure how to go about it. That's why I came. Well, plus it's a lot of money, and I didn't want anyone thinking it was me."

I nodded, understanding. "Well, was there anyone else there when things were taken and money was stolen, anyone besides Lupe?"

"The only other person who was there all the same times was Rosa," Maritza said. "But I hardly think she'd steal."

I nodded in agreement. Rosa could be tough and wouldn't waste a second in throwing someone under the bus to get ahead, but she was almost as dedicated as Maritza and had a lot more than 1000 pesos to lose if she ever stole anything; whereas Lupe had already been on shaky ground, to put it mildly, and had admitted she was in dire need of money.

I shook my head sadly. "So what do you think we should do?"

"I was thinking we could gently question them both, see what they say, and hope Lupe confesses. You wouldn't want to prosecute her or anything, though, right?"

"No." I shook my head. "Not for stealing." *For murder, yes,* I silently added to myself.

"Good." Maritza looked relieved. "They both work tomorrow morning. We could question them after the morning rush, and I'll make sure I'm the only one near the cash register all morning."

I nodded. "What if they don't confess?" I asked.

Maritza shrugged. "I think they will, or we'll be able to tell who's lying. People are never as clever as they think they are."

Lupe's suspicious behavior wasn't doing her any favors, and while I hated Silvia, I needed to try and be rational and acknowledge that Lupe and Esteban were realistically the main suspects in Olga's murder and had motives for Harriet's as well, albeit not as strong. And tomorrow I'd get a chance to ask her about the missing money and hopefully the murders.

CHAPTER TWENTY-TWO

The next day I hung out in the hotel office longer than I should have, waiting.

If only Ana hadn't had the day off. She always made everything feel doable, but her wedding was just a couple of days away. And she was busy getting everything ready for the second time.

Glancing at the clock, I realized I couldn't put it off any more. I gave Furby a pat. He squinted and readjusted himself.

"I'll catch you later," I told Lía.

She looked up from her computer. "Oh, that's right. You have that thing with Maritza and Lupe. Let me know how it goes." Lía's tone was not encouraging.

I sighed. "I just want to get it over with."

The bakery had hit its afternoon lull. Maritza had locked up, so we could discuss the issues with Lupe and Rosa in private without fear of being disturbed. Seeing the main bakery empty, I hurried to the storeroom where I found everyone already seated. Maritza sent me a grateful smile.

I'd thought that we were going to discuss everything individually, but Maritza seemed to have other plans. I shifted nervously. Rosa had a strong personality, and if she became too overbearing, there was no way Lupe was going to confess in front of her.

But Maritza was two steps ahead of me. After she'd laid out the issue, Rosa started ranting and yelling about all the work she'd done for the bakery, and she did not enjoy being accused of stealing.

"We're not accusing anyone," Maritza said calmly. "But you two have been my oldest and most loyal employees. I was simply wondering if you had seen or heard anything that might be helpful."

Rosa immediately calmed. "Well, that girl Andrea worked here for a few days, and she's a weird one. Maybe it was her."

Maritza nodded. "I'll look into it." Even though we both knew it couldn't have been her.

Rosa sighed satisfied. "So is there anything else you need?" she asked.

"No," Maritza said. "But if you hear or see anything else, please let me know."

"Sure thing," Rosa said before rushing out.

Lupe slowly stood to leave as well, although she hadn't uttered a single word. She glanced nervously between the two of us. Wow, Maritza was right. Most people are horrible liars. Lupe might as well have had *I stole the money* written on her forehead.

"So did you see anything, Lupe?" Maritza asked.

Lupe mutely shook her head.

"You know we can work it out if there's something we need to know. Maybe we can even help. You know me. I'm not going to call the police or anything." Maritza's voice was softer than I'd anticipated.

"I would never steal," Lupe said so quietly we both had to lean forward to hear.

"I know you wouldn't," Maritza said, "under normal circumstances, but things have been tough for you. If we're afraid, taking a little money from the cash register doesn't seem that bad. Any of us could find ourselves in that situation."

Lupe shook her head. "I'm not afraid. It's not like that."

"Then how is it?" Maritza waited.

"I was going to pay it back." Lupe collapsed into sobs.

I was impressed. Maritza was a way better investigator than anyone in the Santa Rita police department. I wasn't sure what to do. Obviously Lupe had to be fired, she'd been on probation after all, but I wanted to find out why she'd been stealing first, and what it might have to do with the murders.

"What happened?" Maritza asked.

"It's Esteban. He's just been drinking so much. He hasn't been bringing any money home, and my check only goes so far. Plus, we have to pay back everything he's lost, or they can come and get our home and everything in it."

"What about Olga's house?" I couldn't help myself from asking. "Couldn't you rent it out or sell it or sell your house that you're living in now?" I was not nearly as patient as Maritza, and I saw Lupe flinch at my questions.

"It all takes time, the paperwork, the courts, everything. That's how I was going to pay it back. I knew it wasn't right, but I was going to just as soon as we had the money in hand. I promise. You believe me, right?" She looked towards Maritza, her eyes glistening with unshed tears.

Maritza nodded. "I believe you, but it still doesn't make it right." Lupe nodded and turned to blow her nose with the tissue Maritza offered.

"I saw you at the mass yesterday," I said, trying to keep my voice light, but Lupe stiffened just the same, and Maritza glanced towards me, confused. I had no idea where I was going with this either, only that I needed to find out something.

"I know you'd never hurt anyone, Lupe, but did Esteban

ever tell you anything about what happened to his sister, anything at all?"

Lupe's face was growing red. "I told you the truth, and now you think I'm a murderer to boot?"

"No, of course not, I wasn't trying to imply–"

"I was sad about Olga dying, but I knew that if anyone saw me, they'd judge me, just like you're doing. I do feel bad. I should have reached out to her more. I'm sure she was lonely. That was it."

Probably recognizing that she shouldn't have just unloaded on her boss, Lupe pushed her lips together and looked down. "So just tell me what you're going to do," she asked quietly.

"Well, I can have Lía get your last check together by the end of the day, and–" I tried to finish, but Lupe interrupted.

"Wait, are you firing me?" Lupe's panicked face ping-ponged between Maritza and me. "But I thought– Maritza said we could work it out that you guys would try to help. I was honest, and here you are firing me after interrogating me more. This is not right." Lupe was hysterical now, her voice almost to the point of yelling.

"Lupe, wait." Maritza put her hand up to touch Lupe's arm, but she was already standing and headed towards the door. "I'll go see Lía for my last check."

Maritza leaned back and sighed. "Why did you have to fire her like that?" Her voice was sad but not accusatory.

Now it was my turn to be defensive. "But I thought... She stole, right? Don't you fire people who steal, no questions asked? That's what we used to do at any job I've ever had."

"What kinds of jobs were those?" Maritza's voice was still soft. She was talking to me like I was Lupe, and I resented it.

"It was... It was in the US. I've never really worked in Mexico before, except here, and grandma always handled everything, but I just– I didn't mean to– I thought– Wasn't she on probation?"

Maritza nodded. "But this is Santa Rita. We're not a big corporation, and Lupe has worked here longer than I have. Plus, she was just honest with us that she's desperate. She needs help. Do you know how hard it was for her to say that? Where do you think she's going to get a job now? How's she going to get money?"

Maritza shook her head. "You're the owner, though. I'm sorry. You're right. I shouldn't overstep. It's whatever you want, and I agree; stealing isn't okay. But next time, it would be nice if you'd give me a heads up before I start promising that we can help. It made me look like a backstabber."

"I thought we were being generous and helping by not calling the police. We could've had Lupe arrested right now, if we wanted to," I said, feeling heat creep up my face.

Maritza shrugged and nodded sadly. I knew she wasn't going to argue with me, which made her silent reproof all the more convicting. I'd never heard of letting an employee call in, quit, come back, steal, and not fire them. I knew Lupe had a sob story, but was that all it took in Santa Rita to keep you on? Apparently so.

"I need some fresh air. I'll be back," I said, breezing past Maritza and out the front of the bakery.

Lupe was probably already in the back office complaining about me to Lía, and I wasn't anxious to see yet another disappointed face pointed in my direction, so I decided to go for a walk. Even though it was early afternoon and the sun was high and hot, the narrow streets and buildings offered plenty of shade. I headed towards the gardens and fountain in the square and wandered along the paths of sculptured bushes and flowering trees until I reached the large stone fountain.

The church stood directly across, empty, another indication of the lies that Silvia loved to tell. She had made Ana wait so long for her wedding to be rescheduled just because she could. Maybe I should head over and see what I could find. After all, Father Tomás had extended an open invitation, and after what I'd heard from Silvia, I felt like she deserved a visit.

The church loomed over the square. I glanced at the small path on the left that led towards the offices and started towards them. I'd just check to see if Father Tomás was in, no harm in that, right?

I knocked gently before opening, hoping if Silvia was in to catch her doing... Well, I'm not sure what. It didn't matter, though. She wasn't there. The front office was empty. I listened and knocked at both priests' office doors. Both were unlocked and empty as well. The only other room was a large storage closet. I couldn't believe it. They'd left everything unlocked and empty. What were the odds? Maybe it was a sign, a sign that I was supposed to snoop. I shouldn't turn that down, I decided. It would be sacrilegious.

I didn't know how much time I had or what I was looking for exactly. I started with Silvia's desk. Opening drawers, glancing at their contents. I even slipped my hand underneath all the papers, nothing. It wasn't likely that she'd keep a murder weapon in her desk, but when was I going to get an opportunity like this again?

The desk itself was covered in mountains of paper, so I started shifting it around, when suddenly I heard the front door click. I froze and quickly straightened. Unfortunately, I had my hands wrapped around two stacks of paper, and Silvia stood there, a scowl on her face.

"Can I help you?" she asked, set down her styrofoam cup of coffee, and shooed me away from behind her desk. "I thought I could go out for a minute and get a cup of coffee, but apparently this town can't be trusted."

"I was just checking for the reservation for my friend Ana's wedding," I said, trying to think on my feet, and knowing, even as it came out, what a lame excuse it was. "You said it was in two days, right? I couldn't remember and was just passing through, and–"

"Yes," Silvia said, cutting me off. "Doesn't your friend remember her wedding?" She laughed the same grating laugh I'd heard before, and it sent my blood pressure rocketing.

"Of course, thanks for the reminder," I said, my tone laced with fake sweetness. "I noticed that the church has been empty every day except for the funeral and regular masses. But I guess it's hard when you know *you'll* never have a wedding, isn't it? That *your* man isn't free to marry you, never will be, and you'll have to be content to sit on the sidelines. It makes it hard not to be bitter."

"What are you implying?" Silvia's voice rose, but it was as much in fear as anger. I took solace in that.

"Just what I said." My voice was low.

"You better walk lightly," she said. "I have more power here than you know, and it's not like you're married either." She laughed again. "You're almost thirty. I'm sure it grates on you."

"Not at all," I shrugged. "I don't care if I ever get married, and I'd never sell my dignity for a little bit of power. Don't you ever get sick of being shoved in the shadows, Silvia?"

Silvia flinched at my words. "Why don't you just see yourself out? Neither of the fathers are in, but I'll make sure to tell them you stopped by."

"Actually, Father Tomás asked me to come, so if you don't mind, I'll wait." I was not backing down. I might have been wrong or too hard on Lupe. I still wasn't sure who was right, but I had the upper hand with Silvia, and I wasn't going to lose it.

"Well, he might be quite a while." Silvia sucked her teeth in annoyance.

"That's fine. I'll wait," I said, hoping I hadn't just backed myself in a corner.

But thankfully the front door clicked and Father Tomás entered, a wide grin on his face.

"Oh Natalia, I'm so happy you came by," he said.

I'd never wanted to hug a priest until that very moment, but I nodded eagerly instead and followed him to his office.

"How is everything?" he asked, closing the door behind us.

"It's fine," I said. Now I'd have to think of something to talk about. Hopefully he wasn't expecting a therapy session or anything close to it because I was definitely not in the mood for that. But thankfully, he spoke first.

"I've decided you're right, Natalia, about Silvia and Father Francisco's relationship," he said, whispering the names. "I don't care about their personal life, but she can no longer work here. I spoke to him about it, and he said he would speak to Silvia today."

"Today?" I asked, worried for the sake of Ana's wedding and my own safety.

He nodded. "I wanted to thank you again for pushing me. I never want to be seen as a hypocrite."

I nodded. What would he think if he knew I was here under completely false pretenses and had just been breaking and entering, in a church no less? But I nodded and tried to think of a way to get out of here before things got any worse. I had learned nothing and just had an altercation with a possible murderer who was just about to get fired.

"So how are things going?" Father Tomás asked. "Is there anything you'd like to talk about?"

Uh-oh, he was going into full-on therapist/clergy mode. I needed to get out, fast. "Well, I actually uh… well, I wanted to talk to you about it, but I just got a text. There's an issue at the hotel, so maybe we could talk another time." What kind of a lame excuse was that? But it was all I could think of.

"Of course," he said. "I hope everything's all right."

"Yes, I just need to uh… I need to translate something, but I'll be by soon."

Father Tomás stood to show me out, but I waved him back. "I'll be fine. Thank you for your time. See you at the wedding."

I tried, I really did, to exit the office without having any more words with Silvia, especially when I knew what was coming for her later, but she didn't let me.

I had my hand on the door handle when she said, "I hope your friend's wedding isn't delayed again. That would really be a pity."

I breathed, ready to leave without saying a word, but I couldn't help myself. "I guess it won't be delayed unless you murder someone else in the chapel, right?" I said, turning to face her.

Silvia stood slack-jawed, and I sauntered out victorious. It was a risk calling her out personally, but there were times you had to stand up to people. Whether she was the murderer or not, if she knew that I suspected her, maybe it would encourage her to lie low and stop with the power plays.

Maybe, or it might encourage her to come after me. Anyway I wasn't afraid of Silvia. Well maybe a little bit, but right then I was more angry than scared, and I enjoyed seeing her shook, even if it was just for a moment.

I entered the lobby eager to tell Lía about my argument and hopefully offset whatever issue with Lupe I'd created, even though I still didn't quite understand what I'd done wrong.

But there was Sara standing in the middle of the lobby with Ana and Carlos looking serious. What a gut punch. This couldn't be good.

Ana spoke first. "Sara said she wanted to talk to us and explain everything. She wants you to be there too. She said it's important that we understand. Carlos explained the situation to her and–"

"I don't want anyone thinking I'm a murderer, so let's just have this over with here and now," Sara said, looking both contrite and indignant at the same time, not a combination you usually see.

"Sure, of course, where would you like to talk?" I asked.

"I was thinking the cottage might be a good place. My mom said this is a rather delicate matter," Carlos said quietly.

"That's fine," I reluctantly agreed.

We all solemnly proceeded to the cottage, Furby following at our heels.

"He's like a dog," Carlos said. Furby gave an indignant yowl and intertwined himself around my ankles as I tried to unlock the door. "Sorry, didn't mean to offend." Carlos laughed, cutting the tension.

After having met both his parents, it made sense now why Carlos was so excellent at brokering peace and lightening the mood. He'd had ample practice.

Once we were all settled with a pitcher of horchata water on the table between us, Sara took a deep breath.

"I just need to get this out," Sara said. "I did lie to you, Carlitos, and I'm sorry."

"You lied?" Carlos looked shocked, but really was it that shocking? I waited for her to continue.

"I told you that at my last physical everything was fine. I didn't want to worry you, and maybe I didn't want to admit it to myself either. But I was diagnosed with an autoimmune disorder and prescribed that medication. I don't want to get into specifics." She looked pointedly at me, and I didn't blame her. I wasn't interested in hearing about Sara's medical history, just if she had a legitimate reason for that medication.

Sara continued, "I've been walking in the mornings. The doctor said it would help to stay active. I also haven't been sleeping that well, and it helps me think."

Sara adjusted her watch before continuing. "I did argue with Olga at the rehearsal dinner the night before she uh was–" Sara cleared her throat. "I felt bad about it, but I never went to church that morning. The closest I got was to the fountain. I would certainly never poison anyone. I'm sure when the autopsy comes back, it won't be my medication they find in that girl. She was annoying. God rest her soul." Sara made the sign of the cross. "But I would never…"

Sara turned towards me, and I tried not to fidget. "I haven't been gracious with your mother. I can understand why you wouldn't like me. I don't like her much either, but you haven't done anything to me, Natalia. Well, at least until you went through my things and accused me of murder at a funeral that is."

She was still bitter about it, and I couldn't really blame her. "Sorry about that," I said quietly. "My tongue got away from me. I shouldn't have said those things." This seemed to be a common theme with me lately. Maybe I needed more sleep or less people around. I was leaning more towards having less people.

Sara accepted my apology with a nod and continued on, "I know Luis and I didn't have the best marriage." Now it was Carlos's turn to look uncomfortable. I felt bad for him. I needed to find some way to stop her. She'd said all she needed to say, at least for now.

I put a hand on Sara's arm. "You don't have to explain everything. We understand, and I'm sorry. Things have just been crazy around here lately, and I took it out on you accusing you like that. I shouldn't have, and I'm sorry. I really am."

Sara nodded but didn't take the hint. I sent Ana a silent, pleading look. I'd tried. I really had. I should at least get credit for that.

"I've just been thinking about *what if* lately. All the problems Luis and I had pale in comparison to being sick." Sara continued on for a good 20 minutes, going into details that none of us wanted to know.

Was this my penance for embarrassing her? *I'll never do it again, God. Just please make her stop*, I pleaded, which thankfully, she eventually did, and I still don't know how I got her out of my house. But within an hour, Carlos and Ana were walking a much happier Sara back to her room. Maybe she'd be less tense now that she'd gotten all that stress off her shoulders. I hoped so anyway.

CHAPTER TWENTY-THREE

I showed up at the bakery the next morning at 4:00 a.m. much to Maritza's surprise.

"What? I wasn't expecting you to come to work today," she said.

I shrugged. "I felt bad about yesterday. I should have talked to you first before I rushed forward like that with Lupe, made sure we were on the same page."

"Natalia, it's your bakery. You're allowed to do whatever you want. You don't have to ask my permission." Maritza laughed. "But I'm happy you came in all the same. We have a big day today. Would you like to work on some of the cakes while Rosa and I handle the daily breads?"

I nodded. Those were my favorites. I loved mixing the bases in various mixers, pouring them out, and then baking them all simultaneously. It was astonishing how much more productive you could be in a commercial kitchen, and with Maritza at the helm, all I had to worry about was my little corner of the kitchen, and she and Rosa would handle the rest.

"Are you going to redo Ana's wedding cake today?" I asked. "I can't believe her wedding is tomorrow, again."

"I know," Maritza agreed. "I was pretty far behind, but you've been a life saver handling all the smaller cakes." She grinned. "I just hope everything goes off without a hitch."

"Yeah, no more dead bodies in the chapel would be a nice start," I joked.

"You're right about that," Maritza agreed.

The morning had flown by, and although I was wide

awake, my feet were aching. I leaned on the counter for relief.

"Take a load off. Rosa and I can handle it from here," Maritza said, indicating the coffee maker and empty tables.

I didn't need to be told again. Standing for hours on end in concentration was more of a strain than walking. I eagerly grabbed a cup of coffee and an assortment of pastries before sitting with a contented sigh.

A few customers were enjoying their morning breakfast and others were picking up a bite on their way to work, but otherwise it was still pretty low-key this time of morning. The first rays were just peeking through the window, and the cool morning air filled the bakery.

I glanced out on the cobblestone sidewalk with the brightly painted ceramic planters overflowing with flowers. Across the street an old man, probably in his eighties, was selling tamales. I thought about dashing across to buy one. Pastries are nice, but a juicy tamal de rajas would really hit the spot right about now. I left my bag of pastries and coffee on the table and went across to buy two tamales. The pastries would be just as delicious later, I rationalized.

After receiving my change, I turned to head back across the street towards the bakery when I was stopped in my tracks by a maliciously grinning Esteban. Being so early in the morning, I expected Lupe's husband to be at least somewhat inebriated, but he was sober from what I could tell.

"Good morning," he snarled.

"Good morning," I replied quickly and stepped to go around, but he blocked my path yet again. I stifled a groan. This man was going to make me interact with him whether I wanted to or not.

"So you called my wife a thief and then fired her for it,

huh?" Esteban said loud enough for any passerby to overhear.

I shifted uncomfortably. "This really isn't the time or the place to–"

"Answer the question." He jabbed his finger in my direction.

Murderer or not, I wasn't going to be cowered by this bully. "Your wife," I said, matching his volume as much as possible, "admitted to stealing money from the bakery, so yes I think I had every right to fire her at least for the time being. But I feel bad for her because she was put in an impossible situation, so it wasn't entirely her fault. So we might revisit that situation soon."

"What do you mean it wasn't her fault?" Esteban asked.

"Apparently her husband is a drunkard and a gambler and forces his wife to take care of him after he screws up." I gave him a pointed look. "Excuse me." I stepped around Esteban and hurried back to the bakery. I really shouldn't have been that forthright, but he'd caught me hungry after a morning of working. I was only human after all.

I settled back in at my corner table and unwrapped the corn husks from the soft, savory filling. "Finally." I sighed.

I had the first bite to my lips when Claire and Jessica strode in. I swallowed all the off color words that came to mind along with my bite of tamal and scrunched down in my chair, hoping they'd pass by.

Of course in a nearly empty bakery that wasn't likely, and Jessica gave me a wide smile and pulled Claire in my direction. My hopes of eating a tasty tamal in private were shattered, but I pasted on a smile and inched out the chair next to me for them to sit.

"You want a pastry?" I offered the bag. "I think one or two of them might be vegan."

"Well, that definitely isn't." Jessica wrinkled her nose at the sight of my tamal. I shrugged. "No, they're not," I agreed. "But they're definitely tasty."

"If you think suffering is tasty." Jessica flipped her hair behind her shoulder and opened her mouth ready to launch into another speech about animal welfare when Claire stopped her.

"I'm going to get some pastries for us. We shouldn't eat Natalia's after how generous she's already been. Would you like anything?"

Jessica's hand was already halfway in the bag. She pulled it out like a snake had bitten the end of her finger and scowled at Claire. "That's true. Just grab an assortment. Would you like anything, Natalia, anything without suffering?"

I shook my head and shoved another bite into my mouth. "That's okay. I am experiencing no suffering over here." *Except from this self-righteous busybody trying to disrupt my morning reverie.*

"Well, that's because you're not aware..." But Jessica was stopped short by Claire's glare across the table.

"Why don't *I* go get the pastries," Jessica offered and strode towards the shelves of baked goods.

Claire sat down with a sigh. "Sorry about her," she said. "She's been in quite the state."

I nodded, my mouth full. "I'm sorry. She's probably still upset about Harriet. I shouldn't try to egg her on."

Claire nodded. "Jessica isn't great at showing her emotions, but she and Harriet were really close."

I felt bad for Jessica, but I wished she'd go grieve someplace else where I wasn't trying to enjoy my breakfast.

Jessica returned with two cups of coffee and a bag heaping with vegan pastries. "I couldn't pick one, so I just bought a little bit of everything." She smiled. "Did Claire tell you we're leaving tomorrow?" Jessica asked.

"Really?" I was not expecting that and tried to hide my relief. Having Jessica out of the hotel on the day of the wedding would make my life much easier.

Jessica nodded, still chewing. "I forgot but I have a check-up with my cancer doctor."

"It's a really long waiting list to change the appointment," Claire put in. "We could come back afterwards if we're needed for anything... about Harriet." She whispered the last part.

I nodded. "Well, I wish you well with your check-up. It's not serious is it?"

Jessica shook her head. "Not anymore, it's just routine. But I like to stay on top of stuff like that. I never want to go back to how things were. Did I tell you how changing my diet cured my cancer?"

Jessica was ready for another pseudoscience lecture. I eagerly nodded, trying to cut her off at the pass. "Yep, you said eating vegan, right? I'm really happy for you. Being cancer free is a huge accomplishment. You should have a party or something. Are there any good vegan party foods?"

"Of course, there are." Jessica was insulted by the question and started giving a list, with detailed preparation instructions on how to make various vegan party foods, just as I'd hoped. It was still a lecture, but at least I was getting recipes and not unsubstantiated medical advice. It was much easier to nod along to, and I could enjoy my tamal in peace without getting too irritated.

"Well, I think we should probably go get ready." Claire

nudged Jessica. "I have some paperwork I need to get to. Can we still use the multipurpose room?" she asked.

"Sure, I told them to leave a corner for you, but people will be in and out decorating for the wedding tomorrow if that doesn't disturb you."

"Not at all, thanks for everything," Claire said. "I'm sure you'll be glad to have us out of your hair."

"Not at all," I lied.

Jessica glanced at the clock on the wall. "We have plenty of time."

But Claire shook her head forcefully. "I have paperwork that can't wait."

"You can do it on the plane, Claire."

"No I can't, and you need to pack." Finally Claire was able to drag Jessica from the bakery. Claire caught my eye, and I sent her a grateful smile.

"This was my last chance to convince Natalia to change her diet. If she gets cancer, it's on your conscience," I heard Jessica chide as they left.

I shook my head in bemusement. Having cancer so young must've been hard on Jessica. It had definitely taken its toll on her psyche that's for sure.

I dawdled over my breakfast, enjoying every last morsel, and even an additional pastry. It was all an attempt in putting off the inevitable, talking to Lía. I hadn't spoken with her since I'd unilaterally fired Lupe, and after seeing Esteban, I could only imagine what kind of state Lupe had been in when she'd gone to Lía's office yesterday. I didn't know for sure what Lía's feelings on the subject were, but I could guess, and none of them were good. I knew it was cowardly and childish to put it off, but I did it anyway, at least until I'd practically licked the corn husk clean and had no other option but to finally face Lía and hear about the fallout from Lupe's firing.

Furby sat waiting on the front desk and offered his cheek to scratch as payment for entering. I'd hoped that Lía had decided to work from home today what with the wedding just a day away, but no such luck. The office door was slightly open, and I could hear her clicking away. I already knew Ana wouldn't be in, but I wished she would. She made an excellent buffer. I'd never had Lía angry with me before, and she wasn't one to yell or insult, but she'd act disappointed, which was so much worse.

Furby turned and settled down on the lobby keyboard. Miguel must've been on a bathroom break, and whenever anyone left the desk unattended, even for a moment, Furby made it his own. I decided to take a page from his book. Furby never cared what anyone else thought. He just waited to be adored and loved and knew this was his domain. This was my hotel and bakery. They had been left to me, and I was still the primary owner. I needed to follow Furby for once, well minus the arrogant wanting to be adored part. I'd just settle for being comfortable in my own skin and not cowering from criticism.

"Hi Lía," I said, breezing into the office. "How's it going?"

She glanced up, surprised. "Okay, I guess. I wanted to ask you about–"

I sank down in the chair opposite her. "About Lupe? Was she upset yesterday?"

"Upset? I'd say that's one word for it," Lía said. "She came in here crying and making such a fuss that I had to assure some guests in the lobby that no one else had died, and then I had to figure out from her what had happened."

"Are you mad? Sorry, I didn't..." I stared at my hands, all confidence fading and trying to conjure it back.

"Mad? No, not really." Lía wrinkled her brow. "I just would've appreciated a little warning before you sent a hysterical Lupe over to me and maybe not fired her two days before Ana's wedding with a hotel full of guests." Lía chuckled to offset her criticism, but it didn't help.

I looked up. It wouldn't be very professional to dissolve into a puddle of tears, especially when I'd been at fault, but I really, really wanted to.

"Are you okay, Natalia?" Lía asked. "Maybe once Ana gets back from her honeymoon you should take a vacation yourself. I think you're a little stressed out."

I swallowed and ignored Lía's words so as not to burst into tears at that exact moment and gave a dry laugh to extricate the lump in my throat instead. "I think we're all a bit stressed with family in town and well... everything that happened. I should've warned you about Lupe. I didn't expect that Maritza wasn't going to fire her. I assumed that if someone stole, it was a no more questions asked policy."

There was nothing else to say. It was just one of those times that it became evident that living in Santa Rita was not the same as being raised here. Whatever I assumed was the same, that was the thing that was going to be different.

"Lupe shouldn't have stolen. I think we all agree on that, but now how is she going to take care of herself? We've made everything worse for her," Lía said sadly.

The logic. I couldn't follow it. Was there any? I stared at Lía, usually practical and level-headed, but this line of thinking was so out of left field, I didn't even know how to respond.

"What are you trying to say, Lía?" I finally asked after trying to decipher her implication and coming up short.

"I think we should hire her back." I appreciated Lía's

directness, but I was not expecting that.

"Really? But she stole."

"I don't think she'll do it again," Lía insisted. "It's up to you, Natalia. I'm not trying to–"

"Lía, you're part owner too," I said, sensing Lía's unease at speaking openly.

She nodded gratefully. "We need Lupe, and she needs us. I think we should offer her her job back. I asked Maritza about it, and she agrees. She has to redo the wedding cake today, and she'd appreciate the extra set of hands. But if you don't want to, I understand."

Lía said she'd understand, but I knew none of them would. It was just another heartless-gringo aspect of my personality that they'd look at in pity, and no matter how much I explained the reasoning, they'd never understand.

I nodded. "If you want to hire her back, that's fine. I know things work differently in Santa Rita than the rest of the world." I couldn't resist that last passive-aggressive jab.

Lía smiled shyly. "If that's what you think we should do, then I think you should be the one to hire her back."

"Me? Why?" I asked.

"Because if Maritza or I do it, it looks like we're not all on the same page. If you do it, it looks like you're being benevolent and giving Lupe a second chance, and she won't hold so much resentment towards you."

I remembered Esteban's angry face shouting insults at me in the middle of the street and thought about telling Lía but decided against it. It would just be another example of why I shouldn't have fired her in the first place. I nodded silently. "Tell her to come by around 1:00, and I'll talk to her," I said.

Lía nodded. "Are you sure?"

I nodded again. "I need to finish some things first, but I'll be back in time."

"Are you sure you're okay, Natalia?" Lía asked again.

I nodded and faked a smile. "I'm just a little tired."

The *things* I needed to finish were just to wander around town absent-mindedly trying to get myself together. I wanted to clear my head before I was forced to deal with Lupe, who probably wouldn't be as emotional this time around, but the tension would be thick.

I bought a zapote flavored ice cream and settled on a bench in the square to eat it. Zapote was my grandma's favorite flavor, and I hoped its sweetness would offer some of the courage that she and Blanca possessed, but I'd been left out of that genetic exchange.

Silvia stalked through the square going somewhere. Wherever it was, she wasn't happy, and then I realized too late that her object was me. She was hurriedly barreling towards me, and I had no mode of escape.

"So you thought you could get me fired?" Her spittle flew everywhere, but I leaned back to prevent it from falling directly on my face.

"Calm down. What are you talking about, Silvia?" I asked.

"Oh, don't play dumb. That goodie-goodie priest went to Francisco and told him to fire me because of you, and he was going to do it too. But if you think I'm that easy to make go away..." She laughed. "Do you have *any* idea what I've had to do to get this job? If Olga couldn't get rid of me, do you think you can?" She laughed again. "Try again, honey, but it won't work." Silvia turned and sauntered away.

What was that? I glanced around to see if anyone had overheard her, but the square was blessedly empty at the bright noon hour.

How was it possible that I was being blamed for two people being fired when no one had actually lost their job? And what had Silvia meant by that, what she'd had to do to get this job? Was she just referring to having to endure a long-term relationship with an older priest in a conservative town that was more eager to blame the woman than the man who'd actually made the vows of celibacy, or was she referring to something much more sinister?

I shook my head and tried to stop my heart pounding. I needed to head back and deal with Lupe's situation. I groaned as I stood up and saw Father Tomás striding towards the church. I called out to him. He waved and gave a sad smile.

"Sorry, Natalia, I'm in a hurry. We can talk later, okay?" He smiled broadly, but I knew better.

"Coward," I mumbled under my breath but pasted on the same fake smile he had.

He'd used me as an excuse for firing Silvia, and now I was the one being blamed, and his conscience was clear because he'd *tried to do the right thing.* I'd been right the first time. Father Tomás was a politician. It's just that he worked for the church instead of the government.

I wished I had a little bit more of that political spirit and less of a transparent one, at least for the next half hour talking to Lupe. Maybe I should try practicing that wide, fake smile in the mirror more often. The problem was you couldn't pretend not to care, in the mirror or otherwise. I tossed the ice cream paper in the trash and turned towards the hotel. Maybe Lupe would arrive early, and we could get this over with faster, and I could disappear for an afternoon of baking and forget that anyone in this town hated me.

CHAPTER TWENTY-FOUR

My conversation rehiring Lupe was just as awkward as I'd feared it would be. She sat across from me, glaring with an occasional sniffle, although I never saw a tear. I mumbled my way through an awkward speech, praising her long time working for us, explaining that we had decided to give her another chance. Lupe obsequiously nodded, but I could see her seething underneath. Had I rubbed it in too much? I was beginning to doubt every decision I made. Maybe Lía was right. I needed a vacation.

"See that didn't go so bad, did it?" Lía asked brightly after Lupe left.

"No, not at all." I tried to match her level of brightness and pulled out my phone to text Nico.

Today has been the worst. Please tell me we can have an early dinner.

Nico must have been in a similar mindset because he answered moments later. Absolutely, I'll be there as soon as I can. I've missed our dates. You've been so busy lately. He signed it with an emoji with heart eyes. So corny, but I ginned anyway.

"I'm going to go work on some recipes," I told Lía, but really I just wanted to get away from everyone and bake. Everyone but Furby, that is, I scooped him up and headed back to the cottage. He yowled at the indignity of being foisted from his perch but quickly settled into the crook of my arm. The best part of owning your own business was heading out of work whenever you wanted, and after going in at such a godawful hour, I deserved a little break.

By the time Nico made it over, I'd already whipped up a

plate of chocolate dipped shortbread cookies and some simple hazelnut cupcakes with a light whipped frosting.

"Let me know what you think," I told Nico, setting the desserts in front of him while I tackled the pile of dishes, the only downside to baking.

"Isn't it a sin to eat dessert before dinner?" Nico asked around a mouthful of cookies.

"Not in my kitchen. Dig in. Tell me what you think. Be honest."

Nico massacred his dessert in no time. "That was great," he said.

I smiled. "Could you be a little bit more descriptive? I tweaked the hazelnut recipe, and I thought the lightness of the cake would go well with the chocolate shortbread."

"Yes, that exactly," he said. "It wasn't too heavy or too sweet. I like them both together."

I leaned over and gave him a kiss. "Well, maybe you're not ready to be a food critic, but you're welcome in my kitchen any time."

He laughed. "Well, how about we go get some real food before I overdose on sugar and demolish all these cupcakes?"

"Sounds great. Let me grab my purse," I said and offered an outraged Furby a pat on the head, but he declined.

We found ourselves at our favorite taco hotspot, Pancho's Tacos. It was still a little early for most people, so we didn't have to wait long for either our order or a table.

"I'm glad you weren't too busy tonight with Ana's wedding tomorrow and all. I really needed this." I said once we were settled with our food.

"It sounds like you had a pretty rough day. You want to talk about it?" Nico asked as he spooned onions and cilantro onto his tacos.

I shook my head. "Well kind of. Apparently Maritza and Lía didn't want to fire Lupe even though they caught her stealing, and then I became the bad guy because I assumed that you would automatically fire someone for stealing. Just when I start to feel like I might belong somewhere, something always happens that throws it all out of whack, and whatever I assume is the right thing is actually wrong."

"I still feel that way," Nico said. "It's a human thing. I know you're sensitive to being an outsider, and there are differences, but that's what special about you. You always have a unique perspective, a more objective one, I'd say, because you're aware that there's not just one right way to do things. But you worry about it too much. It's not that deep, and Lupe should be happy you didn't fire her. Santa Rita isn't the moon. A lot of people would've fired her, not just you."

"Really?"

Nico nodded. "It's not always so black and white. It's opinion. Plus, she might not be just a thief. She could be a murderer too."

I nodded. "I completely dropped the ball with the murder investigation. We hit a wall, and the police still don't care. Olga's been buried, and no one's even calling it what it was, and there's been radio silence about Harriet's cause of death."

"I know," Nico said. "Esteban's still my number one suspect, at least with Olga, but Lupe might've helped."

"Especially with Harriet," I said. "I know it's sexist, but I just don't see Esteban poisoning anyone."

Nico nodded. "He's not that thoughtful of a guy. That

could've been Lupe for sure."

"Or Silvia and Francisco," I added. I explained my run-in with Silvia to Nico.

"Wow, you did have an awful day," he said. "But why would she blame you specifically?"

"Because of Father Tomás." I sighed. "I told him how hypocritical it looked, and apparently, he used me as his excuse when bringing it up to Father Francisco. It didn't help that she caught me going through her desk when she wasn't there, and we had a little bit of an argument yesterday too."

Nico raised an eyebrow but nodded. "Father Tomás wants to be good, and he's a nice enough guy, but he doesn't have the kind of backbone to be truly good because actually good people, or at least people who stick to their morals, are not always liked. They care more about the truth and being good than in being liked or being nice. Like you, Natalia." He smiled, and his dimples that I loved so much appeared.

My face felt hot. "You really think I'm good?" I asked.

"Of course." Nico popped another bite of taco in his mouth. I had to wait for him to finish chewing to continue. "You fired Lupe because you thought it was the right thing to do. You're trying to find the murderer because you want justice even if it puts you in danger, which it does, and I wish you wouldn't." He smiled. "But I love that about you, and even though I want to keep you safe, I know I can't change you, and I'd never want to."

My cheeks felt so red now, I had to hold my face over my cool cup of soda and took several giant sips. "I never thought of myself that way. I just thought I needed to control my temper."

"Well, you need to do that too. It's nice to have a little balance sometimes, just like I can't puff up your ego too much, and now I need to bring you back down to earth." He laughed, and I joined him.

"I thought I'd miss not having Ana tonight to talk over theories with, but you've pleasantly surprised me," I said, and it was Nico's turn to blush.

"I'm glad Ana's not your only sleuthing partner."

"Me too," I said. "Plus, we get to make out after *our* sleuthing sessions."

"I didn't know that was part of the crime-fighting package, or I would've done it more often, and I wouldn't have eaten all these onions," he said.

I laughed. "I have a new toothbrush you can use. So you really still think Esteban is the main suspect?"

"I do but with Lupe. I don't think he would've done it alone. He's not that bright," Nico said.

I nodded. "I don't have any way to tie Harriet to Silvia and Francisco, but it's possible she asked them the wrong things too, and Silvia does have a temper."

"That's true," Nico agreed. "But it all comes back to the toxicology report. Ana told me about Sara's reasons for the medication, but if Harriet was poisoned with her medicine then... Well, all of her explanations were just an act."

I nodded. Sara had seemed sincere, and her reasons had made sense, but we still didn't have any concrete proof that she *hadn't* poisoned Harriet besides her word.

My head was spinning. "Sara is the only one we have some type of evidence against, even if it's just circumstantial."

Nico nodded. "Well, the location of Olga's murder doesn't bode well for Francisco or Silvia either."

"That's true, but it was a public space. Anyone in town

would've known she liked to open the church early to pray, including Esteban," I said.

"The fact of the matter is if you don't get any more concrete evidence, you might just have to resign yourself to the fact that without the support from the police, the murder will remain unsolved." Nico shook his head sadly.

"You might be right." I shrugged. But I couldn't resign myself to that. I wouldn't. "We just need some more information about Harriet. That's the smoking gun."

"I agree, but now that we're done with the sleuthing part, can we move onto the kissing part?" Nico asked, wiggling his eyebrows.

I laughed. "I guess so. There's nothing else to go over."

Nico and I walked back towards the hotel. I leaned into the crook of his arm. The uneven cobblestones of the sidewalk caused me to lean more into him as we walked.

"Let's go around back," I said. It was a little bit longer, but it avoided the risk of running into any guests in the lobby, and some of Luis's extended family was supposed to arrive for the wedding tomorrow, not to mention Harriet's parents were due in, none of whom I wanted to talk to in the middle of my date with Nico.

Furby greeted us as though we'd left on an expedition instead of just to grab a quick bite to eat. We'd snuggled on the couch and had just started into the kissing portion of the investigation when my phone buzzed. I stopped to glance at the screen, and Nico sighed.

"Can you turn that thing off? How can I think properly, if I can't kiss properly?"

Nico's dry humor made me smile. "Hold on just a second. It's Lía, and I think it's important."

She'd sent a text. I hope you're not mad about earlier. You know you're the best. Good news. Eduardo's friend called. Harriet wasn't poisoned with Sara's medication. There was rat poison but not enough to kill her and some heart medication. It's all really weird. Give you more details tomorrow. Sleep well!

"Well, I don't think it was Sara," I said.

"Why not?" Nico asked.

"Lía said, according to her source, Harriet died from an overdose of some kind of heart meds, but there was also a bunch of rat poison too."

"But when?" he asked.

"I'm not sure, but they could've put a cocktail of poison into her food at the restaurant," I pointed out.

Nico nodded. "That's true."

"At least we can rule Sara out. That's a relief. I hated thinking that Ana was marrying into a family with a murderer so close by."

We discussed our same culprits over again but couldn't get any further. We'd struck one off the list but still didn't have anyone to inch up.

"Well, tomorrow's the wedding. I guess we should get some sleep." I pointed to the clock that read midnight on the wall.

"Yeah, I don't think Ana will be very happy with us if we arrive with dark circles," Nico said. "You can use makeup, but I don't think I'll look very good with concealer under my eyes."

"Don't be silly. Lots of guys are wearing makeup," I said, smiling, thinking of Nico applying under eye concealer.

Nico shook his head. "I don't think that would be a very

appealing look for me. I can slap paint on a chest of drawers, but my face? My talents don't lie in that area of expertise."

I laughed. "Yeah, I think you're right."

Nico stood to leave. "Lock the door, and don't let anyone in, no matter what. Please, Natalia."

I had to stop myself from rolling my eyes.

"It's not a joke," he said.

"I know it's not a joke," I agreed. "But like you said, we may never know exactly who it was. Are we going to live the rest of our life in fear in the meantime?"

"I guess not," Nico agreed. He bent down and offered a long kiss before leaving, brushing his hand against my face. "Just please don't be stupid."

"That's what you always say. Do I have a tendency to do stupid things or something?"

I was attempting sarcasm, but he took my question seriously. "Not stupid things, but let's say, not well thought out things," he said.

I couldn't argue with him there. We kissed again before he turned to leave. I should have started to get ready for bed, but I had to learn more about rat poison and different types of heart medication. I went to flip open my laptop to research, but I'd left it in the office. I groaned. I should just leave it there. After all, surely Lía had locked everything up, but Andrea would be at the desk, and I felt nervous leaving my computer potentially out with a ditz at the helm.

"I'll just dash over and get it before I put on my PJs," I said to Furby. I attempted to open the door quickly, but he dashed out ahead of me. Oh well, Furby never liked to be left behind, he'd follow me back home just as quickly as we went out.

I ran towards the back door of the hotel and quietly entered. My conversation with Nico was scrolling through my head when suddenly something clicked. Something I hadn't thought of before, and as my brain started ticking through the questions, I decided they couldn't wait. There wasn't time.

Instead of turning right towards the lobby, I headed up the stairwell to the rooms on the second floor. Claire, I needed to talk to Claire. I knocked hesitantly on her door. There was no answer. She was probably already asleep. After all, they were leaving tomorrow early. Maybe I shouldn't disturb her after all. I turned to leave but decided against it and knocked louder, still no answer.

What if something was wrong? Should I go to the front desk and get a key? I hesitated, not sure what to do when I noticed one of the small overhead lights was on in the multipurpose room sending a sliver of light under the door. That was odd.

I went to switch it off, opening one of the wide swinging doors. I turned to the wall to flip it off, but there was Claire. I'd found her after all. But unfortunately she was tied to one of the chairs, her mouth gagged, and Jessica stood over her, a hammer in one hand and a knife in the other.

CHAPTER TWENTY-FIVE

It took me a moment to register what exactly was happening. Was this some kind of joke? But the look on Jessica's face put that idea away quickly.

"Come over here!" Her voice had taken on a harsh quality I'd never heard from her even when she'd been angry.

"Jessica, what are you doing?" I fumbled for my phone trying to buy time, but Jessica gestured to my hand.

"Stop doing that and get over here I said." She pressed the knife closer to Claire's throat, and I heard a small whimper escape from her bound mouth.

"Okay, okay," I said, putting my hands up and stepping closer.

"Stop there." Jessica pointed the knife at me. "Slide your phone over and stand against that wall away from the door. Move slowly."

Claire struggled against the ties and tried to speak, but Jessica pointed the knife at her, and immediately she stopped.

I moved slowly, pulled the phone out of my pocket, and slid it carefully across the floor. Jessica stomped on it. I heard the screen crunch, and I flinched and felt guilty for having a more visceral reaction to having my phone smashed than seeing a friend at knifepoint.

"Can we just talk about this, Jessica?" I asked. "Whatever the problem is, we can talk about it."

Jessica let out a hollow laugh. "But it is too late. It's too late for everything. It's been too late since we got here."

"What are you talking about?" I immediately thought about her cancer. Had the diagnosis been grim? "Jessica, if you're sick, there's still hope. There's–"

"I'm not sick." She laughed again, seemingly pleased with herself. Maybe that would be the trick, use her ego to buy time.

"You're not sick?" I asked, trying to encourage her to talk.

"I never was," Jessica said with a dramatic pause. She waited for my reaction, and I obliged with a wide-eyed stare. It wasn't difficult to fake. I really was shocked.

"But you said that–"

"All lies, it was Harriet's idea. She's a genius at marketing, you know. She helped me fake it and grew the channel like crazy."

What a horrible thing to lie about? But it had helped them earn a lot of money for their channel early on and grew their brand of eating vegan. But I still couldn't believe Claire would've gone along with that.

"But Claire said you were–" I looked over at them. Claire furiously shook her head and looked at me, pleading.

"Oh, she never knew," Jessica said, gesturing with the hammer, the knife still hovered over Claire's throat. "We couldn't trust Claire. She never would've gone along with it. But Harriet knew, and that's why she had to go."

I was confused now. "But why did Harriet have to go now?" I asked. "Weren't you in on it together?"

"Yes," Jesica said, impatient. "But she wanted a raise, and when I wouldn't give it to her, she threatened to blow the whole thing up and expose everything if I didn't pay her a load of cash. I kept putting her off. That's why we came here." Jessica smiled, obviously proud of herself. "I'd heard about all you'd done when the vegan enthusiasts came and mentioned it in one of their articles and what an out of the way little town it was.

"They kept saying over and over again how incompetent the police department had been, and I thought, what better place to do it. I put poison in Harriet's smoothie every day, but it wasn't working, and we were running out of time. She was getting more and more insistent that I pay, so I added the last large chunk at the restaurant plus the medication I brought as a last resort that I'd managed to take from my grandpa before we left. I did it at the restaurant in case anyone thought to check the cup, but of course they didn't. The perfect plan. We come on vacation. I get rid of my little problem and go home. I wasn't expecting *you* to play detective again."

For the first time, I saw fear in Jessica's eyes. She only had a knife and a hammer, and she hadn't planned on me walking in on this little scene. I didn't want to make any sudden movements and risk Jessica harming or murdering Claire, but if I could just buy time, I had to get an opening.

"So that was the plan all along?" I asked, trying to sound slightly impressed without overselling it.

Jessica nodded proudly. "I never meant to do anything to Claire. It's just when she started to go through Harriet's computer and found our messages." She shrugged. "She asked me about it and wouldn't listen, wouldn't go along, and then she tried to get away. What else was I supposed to do, let her turn me in?" Jessica did seem regretful to have her friend tied up, but she'd still done it.

"So Harriet's family?" I asked, wanting to get Jessica's attention away from Claire.

"I never even talked to them." Jessica laughed. "Without actual family, everything would get slowed down even more, and by the time they were contacted, I'd be long gone, and in a town like this, they'd probably lose or destroy most of the evidence by then if they haven't already."

I opened my mouth to argue, but it was true. Whenever things could be ignored, put-off, neglected, Santiago and most of the local government were masters at deflection.

"But Olga, you didn't..." I wasn't sure what to ask. Certainly Jessica had no reason to murder Olga, so did that mean there was still another murderer running around Santa Rita?

Jessica laughed again. "She was just practice."

"Practice?" This lady really was insane.

"I saw her in the church that morning, and she started yelling at me about something. I don't know. I couldn't understand her, probably saying I shouldn't touch the crucifix or something, and that's when I thought it would be a great test-case. I had my hammer with me in case I got a good opportunity alone with Harriet and decided to use it on Olga instead. There was no way anyone would suspect me of murdering a stranger, and I could see the police force in action and decide if I should put things off with Harriet or go ahead, and once I saw how stupid they were, walking all over the crime scene and calling it an accident, I realized Santa Rita was the perfect place to work my magic with Harriet." She shrugged.

I'd never heard anyone call murder magic before, but Jessica was getting more and more agitated. I wasn't afraid for myself yet, but I didn't want her to add any more victims to her list. She'd already shown herself to be completely unhinged. I needed to get her attention on something she loved to talk about. It was a risk, but I decided to go for it.

"But Jessica, you're always talking about not murdering animals. I can't believe you'd actually harm a person. This is a joke, right?" Maybe if I gave her a possible out, she'd take it.

But no such luck. She wasn't falling for it "Animals are innocent. They deserve to live. People are not."

"But Claire's innocent," I pointed out, hoping it didn't backfire.

Jessica paused. "I know. It's unfortunate."

Unfortunate was not what I'd call it. I shook my head. The door clicked open, and Jessica spun, ready to charge, but it was just Furby. He yowled impatiently at me, probably wanting to go to bed and wondering what was taking me so long. Jessica smiled at the sight of him, and I sprung to move forward and grab the knife, but there wasn't enough time. Jessica jumped back and held the knife once again to Claire's throat before I could even move a few steps towards her.

"Ha-ha, nice try. Why don't you have a seat here?" She pushed out one of the other chairs from a large table with her foot and gestured with the hammer.

This girl really was crazy. Did she think I was just going to sit down and let her tie me up and slit my throat too? I saw movement out of the corner of my eye but didn't turn towards it, hoping not to distract Jessica.

But of all the people, it was Andrea. Just my luck. I stifled a groan. "Your cat is making so much noise," she said to me, annoyed that she'd been forced to stand up and come upstairs. "Isn't there supposed to be a reception here tomorrow?" Andrea glanced around the room but still didn't seem to notice the crazed maniac with a knife along with her hostage bound to a chair.

Jessica's eyes went wide and glanced between Andrea and myself. She hadn't understood a word of what Andrea had just told me.

"She just called the police," I told Jessica calmly. "Just put the knife down. The fewer people you hurt, the less time you'll–"

But Jessica was already lunging towards Andrea, knife in hand. What had I just done? I grabbed the only thing close to me, the chair I'd been edging toward, picked it up, legs out, and started charging towards Jessica, screaming at Andrea, or anyone else who could hear, to get out of the way and call the police. Andrea looked surprised, but not as surprised as she should be at seeing a lunatic run at her with a knife. I kept screaming, battering Jessica with the chair. I managed to knock her down, and tried to kick the knife out of her hand. She stabbed at me but couldn't get leverage from the floor. I stepped on her hand, forcing her to drop the knife. She'd thrown the hammer at my head in her last futile attempt, but missed.

Luckily, Blanca had heard my screaming and came running, along with half the hotel, but Blanca was the only one who jumped into action. Everyone else just stood, staring blankly with sleep-filled eyes. Blanca jumped on top of Jessica and screamed at Andrea yet again to call the police. Thankfully, she finally listened, along with some of the other lookie-loos who disappeared, presumably to do the same. I sat on Jessica's legs, while Blanca pinned the rest of her body, until the police and paramedics finally came.

Claire was badly shaken but otherwise physically okay. When Santiago arrived and saw Blanca and I on top of Jessica, her eyes wide and screaming in a way that didn't need translation, he gestured for one of his officers to handcuff her, so Blanca and I could dismount.

"We'll need a statement." He sighed and rubbed his rumpled bedhead.

Blanca was all too eager to give her statement, not embellishing, but definitely playing it for all it was worth.

"Hold on," he said, putting up a hand. "Let's go down to the office. This needs to be official."

I restrained from rolling my eyes. Since when did Santiago want to follow procedure? When it benefitted him, and allowed him to be lazy, that was when.

I dreaded having to tell him everything Jessica had said about choosing Santa Rita because of the incompetent police force. He already hated me, and this wasn't going to help.

Ana's wedding had to be postponed another two days in order to clean up the hotel, and the police had to speak with everyone who had been around or near the attempted murder scene. At least this time no one had been actually injured, except for Jessica who'd gotten some minor injuries from Blanca jumping on top of her, and maybe a few bruises from me hitting her with a chair and stepping on her hand.

Santiago hadn't been happy to hear my version of events but had perked up a little at hearing Jessica had lied about the cancer diagnosis, after I'd explained to him exactly what Youtube was and that yes you could make money with vegan videos and showed him her Go Fund Me page as well.

"So she also committed fraud. The US government will probably want to extradite her for that," he said, upbeat at the prospect that this would be transferred to the national or international level immediately, and someone else might do his job for him. Claire had left for home as soon as she could. I couldn't say I blamed her. Her vacation had turned into a nightmare.

Ana took it all in stride. I was impressed. "The important thing is that Carlos and I get married. It doesn't matter when. It would be nice if it happened some time, though." She shrugged. I wanted to give her a hug, but I could tell she was hanging by a thread, and I didn't want to push her over the edge.

CHAPTER TWENTY-SIX

A na did get married and was a beautiful bride in her traditional lace covered dress and veil, exactly like she'd wanted, and I had to admit Father Tomás did a great job with the mass. There wasn't a dry eye. He might be a master with words, but I was still bitter about him throwing me under the bus, especially watching Silvia gloat from the sidelines, smirking in my direction, every chance she got during the ceremony.

"I hate her," I muttered under my breath to Nico as we exited the church. "I've never wanted to punch someone in the face so much before in my life, her and her toad-priest boyfriend."

Nico smothered a laugh. "Let's just have fun. It's a party after all, and we're all here to celebrate."

"That's true," I agreed.

Everyone in Santa Rita was eager to finally let loose. My mom's husband, Theo, had even chartered a plane to celebrate with us, and I met him for the first time. He wasn't exactly a charmer, but my mom had done way worse in the past. He eagerly explained in broken Spanish to anyone who would listen how brave Blanca had been to catch a murderer and save her daughter. Most people just nodded politely, including myself. I couldn't deny that Blanca had been pretty badass, and they were a cute couple. Irritating, but cute. I did like that he was so proud and concerned about her, though.

"Your mom's no joke," Nico said, following my line of sight.

I sighed. "She's not easy, but she can be helpful. I'll admit that much."

"I brought you some chicken mole." Nico handed me a heaping plate. "Ana said they're going to start the dancing soon, and after that, I don't think there will be anything left until they cut the cake."

"Thanks." I smiled. I was hungrier than I'd realized.

I was able to shove most of the food in my mouth before the DJ announced that the first dance would be starting soon.

A sea of children ran screaming in Ana's direction. A gaggle of girls formed around her, touching the end of her dress with less than clean fingers. But instead of shooing them away, she gestured to the heels she'd discarded next to her chair.

"You can try my shoes on if you want, just take turns and be careful. We don't want any broken ankles." The girls giggled in excitement, each hobbling a few steps in the heels before another begged for her turn.

"Let me use the restroom. I'll be right back," I told Nico and slipped out and down the hallway.

Blanca's low, angry voice took me by surprise. What was she doing out here? Was there trouble in paradise, I wondered, but she was speaking in Spanish, so definitely not talking to Theo. It was a different man, but I couldn't see him. I edged forward slowly, not wanting to be discovered, but also curious.

"She doesn't need to know," Blanca said in an angry whisper.

"But don't you think she deserves to." The man's voice was low as well. I didn't recognize it.

"Listen, it's just better that she doesn't. I left here all those years ago, and I'd prefer if you'd just respect me on this. What are you going to do anyway? It's too late for you to be her father."

My breath caught. Blanca was talking to my father, right here. I had to see him. I needed to know, after all these years. I moved forward once again but misjudged the distance, not realizing they were right around the corner, and I bumped Blanca's shoulder. She gasped in surprise, and the man pointed and smiled but not a nice smile. It was a smile that made me shiver. Rubén... Rubén Sanchez, the head of the police department, was my father. I wanted to vomit, hit somebody, scream. That meant that idiot Santiago was my half-brother. How could I be related to these monsters?

"Natalia." Blanca reached out to touch my arm, but I moved away.

"Let's not talk about this," I said. "It's Ana's wedding. Let's just be happy." I turned to go back into the reception.

"See what you did," I heard Blanca say as I left. "You should have just left it alone."

"She's a detective like me. It's in her genes. But she's much better than Santiago is." Rubén responded.

I really was going to be sick. I didn't care to hear any more. But this was supposed to be Ana's day. I couldn't let it show that I'd just found out the horrible truth. I thought I'd always wanted to know, but now that I knew, I wish I didn't.

"That was fast." Nico smiled. "You ready for the dance?"

I nodded mutely, realizing I hadn't even bothered to use the restroom.

"You okay?" Nico asked. Everything in the room was loud and swirled around me. I'd talk to him about it, but not now, not here. I bit my lip to stop from crying.

"What's wrong?" he asked.

"Are you sure you want to be with me if my family is

absolutely nuts and horrible?" I asked.

Nico pulled me in for a hug. "Your mom's not that bad. I–"

"I'm not talking about Blanca," I said.

Nico furrowed his brow. "Well, I don't care who you're related to. I'll marry you just the same." He reached over and kissed me. "Now let's have some fun and stop moping."

I laughed, seeing how excited he was. Nico was right. It was time to celebrate. Heading towards the line of people, it finally sunk in.

"What did you just say?" I shouted over the music.

"I said I want to marry you no matter what," Nico shouted back in my ear. "Now come on. Let's dance."

He pulled me with him, winding our way around the room. As upset as the news that Rubén Sanchez was my biological father had been, it paled in comparison to how happy dancing with Nico, my future husband, made me. I was actually more upset that I was related to Santiago than Rubén. I'd always assumed my bio-dad was a loser.

"Faster, Natalia," Nico yelled, pulling me along with him to the rapid tempo.

"Okay, okay." I laughed in spite of myself. Nico leaned down as we rounded the corner and stopped to kiss me. "I love you," he whispered in my ear.

"No matter what?" I asked.

"No matter what," he said, not even pausing. And we continued forward, Nico holding me against him as we danced.

A NOTE FROM THE AUTHOR

Thank you so much for reading *Sanctuary for Murder*. As a new and independent writer, I would love to hear from you. If you can leave an honest review on Amazon or Goodreads, I'd really appreciate it. It means more than you know and helps Amazon to show it to more people. I cannot express how much I appreciate everyone who takes the time to leave one. Please feel free to email me at authorlaurengarcia@gmail.com and let me know about your experience with the story. Also, if you'd like to join my mailing list and receive a free copy of my new novella *Consultation for Murder* let me know, and I'll be happy to add you and send you the novella.

I first got the idea for this story after finishing *Check in for Murder*, the first in the series. I wanted to build on the Vegan Enthusiast Club and incorporate the Youtube aspect. I just thought that would be fun and that it was a funny name.

Although none of my characters are based on real people, I got the idea for the Francisco Silvia relationship based on attending a church street fair in our town with rides and games and food when suddenly a priest with a woman coming out of the church caused the people to part in front of them, and everyone was staring. The woman cut in line and ordered food for the priest. I asked my husband who that woman was, and he told me it was probably his mistress. A woman nearby who was selling elote, a corn street food snack, overheard and nodded and said that she definitely was and knew that because she was her neighbor. I was surprised how well known it was, and that's where I got the seed of an idea that I pulled out several years later.

Obviously there are a lot of kind priests and so many lovely, faithful Catholics. There are also a lot of super nice vegans. I hope it's clear that the focus was on the hypocrisy and not meant to demean, insult, or look down on anyone's religious or ethical beliefs.

This is a complete work of fiction. The town of Santa Rita and everything in it is a fictional amalgamation based on small towns throughout the mountains of central Mexico. All characters are pure works of fiction and do not represent actual people, either living or dead.

Language use can be a tricky thing when setting your book in a location where the dominant language is not the same one that the book is written in. A lot of the characters are presumed to be speaking in Spanish, and some authors might choose to include common Spanish phrases to add the flavor of the language. However, as a reader, I don't normally enjoy this tactic and simply skip over words from languages I'm not familiar with. I chose not to include any Spanish words in the English version unless they are referring to places, regional foods, or where it just felt necessary for understanding. A glossary of the Mexican foods and pastries mentioned is provided to help improve clarity.

A GLOSSARY OF FOOD TERMS

These are general definitions but types, styles, and names of food can vary a lot. These terms and definitions are based on the region in Mexico where the book takes place.

Atole- A traditional hot, thick drink made from cornmeal. It comes in many flavors, including but not limited to, chocolate, vanilla, a variety of fruits, or plain.

Besos (kisses)- Two dome-shaped sweet breads joined together by a thin layer of jam or cream, often covered with a thin layer of sugar on the outside as well.

Bolillos- A savory bread, usually bought daily, similar to a French baguette and in some places is called french bread, but it's shorter, fatter, and usually less crispy on the outside. This bread is called by a variety of names in other regions of Mexico and throughout Central America.

Carnitas- Literal meaning is "little meats" and is slow-cooked or braised pulled pork until very tender.

Horchata- A cold, sweet rice milk beverage flavored with vanilla and cinnamon. You can often find this drink sold in ice cream shops throughout Mexico too.

Mole- An ancient, traditional sauce in Mexico from the Nahuatl word (molli). There are dozens of different varieties but all generally include a mixture of fruits, nuts, chili peppers, and different spices all formed into a thick sauce.

Nopales- They are the pads of the prickly pear or nopal cactus stripped of spines (of course) that can be eaten raw or cooked.

Piedras (stones)- A large, very dense sweetbread in a variety of flavors, normally eaten with a hot drink.

Rebanada (slice)- A thick slice of white sweet bread covered with a thin coating of buttercream or butter and sugar on top. These can also be dipped in chocolate.

Tacos de Canasta (Basket tacos)- These are tiny steamed tacos filled with a variety of fillings like potatoes, beans, chicken, meat. It is a popular street food.

Tacos al Pastor (shepherd tacos)- Traditionally made with pork marinated in various dried chiles, spices, pineapple, and achiote paste cooked on a rotisserie, thinly sliced, and served with corn tortillas, finely diced pineapple, onions, cilantro, and a variety of salsas.

Tamales de Rajas- Tamales are pretty well-known, a corn masa steamed with various fillings and wrapped in a corn husk or banana leaf. Rajas tamales are filled with poblano peppers and cheese, all cooked inside the tamal.

Tlacoyos- This is a pre-hispanic dish that has a thicker dough than traditional tortillas, oval shaped, and can have a variety of fillings such as chicharron, beans, cheese, and can be fried or toasted.

Zapote or Sapote- A very soft, sweet fruit that is often incorporated into drinks, ice cream, desserts, or can be eaten by itself. There are many varieties and names that this fruit can go by throughout the Americas.

ABOUT THE AUTHOR

Lauren is a writer and English teacher and lives in a small town in Guanajuato, Mexico with her husband, son, and lovable husky, Susi. This is her first cozy mystery series. When she's not writing, she can be found reading way too many books and baking delicious, but not usually beautiful, desserts. She studied creative writing at Northern Kentucky University and second language acquisition at the University of Cincinnati before making her forever home in central Mexico almost 10 years ago.

BOOKS BY THIS AUTHOR

Check In For Murder: A Natalia Hernandez Mystery: Book 1

Natalia didn't expect to land in the middle of nowhere central Mexico as a hotel and bakery owner, but when her grandma dies and leaves them both to her, that's exactly where she is. The joy doesn't last long, though, when one of the hotel's guests is murdered, and the head baker is carted away as the prime suspect.

Several residents in the tranquil, mountain town had more than enough reason to off the out-spoken Clemencia, and the police seem determined to pin the crime on an innocent woman.

Time is running out for Natalia to revamp the hotel, solve the murder, and regain the town's trust. With a murderer on the loose and the gossip mill running rampant, no one is willing to set foot in either the hotel or the bakery. If Natalia can't solve this murder in time, she'll be forced to return to her dead-end job as a failure and leave the only place that has ever felt like home.